Also by Leia Stone

Fallen Academy
Fallen Academy: Year One
Fallen Academy: Year Two
Fallen Academy: Year Three
Fallen Academy: Year Four

Gilded City
House of Ash and Shadow
House of War and Bone
House of Light and Ether

Kings of Avalier
The Last Dragon King
The Broken Elf King
The Ruthless Fae King
The Forbidden Wolf King

Wolf Girl
Wolf Girl
Lost Girl
Alpha Girl
Mated Girl

FALLEN ACADEMY

YEAR ONE

LEIA STONE

Bloom books

Copyright © 2018, 2025 by Leia Stone
Cover and internal design © 2025 by Sourcebooks
Cover design © Covers by Aura
Cover images © Urfingus/Depositphotos, _Vilor/Depositphotos, alpinist_den/
Depositphotos, paulfleet/Depositphotos, Studiotan/Depositphotos, upetrovic.
hotmail.com/Depositphotos, GraphicCompressor/Adobe Stock, luuuusa/
Adobe Stock, SWEviL/Depositphotos, SSilver/Depositphotos

Sourcebooks, Bloom Books, and the colophon are registered trademarks of Sourcebooks.

All rights reserved. No part of this book may be reproduced in any form or by any electronic or mechanical means including information storage and retrieval systems—except in the case of brief quotations embodied in critical articles or reviews—without permission in writing from its publisher, Sourcebooks.

No part of this book may be used or reproduced in any manner for the purpose of training artificial intelligence technologies or systems.

The characters and events portrayed in this book are fictitious or are used fictitiously. Any similarity to real persons, living or dead, is purely coincidental and not intended by the author.

All brand names and product names used in this book are trademarks, registered trademarks, or trade names of their respective holders. Sourcebooks is not associated with any product or vendor in this book.

Published by Bloom Books, an imprint of Sourcebooks
P.O. Box 4410, Naperville, Illinois 60567-4410
(630) 961-3900
sourcebooks.com

Originally published in 2018 by Leia Stone LLC.

Cataloging-in-Publication data is on file with the Library of Congress.

Printed and bound in the United States of America.
LB 10 9 8 7 6 5 4 3 2 1

To Hawkwind. Never lose your wild imagination.

CHAPTER 1

My mother pushed open the door to my bedroom, allowing the light to leak inside. It took a second for my eyes to adjust to the sudden brightness, and when they did, her troubled face came into view. I'd been sitting in my dark room all day, avoiding the inevitable.

"It's time," she announced with resignation.

My gaze swept over the hard lines around her eyes—from years of worrying—then at her tearstained cheeks, but what stood out most of all was the red crescent moon tattoo on her forehead.

The symbol of a demon's slave. The symbol of my future.

Nodding, I lifted myself off my bed with heavy limbs, and an even heavier heart. My mother stepped to the side as I passed her, and I made my way out into the living room.

Mikey, my younger brother, sat on the couch, staring at the smooth plaster walls as if by his sheer will, he could change the present. Nothing could change what I was about to do, what I was about to become. My fate had been written a long time ago.

"I wish I was the firstborn," my little brother muttered in a hollow voice that made my throat pinch with emotion. My normally goofball brother was near tears, and it *killed* me.

I didn't wish he were born first. I was glad it was me. My brother was too soft emotionally to live the life of a demon's slave. It was better this way.

"Today I wish I never had children," my mother said gravely.

I knew she didn't mean it. She just wanted to protect me from this, and wishing me out of existence would do that. That's how bad times were. Since The Falling, none of us had any hope at a normal life anymore; all we could do was wish things were different or accept what was.

My mother wiped her leaking eyes and straightened. "Maybe you'll get Necromancy like me and get a more prominent post. Then we could work together after your academy studies." Her mood instantly brightened at the thought.

I nodded, although it was highly unlikely. When the angels fell from Heaven and warred on Earth with Lucifer and his demons, powers flared out like the aurora borealis, infecting most of humanity. The Falling turned most of us into some sort of supernatural creature and left the rest human. Your gift depended on whether an angel or demon's power touched you during the fight. It was completely random and had nothing to do with whether or not you were a good person. My mother was demon gifted with Necromancy, and reanimated the dead for a living. It was the only reason we weren't living on the streets, like half of the human population. But they weren't really alive; the... things she reanimated were akin to zombies. I shuddered, thinking of the times she'd brought her work home with her.

"It won't be Necro, Mom. It's random. She could be a Gristle for all we know." There was my sarcastic Mikey, back in action.

My mom reached back and swatted his head. "Just be quiet," she chided. Her normally vibrant blond hair was dull and greasy. She'd no doubt stayed up all night worrying about this.

I laughed dryly to lighten the mood. If I was a Gristle, that would actually be the perfect shitty topping to my already shitty life. It meant having the magical ability to make trash disappear. Gristles smelled like crap, literally, and they were the bottom of the barrel as far as magical society was concerned.

I was five years old when The Falling happened. My mom said that when the magic hit me, my body hovered in the air for a full five minutes, and she had to pin me to the bed to keep me from floating away. Mikey was four, so he wouldn't really remember, but she mentioned his skin had turned green for over an hour.

Stepping closer, my mother smoothed my bright blond hair down. "I'm sorry. I should never have taken the deal wi—"

I cut her off with a wave of my hand. Quite frankly, I was sick of the apology. My dad had been dying of cancer, and the whole family agreed that my mom would sell her services to the demons, becoming a lifelong Necro for the baddies. We just hadn't read the fine print, which stated your firstborn was also a lifelong slave to the wicked.

I'd have been fine with it, if my father hadn't been hit by a bus six months after the demons took his cancer. *Six months* of extended life was all that my mother's and my lifetime enslavement earned him. Life was jacked up, and I'd learned not to depend on sunshine and rainbows. The unicorns of my childhood dreams were dead and slaughtered.

Now summer was over and I was eighteen. Today I would go to the Awakening, a magical ceremony put on by the fallen angels to fully ignite our powers, to reveal what gifts or curses we held. Angel blessed or demon gifted—at least for those of us who had them. When The Falling first happened and all of the powers were unleashed on the humans, no one was sure who got hit or with what. When the angels realized what they'd done—mutated humanity—they contained all of the powers given to anyone under the age of eighteen. They couldn't take them back, but they could at least keep them at bay so we could have a childhood.

Once my power was determined, I would exit stage left, get my demon slave tattoo, and enroll in the notoriously dysfunctional and scary Tainted Academy while the others exited stage right and enrolled in Fallen Academy with the rest of the free souls. Fallen Academy was an exclusive college for those who weren't demon-slave bound, mostly the angel blessed. The supernaturally gifted would be trained for four years, and then be drafted into the Fallen Army, receiving good payment for their service to the light. We were still at war, after all, and I was about to sign up for the wrong side. My lifetime service to the demons would start today, and I felt sick thinking about it.

"I should get going. I don't want to be late," I said abruptly. That would result in my entire family being slaughtered by demons. They were greedily awaiting their new slave, a fresh eighteen-year-old to torture and wear down over the rest of my life.

My mom fell into a puddle of tears then and I just couldn't deal with it. I needed to stay strong or I was going to lose it.

"Love you guys. See you after," I added, ignoring my mother's weeping as I walked hastily to where my coat was hanging by the door.

"Brielle." My mother's voice carried so much emotion that I knew I wouldn't be able to turn around or I would completely fall to pieces. "I'm so sorry. Forgive me?"

The apology was old, but this was new. Did she think I blamed her? We'd all agreed that the healer demon we went to had tricked her. She had no idea a blood oath included her firstborn. I was twelve years old and mature enough to know what I had encouraged her to do. We all did it for my father.

That time I did turn around.

"Of course I forgive you, Mom. It's the demon scum that will never get my forgiveness." I hated them. Rage built in my chest as I grieved for my future. The future I would've had if they hadn't tricked my mother into giving up my life to save my father's. If he'd still been alive, it would've been worth it, but six months? It wasn't enough.

My mom just stood there and nodded. "Your father would—" She couldn't finish as the sob escaped her throat. I needed to get the hell out of there. It was too sad.

When the bus hit my father six years ago, I'd begged my mom to reanimate him so I could talk to him, tell him how much I loved him, and get bear hugs from him again. She refused, and at the time I'd hated her for it. As I grew older and interacted with the reanimated more, I understood why. They were zombies, shells of their former selves. Besides, he'd made her promise that she never would.

Suddenly, my mother and brother were both bearing down on me with their arms around me, squeezing tight. "Maybe you'll be a dud and useless to everyone," my brother mumbled into my hair, and then we all broke apart laughing.

I punched his arm lightly. "There's only room for one dud in this family, and you've taken to that position beautifully." He just grinned and shook his head.

A dud was a nonmagical being. A human. They were rare in Los Angeles, since The Falling started there, but it did happen. Maybe I *would* be a dud, but I was sure the demons could find use for a human, and I was also sure my brother had magical abilities as well. That night of The Falling, when I was floating up in the air above my bed, I had a vivid memory of my brother lighting up like a Christmas tree, bright green.

Neither of us would be duds.

After that night, adults' gifts started showing immediately, but our gifts had been locked down. Could you imagine a five-year-old Gristle eating up trash on the street? At least that part had been fair. We'd been given somewhat normal childhoods—if growing up with demons and fallen angels roaming the streets was normal. At least we weren't being made to raise the dead at seven years old.

"I love you guys. Everything's going to be fine," I reassured my family with as much strength in my voice as I could muster.

A heavy sigh escaped my mom, and she reached out to touch my cheek. "You're wise beyond your years."

My throat tightened as unshed tears lined my eyes. My father used to say that to me. In fact, they were the last words he shared before he left for work and was taken from us.

"I can't be late. Gotta meet Shea." I grabbed my hooded parka, and headed toward the door.

We lived in Demon City, the place of demons and their slaves, but the Awakening ceremony was all the way in Angel City. Those who enjoyed normal humanity, the free souls, and the angel blessed lived there. Both Demon City and Angel City used to formally be called Los Angeles, having been split apart and renamed after The Falling.

I was going to have to run if I wanted to make the 5:15 pm bus. I slipped my gray parka on and pulled up the hood. It rained 90 percent of the time in Demon City. No one knew why—maybe it was the concentration of so many demons—but the sun barely shone there.

Without another word, I grabbed my messenger bag and slipped out of the fourth-floor apartment I shared with my family, and my best friend Shea. She was meeting me at the bus stop, going right from work to the ceremony. Being late to an Awakening ceremony was not an option. The ceremonies were done each year on the day before classes started at Fallen and Tainted Academies, and Shea and I had birthdays only sixteen days apart, so we were going to be in the same one. Shea was also destined to be a demon slave, except for all the wrong reasons. Her mother was a drug addict and sold her lifelong labor to a demon for a day's worth of drugs. Shea was her firstborn, so she went right along with it. She had moved to Demon City about the same time we did and had seen me through more than some who had known me my whole life. When her mom bailed to go to Vegas, my mother took her in.

I burst through the stairwell door and took the four flights down three steps at a time. Shea was the long-distance runner, while I was more of a "sprint and then collapse panting on the ground, willing myself to die" kind of person. With a giant leap, I crashed through the door that led outside. Sitting right next to the stairwell door was Bernie, in his usual spot, Maximus curled up at his feet, his tail thumping when he smelled me.

"Who's there? Is that you, Bri?" Bernie sniffed the air. It was pelting rain, but somehow he always knew it was me.

I grinned.

Bernie didn't have a home and was legally blind, but he was sweeter than sugar. The nicest man I'd ever met. He once tried to offer me his only coat when I was cold.

Pulling a blueberry muffin from my bag that I had stashed there earlier, I plopped it in his hand. "I have my Awakening ceremony today. Can't talk now, but I'll come by later and bring you dinner."

He patted my hand and smiled, showcasing missing teeth. Ripping a piece of the muffin off, he gave it to Maximus.

"May you be angel blessed," he said and nodded to me.

Angel blessed. Yeah right. Odds were unlikely, seeing as my mother was demon gifted. And it wouldn't matter anyway, because I was going to Tainted Academy whether I was angel blessed or not.

"Thanks, Bern. I'm late," I told him again. I cherished our chats, but I really couldn't be late.

"Run like the wind, child!" he shouted, shooing me. Maximus barked for full effect.

Turning on my heels, I dashed out into the pelting rain and nearly slammed right into a tiny Snakeroot demon. I was able to sidestep him at the last minute but still got a whiff of his natural scent—sulfur, acid, and raw sewage. *Yuck*. Their red, beady eyes and threaded, black horns gave me the creeps, but they were beauty queens compared to other demons I'd seen roaming around the hood. The top of my left foot was scarred from a Snakeroot demon. Long story, but it was Shea's fault.

As I turned the corner onto Rosecrans Boulevard, I grinned when I saw Shea's dark brown, curly ponytail hanging out the bus's front door, her boot on the curb. "I said hold the bus for one more *goddamn* minute!" she roared.

My best friend was half Black, half Puerto Rican, and she didn't mess around. You either did what she said, or you did what she said.

"I'm here!" I yelled.

Shea turned to meet my eyes and shook her head. "Always late."

I just smiled, and we both rushed onto the bus to meet the glare of a demon slave woman who sat behind the wheel, her red crescent tattoo glaring on her forehead above hateful eyes.

"Next time I'll shut the door on your pretty foot!" she snarled at Shea.

Shea shrugged as if she didn't care. She really probably didn't. A broken ankle would get her out of work detail for a few days until a healer demon could fix it, and that would be awesome. After Shea's mom ran off when she was thirteen, it left her slave contract broken, which meant if she ever stepped foot in Demon City again, she was dead on arrival. They had better things to do than go chasing after a junkie to make them live out their contract. So instead, they'd made Shea pick up her mom's post. She'd been working for demons ever since.

"How was work?" I made small talk, trying to get my mind off what was about to happen. Shea and I would both officially be slaves to the demons. *Forever.* We didn't have our tattoos yet. The demons couldn't technically do that to us until we had gone through the Awakening. She'd been working off the books for the

Grimlock demon who owned her contract. It kept her alive and fed, so she didn't complain much.

She shrugged. "The usual. Master Grim had me interview some new 'dancers' for his club, and after that I scrubbed the leather seats with bleach and water. Fun times." The way she did air quotes around the word dancer always cracked me up.

"How exactly does one interview a 'dancer'?" Grim, her boss and the demon who held her contract, was also the owner of five strip clubs in Demon City. He made big money and had more slaves than I'd ever seen. Shea was his personal assistant.

She pushed her breasts together, batting her eyelashes, and I laughed even more. Even when the world had gone to shit, Shea could always make me laugh. "That's it? A nice rack and you're in?"

Hmm, maybe that would be my backup plan if my new post didn't pay well. Necros made good money, but if I was a Gristle, I was screwed. My boss would barely pay me enough to eat. My mom wouldn't be able to work forever. Necro work was hard and soul-draining, so I'd have to eventually take care of her, Mikey, and maybe even Shea too.

Shea's face fell and clouded over. "It's sad. Most of the girls are barely eighteen. Some have kids to support or contracts to fulfill. I'm lucky Grim doesn't make me dance. I'm surprised he hasn't noticed that I was blessed with incredibly amazing boobs."

I grinned. "And a nice booty."

She chortled, turning to look behind her. "It is nice," she agreed, making me smile wider.

"Are you nervous?" I inquired, changing the topic. "What if we're both Gristles?"

Shea shrugged and reached over to hold my hand. "Then we'll be the best damn Gristles Demon City has ever seen."

I smiled again but it didn't reach my eyes. On a day when we were supposed to be getting special powers and new careers, we were selling our souls to the wrong side.

"Do you think the war will ever stop, that one side will win? That the fallen might win?" I asked her. The sunlight was shining up ahead as the bus made its way to the border of Angel City. The place I had once lived, until my dad got sick. I barely remembered it now, but I recalled that the majority of people were happy.

Shea's gaze followed the rain streak down the window, her blue eyes looking out beyond her bronze skin. She let go of my hand. "I dunno. I try not to hope anymore. It only leads to disappointment."

Wasn't that the damn truth. We could pass for normal on the streets now, but after today, a red crescent moon slave mark would mar our looks for eternity. Would show everyone who we were, and what we'd signed up for.

The bus slowed as it reached the border gate, and a

security guard stepped out from behind the tall cement wall that closed off the two warring cities. After a few words and a scan of the driver's badge, we rolled on through. The sunlight burst through the windows and heated my chilly skin. Driving into Angel City was an immediate mood lifter. I took a deep breath as I felt the tension in my shoulders recede.

Shea chuckled. "You love this place."

"Don't you?" Angel City was the normal side, the side with the good people.

"It's not home to me like it is to you," she added with a shrug. "I don't feel any different about either side."

That was true. Shea was from New Orleans, and after moving here, she'd only ever known Demon City as home. She loved the rain and gloomy days, whereas I was dying for a sunny day at the beach.

The bus stopped in front of the Awakening Center, and Shea and I disembarked. My hands clung to my messenger bag tightly as we crossed the busy downtown street and made our way to the line of teenagers walking into the open double doors.

"I saw a Lakers game here once with my dad. I barely remember, but we have a picture," I told Shea.

"The Awakening waits for no one!" a slender woman in her twenties called out to us as the last of the kids went through the double doors.

"Why do they insist on dressing us up? This isn't prom," Shea muttered, running to catch up. I didn't want to know what happened if you didn't make it on time to the Awakening. I'd heard stories and they weren't good.

"Because it gives them something to do," I whispered back, then was met with a glare from the female officer holding the door. I looked down at the silver spiral insignia on her jacket. She was a Light Mage. She also had a silver FA patch right beneath it, the logo of the Fallen Army.

The line of my fellow Awakening ceremony companions began to tighten as we walked single file back to the dressing rooms. The fallen angels who hosted the ceremony every year insisted we dress up, and after we had our Awakening, they threw a big catered party for everyone, even the demon bound.

"I heard there's a chocolate fountain at the party after." Shea's eyes lit up as she told me the rumor. She was obsessed with chocolate—and guys, but mostly chocolate.

The Fallen Army officer hung back until she was walking with Shea and me, giving us a side glance as she tsked through her teeth.

Shea pinned her with a glare as we walked. "Can I help you?" she asked her in the bitchiest tone possible. The fallen and all of their officers were high and mighty, acting better than everyone, especially better than us. The demon bound.

The woman shrugged. "It's a shame to see so many firstborns pledge their lives to the demons."

Another woman up ahead had started roll call at a set of double doors. Shea stopped and faced the officer. Her blood was boiling. I could see that in the way she clenched her fists, and I hoped I didn't have to hold her back. If you struck an officer, it was a criminal offense.

How did she even know we were slave bound? She'd probably looked at all of the files beforehand, specifically looking for the ones like us.

"You think we *pledge* ourselves? Wow, you're stupider than you look," Shea spat.

I froze, unsure what the woman's reaction would be. I didn't spend a lot of time around the Fallen Army and their human cohort. I'd heard they were more forgiving than the demon patrol officers that roamed our streets, but I wouldn't bet on it.

"No." The officer stepped closer to my best friend. "What's stupid is that your mothers, the people in charge of your safety and security, pledged your life to a demon for their own gains."

I stepped out of the line, ready to give this girl a piece of my mind, but the officer at the front called Shea's name just then.

"Shea Hallowell. Demon bound."

Shea gave the officer one last glare before stepping in line and raising her hand.

The officer at the front typed something into her tablet and pointed for Shea to step out of the line. There was a small group of three others I recognized from Demon City. All demon bound.

"Brielle Atwater. Demon bound."

The way she said 'demon bound,' like it was dirty, made me hate them more. The self-righteous Fallen Army.

I raised my hand and held my chin high. Yes, my mother sold herself to a lifetime of demon slavery to save my father's life, but what other choice did we have? That's what you did for love, for family. The fallen angels didn't heal the dying—free will, destiny, and all of that bullshit. They said the humans who were terminal were meant to pass, and no one should interfere. Pious bastards.

I stepped out of line and followed Shea to stand with the others from Demon City. Five of us. The rest were free souls and would exit stage right and be recruited to enter Fallen Academy. Mages, the Sighted, Centaurs, and of course, the rare and mythical Celestials were all of the angel blessed powers and were looked at as the 'good ones.' There hadn't been a Celestial in five years. It was said they were endowed with so much angel energy during The Falling, that they were kin to the fallen angels themselves. They were easy to spot with their large, white wings, smaller yet identical to the wings of the fallen. The only difference was that the Celestials could retract their wings at will, and the fallen couldn't.

I saw one once. A fallen. I was nine years old, right

before my dad's diagnosis while he was in the hospital. Raphael, the Archangel of Healing, was going around blessing the sick—he must have skipped my dad. I'll never forget what he looked like, and the way he looked at me, like he could see right through me. It was unnerving.

"Free souls this way. Demon bound that way," the lead officer called out, and we all entered the hallway.

The free souls started walking into a dressing room to the right as we headed left, where a demon slave with the red crescent moon was waiting for us. She had a cattle prod in one hand, and Shea and I raised our eyebrows at each other. She was a slave minder. If one of us chickened out or tried to run, we'd be shot up with electricity.

Icing on the cake.

We were led into a small dressing room—coed from the looks of it—and the slave minder pointed to a rack of dresses and suits. "Get yourself presentable, and then we'll go out into the main reception hall. You have five minutes."

She left the room and closed the door, presumably locking us in from the sound of the click.

"Five bucks says Steph is a Gristle," Ben told the room, and we all laughed as Stephanie gave him the middle finger, but then smacked his butt. Steph and Ben had been dating for over a year now. They didn't live in the same housing building as Shea and me, so I only saw them at school in one shared class, but they were cool people.

Shea started flipping through the dresses. "Reality is we could all be Gristles. No sense in worrying about it."

Steph and I shared a look. Shea was my little pessimist. She never saw the silver lining or had hope that anything would work out. Only on rare occasions did that happen.

James, the fifth person in our group, was quiet, sitting in the corner while staring at the wall. He was one of those perfect guys—smart, utterly gorgeous, and gay.

"What's up, James?" I asked, dropping into the seat next to him as the others spoke in soft voices near the dresses.

"I had a bad dream last night, that's all." He stood abruptly and walked over to get dressed.

I stayed still. James had the gift of future sight. When the fallen angels quickly closed down the powers of anyone below the age of eighteen, there were a few glitches, and not every child's power was caught 100 percent.

James had prophetic dreams.

One day he came into school screaming for everyone to get out and even pulled the fire alarm. We all ran out of the building, and not ten minutes later, a Fallen Army helicopter crashed into the side and blew up our school. He said he'd dreamed about it and just knew it was real. So if James had a bad dream last night, I was all ears.

Absentmindedly, I grabbed a black silk dress in my size, and followed James to the corner of the room where he was disrobing. I started to take my shirt off and James looked at my chest. "Eww, boobs."

A chuckle escaped me as I rolled my eyes, stepping into the dress and pulling the delicate straps over my shoulders. "So...your dream? Should we expect a helicopter crash landing later today or what?"

I could usually make James laugh, as he had a good sense of humor, but this time he was just stone-faced. Dark.

"You need to be careful," James whispered, as I shimmied out of my pants.

I stopped dead. "Okay, elaborate please." What the hell did that mean, and why me? He said *I* needed to be careful. I was already nervous for this ceremony, and now my heart was jackhammering in my chest.

James side-eyed the rest of the group, who seemed to be laughing at Shea's impression of the Fallen Army officer. Then he leaned in closer to me. "You're different. They—"

The door swung open then, and James straightened as the slave minder walked in.

"All right, it's time," she growled, pointing her cattle prod at us.

Frick. Mental telepathy would be a good skill to have right now.

I followed my group out of the dressing room with my knees knocking together in fear. If James said I needed to be careful, I was royally screwed.

CHAPTER 2

We were sat apart from the free souls in alphabetical order, and I was sitting next to the wench with the cattle prod. That meant I couldn't ask James what the hell he'd meant, nor could I even freak out with Shea. I had to just sit there and let my wild imagination dream up wild theories.

After I turned around, I found my mom and Mikey's faces in the crowd. They were standing in the nosebleed section, but seeing their faces only made me more nervous. Now the ceremony was starting, and I was pretty sure I would faint from the amount of adrenaline pumping into my veins.

"You're different. You need to be careful," James had said. If that wasn't an ominous warning, I didn't know what was.

I hadn't been watching the stage, but at the sound of a booming voice, my gaze was drawn upward.

"Welcome, Citizens of Earth!"

A shock ran through me as I saw the fallen angel before me. Archangel Raphael. Standing over six feet tall, with wavy golden hair, and piercing blue eyes, he looked to be in his early thirties; the same as when I'd met him. I had forgotten until now that the fallen didn't age. His long, white gossamer wings glowed so brightly that it was hard to look directly at him. He stood to the right of the stage on pearlescent white tiles, while the left half was tiled in a black onyx stone, where a Grimlock demon stood, glaring at the fallen.

"Thirteen years ago today, a war raged in Heaven, and we mistakenly brought that war to Earth," the angel admitted as the Grimlock demon rolled his eyes. "We could not take back what we had done to humanity, but we could at least let your power lie dormant for a time, until you could come of age. Now is the time to let that power free, so you may train with your assigned academy and earn your rightful place in society."

I'd heard rumors of a kid who fled the Awakening ceremony. He lasted about two years on the road before his powers started to emerge by themselves. He had the power of a Beast Shifter, predominantly demon, although he was a free soul. With no one there to train him, he'd attacked an entire town and then was killed when the Fallen Army showed up to contain the mess. Moral of the story: Go to the Awakening, get your power, and train at your given academy. The powers could only be contained for so long.

The demon stepped forward, casting a long shadow upon the archangel. "When we call your name, you will step up to the stage and walk to the white area. After Raphael unlocks your power, you will exit right, and be enrolled in Fallen Academy if you are a free soul and left to be enrolled in Tainted Academy if you are demon bound." He grinned, giving us all a view of both sets of his razor-sharp teeth.

The angel hit the Grimlock demon with a glare that gave me the chills.

"Let's begin," Raphael announced, and the demon stepped back, exiting center stage to sit at a table with another demon I recognized.

My mom's boss, Master Burdock, a Brimstone demon.

The one who held our contracts sat smugly in his seat, his furry black horns sticking up off his head and going straight up like ears. I'd heard many stories of how he gored those who upset him. He was a cross between a bull and a man, and he was about to be my new master. A demon with the most haunting black, shiny eyes you ever saw.

"Tilly Anderson. Free soul," Raphael announced, and my attention was pulled to the center stage again.

Raphael stood inside of the white half of the stage, and just over his left shoulder was a guy in his early twenties. A Celestial. He was tall, with dark brown hair that was long and spiky on top, with short buzzed sides. The ethereal wings he wore had me spellbound. They glowed at certain angles, and the white feathers looked like they contained electricity as they danced with blue light.

I knew who that guy was. He was the Celestial from five years back. Lincoln something. He'd made it in all of the papers. He was very rare in that he held the power of two Celestials within him, Archangel Michael and Archangel Raphael. They said he'd changed the face of the war, that his demon-kill record was one of the highest, and he'd taken back part of the valley for Angel City. Even though demon and fallen were in the same room for the Awakening ceremonies, the war between them was still waging outside of these walls.

Tilly walked nervously up to the stage, and my heart went out to her. Being the first to be called for something like this sucked. It sucked bad. I leaned forward a little, and turned my head to the right, trying to catch Shea's attention, but the slave minder's hand clamped down on my thigh, forcing me to look forward. I bit my tongue to keep myself from lashing out at her. Tilly looked ridiculous in her large, yellow evening gown. We all did. But the fallen were sticklers for ceremony and respect, so I imagined it was for them.

As she stood before the fallen archangel, I could feel her anxiety from where I sat over fifty feet away. The

Awakening was a terrifying thing. To be turned into a monster at random for the rest of your life—how could anyone look forward to that? I noticed a bunch of other Fallen Army officers waiting to the right of the stage to greet her once she was done. Once her powers were revealed, she would immediately be enrolled in Fallen Academy, the illusive and fancy training school for the free souls. Unless she was a Gristle. That was the only supernatural race that didn't get schooling; you just exited the stage and were given a job working for the city sanitation department.

Raphael held his hands above her head and a golden orange dust began to fall from his palms, saturating her body. We all stared in shock at the golden dust that coated her skin, making her glow like an angel atop a Christmas tree. I saw the appeal of the dresses now. She looked breathtaking. But the beauty was short-lived. Soon, she started breathing roughly, her body lurching forward as she doubled over in pain.

I had never seen an Awakening ceremony, since it was only for the families of those involved and was never televised. Now I knew why. Tilly made a whining noise and then, as if it had never existed, the dust disappeared. She stood shakily and looked out to the crowd. *Holy shit.* Her once-blue irises were black, her skin looked as white as paper, and her canines were more pronounced.

Raphael took one look at her and nodded. "Tilly Anderson. Nightblood. Welcome to Fallen Academy."

I heard weeping in the upper deck, and guessed it was Tilly's mother. Nightbloods couldn't go outside in the day or they had some type of allergic reaction. They were trained and used in the war for their extreme strength and speed, but to the free souls, they were seen as an offspring of the tainted. Nightbloods were demon gifted, along with Beast Shifters, Necromancers, and Dark Mages. Tilly would be feared by those in her community for the rest of her life, and she would probably end up moving to Demon City just to feel normal.

Tilly cast her head down in shame and exited the stage, walking across the white tiles, and down to the waiting Fallen Army to get her new government-issued identification. She would be matched with a Nightblood master teacher for her training.

"Brielle Atwater. Demon bound." Raphael's voice snapped me from my remorse for Tilly.

No. Fricking alphabetical order!

I stood, a wave of dizziness hitting me as adrenaline coursed through me, and my heart rattled against my chest. I walked numbly to the stage, trying not to trip over my too-long, black silk dress.

"You got this!" Shea yelled. I heard the slave minder shush her, but it made me smile the slightest bit, and I walked a little taller. No matter what happened today, I would still go home tonight and be with Shea, my mom, and my little brother. Nothing would change that. If I worked a shitty job for the rest of my life, then so be it. I still had my family.

Before I knew it, I had reached the stage, and stood before the fallen angel.

"Brielle." He said my first name as if we were dear friends. It both made me nervous and comforted me at the same time.

"Yes, sir?" I didn't know what protocol was. I'd grown up around demons, not these nice, winged creatures.

Raphael looked sadly down at me. "I'm sorry for the circumstances in which you find yourself," he whispered.

For some reason, I wanted to burst into tears. What was he doing? Throw the freaking glowing dust on me and be done with it already! Saying heartfelt shit wasn't going to get me through this; it was only going to make me look weak.

I simply nodded, holding back my emotions. Looking past him, I saw Lincoln appear over his shoulder and glare at me as if I was the scum of the earth. That was more like it. More of what I was used to from these people—looking down on me for being slave bound.

I was tempted to give him the middle finger but thought better of it, instead deciding to focus my attention on the huge palms that had just spread out above me. I was standing in the presence of a fallen archangel, a being with more power than I could ever imagine.

Before I could think more on it, the dust began to fall.

It lay on my skin, settling into the pores there, tickling as it worked its way into my body. I felt a zinging sensation as an unseen energy moved up and down my back. The tickling gave way to a burning, and I started to sweat. Would I be a Gristle? Or worse, some form of a demon like Tilly? What if I sprouted horns? I just wanted to be something middle of the road. Not too low but not too high. If you were too powerful, they were calling you to the front lines of the war after you graduated Tainted Academy. I just wanted my life to stay the same.

A red-hot pain shot from my navel to my chest and out through my shoulder blades as I fell forward with a shriek. The pain was unlike anything I'd ever felt before, and the edges of my vision went black as I fought to stay conscious. My back was on fire, and I'd bet my mother's life that I had just endured a pain worse than childbirth. Bile came up my throat, but I swallowed it down. I tried to keep quiet, but at the sight of a bright, blinding light shooting out from behind me, and a ripping sensation down my back, I screamed. I screamed bloody freaking murder.

Dresses? They gave us dresses to get through this? Where's the Vicodin? Morphine? Anything!

The pain started to pulse, giving way from a sharp stabbing to a dull throb. The gasps from the crowd gave me the first indication that something bonkers had just happened. I didn't dare move. My skin felt like it was on fire all over. It hurt so bad that I wanted to scream again.

"Brielle!" Shea shouted, and I heard a commotion in

the seats. I looked up and squinted. Everything was too bright, noises too loud, smells too strong.

"She's angel blessed," Raphael's words were the tiniest whisper, I wasn't sure I'd even heard it.

Angel blessed.

There were only four angel-blessed powers compared to the four demon-gifted things you could become. I looked down at my hands, but other than a shimmery glow on my skin, they looked no different. I tried to stand but felt off-balance. I must've grown horns or something. Or maybe I was a centaur, with animal lower half and human upper half.

Murmurs started on the Fallen Army side and it made me nervous. They hardly broke protocol, but now they were gasping, pointing, stepping closer.

"Get up!" the Grimlock demon roared, and fear flushed through me. Once again, I tried to stand, and that's when I noticed what was wrong. Turning my head behind me, I glimpsed a shimmery set of Celestial wings. They were pitch-black.

Oh shit.

Raphael's hand came out to steady me, and a warm, soothing balm coursed through my body, taking away all the pain. I could breathe a little easier without the throbbing pain between my shoulders.

I had wings. Black freaking wings. I'd never heard of a black-winged Celestial. They were all white. All of them. Always.

"Brielle Atwater. C-celestial." Raphael's voice cracked as he spoke.

I couldn't bear to look at the crowd.

"Come forward and receive your slave mark," the Grimlock demon said, standing at the very edge of the black line on the stage. I tried to release my arm from Raphael's hand, and step over the line when his grip became viselike.

"She's with us," the fallen archangel hissed.

What. The. Frick did he just say?

Lincoln stepped closer to me, and pulled a glowing sword as I stared in shock at the Grimlock demon, whose horns had begun to spew black smoke.

"You will honor the accords, or we will war right now! Give. Her. To. Me!" the Grimlock roared. My mother's master demon stood and walked closer.

Raphael looked pained, his features tightening. "You tricked her mother into the contract. She didn't know it involved her firstborn."

Whoa. How the hell did he know that?

Master Burdock clapped loudly, and in his once bare palms was suddenly a tan parchment. It had tiny golden writing, and at the bottom, a red bloody thumbprint. My mother's.

"It's her fault for not reading the entire thing. Now hand me my slave or bring Hell upon the earth once again," Master Burdock crooned.

Raphael was holding me so tightly that my wrist began to hurt. At that thought, his grip lessened.

"No," Raphael said, and the walls shook with his voice, as if it had been amplified a thousand times.

The Grimlock demon looked at one of the slave minders that stood beyond the stage. "Bring me her mother so I may kill her."

"No!" I lurched forward, but Raphael yanked me back.

"Do *not* cross that line," Raphael whispered.

I looked at him incredulously. "Let. Me. Go!" I demanded, and I saw the hurt cross his face. One rule I knew the fallen were big on was free will. They *had* to honor our free will.

He bit his lip. "You don't understand. It's not final yet. If you take that mark—"

"Let *go*," I said with more authority, cutting him off, and a rising of power crackled within me. At the same time, I heard my mother scream in the stands.

He dropped my arm, eyes wide in shock, and stepped backward a foot.

"Stupid girl," Lincoln spat.

"Screw you," I shot back at him, then stepped out of the white area of the stage and over the line into the black. Where I belonged. The collective gasp from the Fallen Army made me sick. A literal nausea washed over me as I stepped closer to the Grimlock demon, who was practically salivating as he looked at my black wings.

"She knows not what she does," Raphael whispered to Lincoln.

The Grimlock demon stared into my eyes, and I felt the nausea rise to epic proportions. "Kneel to me and honor your contract as a slave to the tainted."

Suddenly I felt regret. The urge to run, to *fly* the hell away from there. *Anything* but take the mark. Then I heard my mother whimper in pain behind me, and I fell to my knees willingly. My mother was a slave, I was a slave, and there was nothing we could do about it. Mikey was a free soul, and I needed to look forward to that.

With lightning-quick moves, the Grimlock's thumb snaked out and touched my forehead, igniting a searing pain. When he pulled away, I knew I bore the red mark. The mark of a slave to the baddies.

"It's done," the Grimlock confirmed with a sigh of relief.

"We still get to train her. You don't have anyone who can contain her powers, and you know it," Raphael added from behind me.

What?

The Grimlock scowled. "For six hours a day. No more."

Raphael must've nodded because the Grimlock told me to stand. When I did, he gave me one last smug look. "Go home," he said, and the mark on my head flared to life with searing pain. It was an order, and orders had to be obeyed.

After the Awakening, there was always a fancy

banquet where you could eat dessert to your heart's content and dance until midnight. It was the one thing we had to look forward to, the one thing the fallen did for us. An apology of sorts for getting us into this mess. I didn't want to go home. I wanted to stay and see what Shea's power was, to dance and eat chocolate, but I knew better than to argue after that scene.

"Yes, Master," I answered through clenched teeth, then turned to face the crowd.

Shea was halfway down the aisle with a cattle prod stuck to her back, and my mother was on her knees with Master Burdock's hand in her hair, grabbing a fistful. As I made my way toward them, she pulled from his grasp and ran to me, wrapping her arms around me.

"What am I?" I whispered to her, because a black-winged Celestial wasn't a thing.

"I don't know baby, but I think it's important," she replied.

Yeah, no shit.

An archangel almost started another war over me. At this point, I'd have taken being a Gristle.

———•·•———

When we exited the Awakening ceremony, there had been a sleek black SUV waiting for us. Courtesy of my new boss; he probably didn't want these black wings riding the public bus and starting a panic. I tried to retract them, to think them back into hiding, but nothing worked, and when I sat on them, it hurt. I just wanted to cry as I laid in the back of the car.

Arriving home, I went straight to my room without dinner. My mom and Mikey tried to talk to me, but I wasn't interested.

Alone in my room with my thoughts, the tears came. I was lying in an awkward position on my bed with pillows under my shoulders so I didn't hurt my wings. They were jet-black, and very…real. Like an arm or a foot, I could feel them. I'd never heard of a demon slave Celestial before. Celestials were so rare, and the ones that did pop up were whisked away into the Fallen Army, and given the highest officer ranking. That asshat Lincoln was second in command next to the archangels, and he was only twenty-two. Celestials were a big deal, I knew, but what could I do?

I replayed that moment on stage over and over again. Raphael had told me not to cross that line. Why? As if I had a choice. I had to fulfill my contract. I wasn't going to sacrifice my mother for my own freedom if that's what he'd expected.

What had me the most nervous was the unknown. What would the demon masters ask me to do for them, knowing I had this power? Would they put me on the front lines of the war? Would they make me kill for them? The thought made me physically sick. I'd always been firmly on the fallen side of things, as they were the do-gooders. No one went hungry in Angel City, no one got killed for making a mistake. Now I was worried I had ranked too high and would have to do awful things, things I wasn't morally okay with, just to survive.

There was a light knock at my door.

"Go away," I told my mom, wiping my tears.

The door opened and I was ready to yell at her when I saw it was Shea and she was holding a box of Cloud Nine Donuts. My mouth immediately watered.

"You didn't," I gaped in awe.

Shea shrugged, stepping in and kicking the door closed with her foot, before setting the donut box before me. She bore the red crescent moon tattoo, just as I did.

"I'm a powerful Mage now, baby. I can do whatever I want." She smirked, indicating the donuts.

"A Mage?" I gasped.

Vulnerability crossed her features before it was gone, and then she nodded smugly.

Well, this day just got crazier.

Mages were second in power to Celestials, and normally went to Fallen Academy, but if you were demon bound, then you went to Tainted Academy to learn dark magic.

"Your school?" I swallowed hard, praying she would tell me that Raphael had fought for her to train at Fallen Academy as well.

"Tainted Academy," she confessed in a hollow voice.

Shit. Mages who studied dark magic turned evil.

They were forced to invoke demonic powers and do awful things. That was possibly worse than what happened to me.

"We're screwed," I stated with finality.

She popped open the box and the sugary sweet smell wafted into the air. "We're screwed, but we have Cloud Nine Donuts."

I gave her a weak smile. This was an old joke between us. The day we met, she asked me what I missed most about living in Angel City. I'd declared Cloud Nine Donuts. These weren't normal donuts. They were filled with magic; the owner was a Light Mage, and all of the donuts had spells on them. The bliss bomb was my favorite. One bite and you were laughing hysterically for ten minutes. Shea preferred the mellow melon. Half a donut and you were sacked out for two hours. Not to mention how good they tasted. "Seriously, how did you get them?" I eyed a bliss bomb. Its red cherry glaze was unmistakable.

The lines were hours long to buy them, and they cost a fortune. Shea had only had them once, to celebrate our sixteenth birthdays. My mom had bought just two donuts for us. She'd had to get the day off work to travel into Angel City, and I was sure she'd saved for months. It was our only present that year. I'd never seen an entire box before. It must've cost a grand, easily.

She smiled. "They were serving them at the banquet. I flirted with the waiter and hid a box under my dress."

Some of them looked mashed together. Now I knew why. "You're the best," I told her, grabbing a bliss bomb as she grabbed a bright orange one I couldn't identify.

"Cheers." We smacked our donuts together and took a bite. The second that tart cherry hit my tongue, I was flooded with euphoria. Joy bubbled up inside of me and I burst out laughing. Shea was chewing hers, looking perplexed.

"I can't tell what mine does," she said, but the second she spoke, we both cackled in laughter. Her voice sounded like she'd sucked in helium.

We spent the next hour overdosing on donuts, the effects only lasting a few minutes. We'd saved the mellow melon for last.

"Ready to chill?" she asked, breaking the lime-green donut in half.

"So ready." I wanted to sleep the day right away and worry about everything tomorrow.

We both sank our teeth into the donut and an immediate calm fell over me. I should've started with that one, the one thing that could tamper my buzzing anxiety.

Shea laid her head at my feet, looking up at me from the bottom of my bed.

"You have black wings," she stated in a dreamy voice.

I figured the donuts were mixing, making her a little

loopy. I was also pretty sure you had to be twenty-one to eat some of them.

"I do," I answered as sleep beckoned me.

I was just about to drift off when Shea's warbled voice reached me. "I won't let you go dark, if you don't let me," she declared.

My throat tightened. It was my biggest fear, turning evil because the demons used me as a puppet for their bidding. Scooching down as far as I could without folding my wing, I grasped Shea's hand.

"I'll kill you before I see you become a Dark Mage," I promised her.

She smiled. "Good."

And then sleep took us both.

CHAPTER 3

THE NEXT MORNING, I WAS WOKEN BY MY MOTHER nudging me with her foot. I cracked open an eyelid and glanced at the clock. It was 5:00 am, not even light out.

"No," I mumbled and rolled over, but a sharp stabbing in my back alerted me that I still had huge angel wings and couldn't just 'roll over' on them.

My mom nudged me again. "Get up. A car just arrived for you from Fallen Academy," she whispered, so she wouldn't wake Shea. "Your classes will be from 6:00 am to noon each day, so as not to interfere with your demon work duties."

My eyelids snapped open. "Are you kidding me?" I glared at my mom, though I knew she was just the messenger.

She shrugged. "Get showered and dressed. That boy from the stage yesterday is waiting in the car outside."

I sat up abruptly and winced as I realized how stiff my right wing was from lying on it all night. *Lincoln's here? In Demon City?* I thought they caught fire when they crossed the border, or something like that.

My gaze went back to my wings. "How can I shower with these things?" I was still wearing my dress from last night.

She shrugged. "Figure it out. I don't think he's keen on waiting."

I groaned and crossed the room quickly to my bathroom. That guy had already been on my shit list, but now he was messing with my sleep.

Awkwardly, I banged around my shower and got myself as clean as possible given the circumstances. After shrugging into skinny black cargos and tying my long, blond hair into a top knot, I stared at my T-shirt options. Nothing was going over my head, so I was going to have to step into it and bring it up. My bra was easy to fasten, but stepping into a tight gray tank top was proving difficult. I had finally pulled the straps up when my mom knocked again.

"He said he doesn't have time to train a princess and he's leaving," she told me through the door.

That motherfricker. I pulled open the door to see my mom waiting with a to-go coffee cup and bagel in hand. I grabbed the breakfast, wished her a goodbye, and slipped into my boots, quickly zipping them up.

He wakes me up at 5:00 a.m., makes me rush through

my first shower with these gigantic wings, and now I'm running!

I hated running. He was going to get an earful. I burst through the door just in time to see a brand-new, white SUV driving away.

He wouldn't dare!

"Morning, Brielle," Bernie's sweet voice came from inside his tent.

Shit! I'd forgotten to bring him dinner last night. I chucked the bagel into the tent. "Morning. Sorry, but I'm late. We'll catch up later!" I shouted and took off, pushing into a full sprint.

Leaping into the road, I did the first thing I could think of—I chucked my coffee cup, and watched in delight as it crashed into the back window of Lincoln's SUV, the brake lights glowing an angry red. I then walked calmly to the passenger door and jerked it open, coming face-to-face with the Celestial.

Lincoln was annoyingly gorgeous. Even now, as he glared at me with those piercing blue eyes and pursed lips, I couldn't deny that he was extremely attractive. That didn't stop me from giving him a piece of my mind.

"Listen, buddy. I had the worst night of my life yesterday, I'm still recovering from a Cloud Nine Donuts hangover, and I just wasted a perfectly good cup of coffee, so you need to chill out."

The corner of his lips twitched, but he remained stoic. "*You* listen, princess. Every minute I stay in Demon City feels like a thousand knives are tearing into my back, so get in the car or *go home.*"

Asshole. I reeled back in shock. Now that he mentioned it, he did look like he was in pain. I thought it was just anger at me. *I guess they don't go up in flames, they just feel like crap.*

"I can't fit in there with my wings," I told him, crossing my arms and staring at the tiny hole he expected me to crawl into.

He rolled his eyes and leaned forward, reaching out to me. I flinched and his face softened. "I need to touch them."

Oh. I leaned into the car and his right hand tenderly stroked the top of my left wing, sending chills down my arms. With a quick, sharp pain at my back, they were gone. Just like that.

"Now, get in," he ordered.

And we're back to Captain Asshole.

I climbed into the car and fastened my seat belt. "You owe me coffee."

He just gave me a side glance but didn't say a word.

The car was brand-new, literally still had the sticker on the side of the window. "Nice ride," I admired.

"I'm glad you like it, because I can't come pick you up every day. Being in this cesspool is too painful. The car is yours to use during the course of your studies. Compliments of Fallen Academy," he told me nonchalantly.

My mouth popped open. "Say what?" The course of my training was *four years*.

"So technically you just threw coffee at your own car." He smiled smugly as he turned onto the 105, which would take us into Angel City.

Jerk. He was just like the rest of them, always judging. Judging my mom for taking the slave mark, judging me for crossing over the line yesterday. I crossed my arms and decided to ignore him the rest of the way.

Ignoring my stomach growling and the lack of coffee in my system proved harder than anything.

As Angel City came into view, I found myself pondering why he'd been sent to retrieve me anyway. Was he going to be my new trainer? He was a baby. I was sure there were other Celestials who were more qualified to train me than someone with five years of experience.

"Why exactly are you, my trainer?" I asked, as the car slowed at the border crossing. One look at Lincoln and the guard waved us through. The second our car crossed over, I saw some of the agitation leave Lincoln's face, but not much.

He gave me a side glance. "I'm the only one who offered."

I scowled. "Bullshit."

He chuckled. "You think everyone was jumping at the chance to train a dark Celestial?"

My skin prickled at those words. "Is that what they're calling me?"

He shrugged. "And worse."

I stared out the window, an instant depression settling over me. My body felt heavy, numb. "What's worse than a dark Celestial?" Dark meant evil. Basically they thought I was a flying demon.

Lincoln hesitated, as if he wanted to protect me from hearing the worst.

"Oh please. Don't suddenly become a nice guy," I told him, and he bristled.

"Fine. I overheard some at Fallen Academy saying you could be some kind of archdemon."

My legs turned to Jell-O with fear. "Archdemon? What's that?"

He took the next freeway exit and my old neighborhood came into view. The happy flowering plants that hung over the balconies reminded me of better times.

Fallen Academy was in the beautiful city of Santa Monica, minutes from the beach. It used to be a Catholic school that they built onto across from a beautiful park. As a kid, I dreamed of going there one day.

I guess I got my wish.

"I don't know," Lincoln said honestly, "but they're hoping they're wrong, or that they can at least train you to be good."

Of all the things that'd been said, that one stung. "I'm not *bad*! Just because of my mother's choice, I'm suddenly the harbinger of evil?"

Lincoln ignored me and turned down a side road that

led to the gates of Fallen Academy. The entire school grounds were enclosed by fifteen-foot-high stone walls.

I wasn't letting him get off that easily.

"I'm not a bad person. My mom isn't a bad person. We just work for bad people." Right? My moral lines had blurred since I'd moved into Demon City to save my father's life.

Lincoln pulled up to the guard gate, and once again they let him through after one look at him. As the gates opened, I sucked in a breath at the sight. I'd never been inside, only seen pictures. The well-manicured grounds and stone buildings had that regal, old-world feel. It was breathtaking.

Turning to face me, Lincoln peered into my eyes. "You were given a choice, and you chose to take the mark. To work for everything that's bad in this world."

So yesterday was a choice? If I hadn't crossed that line, Raphael would've somehow annulled my demon contract? My mother would've been slaughtered.

My mouth opened, aghast. "Weren't you there? They were going to kill my mother!"

He shrugged, pulling up to the curb in front of the main office. "War has casualties."

Then he opened the car door and jumped out, slamming it in my face.

Supreme Asshole of the Year!

I stared at my bagel-less and coffee-less hands as rage boiled within me. I wouldn't last four years with this guy. I wouldn't last another hour. I gave myself five minutes alone in the car, practicing the calm breathing techniques my little brother had taught me. When I was ready, I exited the vehicle and went into the door that Lincoln had gone through.

The second I opened it, a blinding white light filled the space, and I found myself struggling to cover my eyes. Hushed voices cut off the moment I walked in, and the light dimmed to a more manageable level. When my eyes focused on what was before me, I nearly fell to my knees in awe.

"Oh. I thought I was just picking up my schedule," I explained nervously. Lincoln let me keep *four* archangels waiting. I would kill him.

"That's okay, Brielle. Please come join us," Raphael offered, waving me over to where they stood in a large office.

I surveyed the angels before me. I knew the one with the sword was Michael, but I didn't recognize the other two. Either way, I was scared shitless. Were they going to hurt me? Expunge the evil out of me?

"No one is going to hurt you, dear," an angel who stood over seven feet tall with long, blond hair stated.

Oh my God. Mind readers. I was so screwed.

I cleared my throat and stepped into the expansive office. Michael was leaning against a bookcase, watching me keenly, his sword hung from his waist.

Lincoln was standing in the corner, arms crossed and

scowling at me. "Raph isn't sure which one of them has endowed you with their gifts, so there will need to be a little ceremony before you can get your tattoo of light," he explained from where he rested.

Ceremony? Tattoo? I realized then that I knew nothing about this life. These people. I'd been surrounded by demons for the entirety of my teen years, and the Celestials were too rare for me to know anything but rumor. I must've looked panicked, because the archangel with the long blond hair stepped closer to me. His wings were massive and hard to look at for too long.

"I'm Gabriel." He gestured to a dark brown-haired angel, standing in front of the fireplace. "That's Uriel. You've met Raphael, and I'm sure you know Michael, since he's the famous one." He grinned.

"Jealous of the stories, my brother?" Michael joked, beaming.

Oh. My. God. They were so…normal.

"Hey…I'm Brielle." I waved nervously. *Why is Lincoln still scowling at me? Can't he just leave?*

Raphael stood from his seat behind the desk. "I've taken the responsibility of teaching the angel blessed, and standing as guardian over this school, but Michael, Gabriel, and Uriel do not often visit unless it's a special circumstance. They're needed elsewhere, tending to the war."

Oh shit. Am I the special circumstance? My stomach knotted. *I just cussed inside my head. I hope he didn't hear that!*

Raphael's lips curled into a smile. "Normally we would have your Choosing ceremony publicly, but under the circumstances"—he gestured to my back, where my wings would've been had they been out—"we thought keeping it private was best."

I swallowed. I had no freaking clue what a Choosing ceremony was, so I just nodded. "I prefer privacy when at all possible." Especially when it came to being the only freak with black wings.

Raphael nodded. "Good. If you'll step forward and produce your wrist, I'll get it over with quickly." He opened the snaps of a case on his desk and flipped the lid back, revealing a golden dagger with engravings.

My eyes bugged out and I backed up. "Wait, what?"

"You frightened her," Michael said, sounding annoyed with Raphael.

Raphael frowned. "That was not my intention."

"May I?" Lincoln offered. "You have to explain things in detail with humans. They don't trust unconditionally like you all do." He stepped from the corner to approach me.

Did he just tell a room full of archangels that I didn't trust them?

Murder. Dead.

Raphael's brow knotted.

Shit. Kidding. Happiness and rainbows.

Now he was trying to hold in a laugh. Frick, they could *totally* read my mind.

49

"Brielle," Lincoln said, pulling my attention to him. He rolled up his sleeves, showcasing two tattoos, one on each forearm. One was a magnificent sword in a brilliant blue. The other was a pair of cupped hands glowing an orangish yellow. "When I found out I was a Celestial, Raphael made a small cut on my wrist. Two symbols on the knife glowed, indicating I had powers from both Michael and Raphael. Then I got these tattoos to ignite their individual powers within me."

Oh. So that's the Choosing ceremony.

"Okay." I shrugged.

Lincoln nodded and then stepped back into the corner of the room, taking his warmth with him, and leaving me suddenly alone.

"Now that we've awakened your powers, you'll need the tattoo of light to help harness the angel light that lives within you," Michael stated. "That's what this ceremony does. Without it, you would…experience discomfort as your powers emerged. Your tattoos will help you harness the archangel's power you possess, without harming your human body."

Oh. Wow. I hadn't even thought about what powers I might have, beyond that of my freakish black wings and flying. I missed Shea right then. She was the strong one who would stick her wrist out and say, *Let's get this over with!*

I decided to channel her before I lost my nerve, stepping forward and holding out my wrist to Raphael.

"Will that thing show if I'm an archdemon?" I blurted out.

So much for being brave.

Raphael looked shocked. "Who told you that you might be an archdemon?"

I tried to clear my thoughts but I was too nervous. Lincoln popped into my head, and Raphael turned over his shoulder, pinning Lincoln to the wall with his gaze.

Lincoln squirmed. "I merely repeated a rumor."

Michael stood taller. "I've seen rumors start wars."

Lincoln stared at his own feet.

Shit, I got him in trouble. He's going to hate me more than he already does.

"Brielle, let me tell you something." Raphael cupped my hand, and warmth went through my arm. "No one, and I mean no one, is born evil. Even those who turn down the wrong path can always come back from it. No matter what."

I swallowed hard, and my eyes flicked to Lincoln, who was still staring at his shoes. It wasn't lost on me that he'd not answered my question about being an archdemon.

"Ready?" Raphael asked.

The moment my head bobbed in consent, the blade licked across my skin. I hissed as he squeezed a few droplets onto the hilt and then released my hand.

"Sorry, child."

Lincoln was suddenly there, reaching for my arm. "Would you like me to heal it?"

He could do that? Of course he could; he was some hybrid healer-warrior poster child.

"I'm fine," I told him, putting pressure on the cut with my other hand.

Lincoln frowned. "Come on, just let me heal it. You don't have to be so stubborn about it."

I glared at him, giving him my best *I will cut you* look.

"Free will. She said no," Michael reminded Lincoln.

Lincoln grumbled something under his breath and walked away.

The other three archangels started to come forward then, pressing their collective power in on me. It felt like the air had charged with static electricity. The dagger was doing a crazy, glowy thing.

Peeking forward, I saw a sword symbol light up. "Ahh, lovely. Michael, she's one of yours," Raphael said enthusiastically.

A thrill of excitement went through me and I looked over at the archangel with the powerful muscles and sword. Michael grinned, but then his face morphed into a mask of confusion. I followed his gaze just as another symbol lit up, glowing hands. That was the same symbol on Lincoln's arm, Raphael's. I was a dual Celestial hybrid like Lincoln?

I was about to say something when another symbol

lit up, a pen, and another, a flame. Finally a fifth one began to light up, but Raphael covered the dagger with his palm, and shoved it back in the case before I could see what it was. His expression was complete and utter shock, but there was something else there.

Fear.

What on Earth would be so bad that it would scare an archangel?

"She is blessed by all of us," he declared in a haunting tone.

The room started to sway. I didn't know if it was from standing too close to the archangels, or finding out I had *all* of their powers, but it was too much.

I started falling backward and the blackness took me.

CHAPTER 4

THE FIRST THING THAT CAME BACK TO ME WAS sound. I could hear hushed voices talking over me.

"Do you think she's the one from the prophecy?" I recognized Michael's voice.

"I don't know, but I do know she's an innocent child in all of this, and we should do our best to protect and guide her." That one was Raphael.

"Of course!" Michael sounded offended. "I'll try to get word to Metatron, see if he can share any insight."

Raphael sighed again, longer and deeper that time. "Do not bring our brothers into this. Metatron has firmly taken his side. We'll deal with it."

"She's awake," Gabriel said, and my eyes snapped open.

What the hell had they been talking about? I didn't

want to know, but the reason for my fainting had all come back to me. I moaned and sat up, feeling dizzy.

"Brielle, are you feeling all right?" Raphael swam into view.

I nodded. "I guess."

"Of course she's not all right. She's scared." Michael looked concerned.

I straightened my shoulders. "I'm fine."

Michael grinned. "That's my bravery." He winked.

I blushed.

Raphael rolled his eyes. "Let's not start taking credit for everything she does. Brielle, you have to be back in Demon City in five hours, but it'll take that long to get your tattoos of light. Are you okay with proceeding?"

Ever since I'd seen all those symbols light up, something wild had unleashed within me. I figured it was my power, and it frightened me. If the tattoos would help contain that, harness them, or whatever, I wanted them sooner rather than later.

"I'm ready." I stood, hands fisted at my side.

Michael was staring behind me, looking sad and longing at the same time. I spun around, expecting to see Lincoln, but he was nowhere in sight. Instead, I saw my wings. They must have come out as some defense mechanism.

I shifted uncomfortably.

The Archangel of Protection and Strength stepped forward and placed a strong hand on my shoulder. "It was admirable what you did for your mother." His eyes rested on the crescent moon tattoo on my forehead. "Not a wise choice, but admirable."

That close to him, I could feel his power pressing in on me like a heavy blanket. He must've sensed it, because the moment I thought it, he pulled his hand back and stepped away, walking over to the desk where Raphael had four golden goblets set out.

I frowned, stepping closer. "You guys drink? I had no idea." Maybe we were going to toast before getting my tattoo. This school already seemed more relaxed than what I'd heard.

"Blood of my blood," Raphael said, and slashed the golden dagger across his wrist.

My hand flew to my throat as the goblet filled with the thick crimson fluid.

"Blood of my blood," Michael stated and took the dagger from Raphael, doing the same thing.

I started to back up, fully intent on running the hell out of there and never coming back, but on my third step, I slammed into a warm, hard body that smelled familiar.

Strong hands came around my arms and spun me, and I came face-to-face with Lincoln. "You okay?" His voice held genuine concern, which shocked me.

"B-b-b-blood." There was no way I was drinking angel blood. No. Way.

He peered past me and dawning shone on his face.

"Raphael, you have to explain things, remember?" she scolded the archangel.

A human scolding an angel like a friend. What an odd thing to witness.

"Oh, right. I'm sorry. Brielle, our blood will be mixed with tattoo ink, and that will be what's used to help you harness your power," Raphael explained cheerily.

I'm getting angel blood tattoos? Umm, what the what?

Lincoln finally released my arms, looking down at me with pity. "This is the weird part. Tomorrow you'll start your studies, and get your ass kicked like every other student here. Trust me, it's best to just get this part over with."

Four angel blood tattoos? Should I call my mom? I mean, I'm eighteen, but coming home with four tats is going to throw her into a frenzy. Should the blood be tested for diseases? That was probably a stupid question; they were angels, for crying out loud.

I was still standing there in shock when Michael approached me. "It's been an honor meeting you, Brielle. Now I must go and…tend to some things."

"Oh. Right. You too," I answered nervously.

"Peace be with you, child." Uriel offered with prayer-clasped hands, then exited after Michael.

"May we meet again." Gabriel's feathery voice came from behind me, and then he too was gone.

I wasn't sure what to say in return, so I just stood

there covering my arms. My stomach was eating itself after giving Bernie my breakfast and chucking my coffee at Lincoln.

"Is our escort assembled?" Raphael asked Lincoln.

He nodded. "And Marleen is waiting."

"Brielle, dear, would you like something to eat for the road?" Raphael asked from behind me.

I spun around, no longer able to hold it in. "You totally read minds, don't you?"

His cheeks reddened. "You're a very loud thinker."

Lincoln was giving me a smug grin. *Ugh.*

"I'd love some breakfast. Thank you," I grumbled, because I wasn't sure what to say about the 'loud thinker' thing.

Raphael nodded and disappeared into a hallway at the back of the office. When he emerged, he was holding a muffin and coffee. "Cream with two sugars?" he asked.

My eyes bugged out. "How did you…? You know what, never mind."

I snatched the coffee and chugged it just as a loud knock came at the door. Lincoln stepped forward and opened it, letting three insanely hot Celestial guys in. My eyes immediately fell on the one to the left, his wings glowing a pearly white that gave his dark skin a luminescent glow. He seemed to notice my attention on him and gave me a wink.

Oh. My. God.

"Brielle, these four fine gentlemen will be your

Celestial master guides during your studies at Fallen Academy," Raphael instructed.

My master what?

"I'm Darren," the one who'd caught me looking offered. "I'll be your Uriel master guide." He stuck out his hand.

I shook it. "Brielle."

The next guy stepped forward, super tall with bright blond hair and blue eyes. He looked like a Norse god with tight muscles that wrapped around his arms as he extended his hand. "I'm Blake. I'm your Gabriel master guide."

I shook his soft hand and just nodded stupidly. Shea would shit herself if she saw this many hot guys in one room.

The final guy stepped forward. He looked like he was in his twenties, with dark brown hair and arresting green eyes. "Hello, beautiful. I'm Noah, your Raphael master guide." He winked.

My eyes flicked to Lincoln and then back to Raphael. "Can't Lincoln teach me to control my Michael and Raphael powers?" Not that I wanted him to, but…

Noah burst out laughing. "Not if you want to actually learn anything. Trust me, darling, I'm better with the healing stuff. Lincoln doesn't exactly have a tender heart."

Lincoln groaned, giving Noah a death glare.

"Yeah, I noticed that," I agreed, crossing my arms.

There was a chuckle behind me as Raphael stepped forward with a tray full of the blood goblets. "Still working on that humility, are you, son?" he called out Noah.

He shrugged. "Just educating her, sir."

"Yes, well she's only allowed to be here until noon, so we must hurry. I'd hate to imagine what it would be like to send her back to Demon City with half-finished tattoos of light."

Noah shivered as if that would be an awful thing. At that point I had resigned myself to shock. I'd known being a black-winged Celestial wasn't going to be an easy life, but I never imagined my first day at the academy would involve getting tatted up.

Darren eyed the four goblets and then me. "Four. That's so gnarly."

Raphael frowned. "And remind me again, gnarly isn't bad?"

Darren laughed, showcasing a handsome set of straight, white teeth. "Not in this context, sir."

"Right. Let's go." Raphael flung his hand out, the set of double doors in front of us springing open. I stumbled backward and my wings slammed into Lincoln.

"Sorry," I mumbled.

They started to walk outside when Lincoln reached out and tugged on my arm. "Let's put these away for this little trip, shall we?" He said over my shoulder, right into my right ear. His warm breath cascaded down my neck, giving me chills. His fingers trailed the length of my left wing, stroking from the top to midway down. With a shiver, they retracted, and then he walked in front of me.

"Come on, keep up. This is a dangerous mission," he snapped.

Once I could gather my wits from that little wing massage episode, I ran after him.

"Why is it dangerous?" I asked, stepping out into the open atrium to see no less than twenty armed Fallen Army guards taking orders from Raphael.

Lincoln turned to face me. "One goblet of archangel blood will fetch a fortune on the black market. Four? It's extremely valuable."

Oh. "Why?" I hated asking him questions, because each one gave him the opportunity to be a dick, but I was a curious soul, and I needed to know.

He squinted as he glared at me. "Your demon friends buy them to sell to the Dark Mages for dark magic. Don't act like you didn't know that."

Anger ripped through me, and my wings popped from my back as I stepped into his space. "I don't have demon friends, you prick, and I *didn't* know. You don't know anything about me, so how about from now on, you don't assume, and only speak to me when absolutely necessary."

I blasted past him, knocking into him with one of my wings, and went to stand next to Raphael. He seemed like the only sane one in the bunch.

I suddenly regretted letting my wings out, because now the guards were staring at me like I was the angel of death, fascination mixed with fear in each and every one of their gazes. Considering one of the guards was a centaur, half his body a white horse, I shouldn't have been the freak in the group.

Raphael smiled as I approached, seemingly oblivious to the effect my wings were having on everyone.

"This is Brielle, your charge," he told the guards. Each one nodded slightly when I made eye contact with them.

Raphael then turned to Lincoln. "Protect her well and report back to me when it's done."

My eyes widened. "You're not coming?"

He smiled softly. "If I went, it would be like painting a target on your back. It's best if Lincoln and the others take care of you from now on."

I swallowed hard. I felt so safe around him—probably because he was a freaking archangel, but still. I didn't want to go anywhere with Lincoln. He was an asshole who hated me, and treated me like a demon-loving piece of shit.

Raphael's mouth turned into a frown. "Be patient with those who appear to be against you," he whispered in my ear, patting my shoulder. "Not all is as it seems." Pulling back, he gave me a fatherly look, and a feeling of warmth and peace trickled down my arm. My wings drew into my back again.

I sighed. *This is going to be a long day.*

"All right, let's move out. This is a time-sensitive mission," Lincoln barked.

With a flurry of activity, I was hauled into a row of four blacked-out SUVs. Darren sat on my left, Noah on my right while Lincoln drove and Blake sat shotgun.

"Dude, where is Marleen going to put four tats?" Darren asked Lincoln, leaning forward as he made a hard right turn onto 7th Avenue.

Lincoln's eyes flicked to the rearview mirror at me for a split second. "I dunno. She'll figure it out."

Blake was balancing the tray of blood-filled goblets on his lap, each one having been fitted with a lid to keep the contents from spilling.

"Is this a bad time to mention that I'm scared of needles?" I announced.

Noah was the first to laugh, but soon everyone joined in, minus Lincoln. "Don't worry, I'll be there to take your pain, darlin'." Noah winked at me. Mr. Winky wink was a *wink-happy* dude it seemed.

Lincoln groaned from the front seat. "Noah, are you capable of not hitting on a female? I mean, is that within your realm of skill sets?"

Darren and Blake snickered, but Noah just shrugged. "Sure. I don't hit on Mrs. Topeka."

Lincoln took a hard right turn and then I was totally lost. I didn't know the area, but it was looking seedier and seedier the more we drove.

"She's the seventy-year-old librarian!" Lincoln countered.

That time I smiled. I was gathering from their banter that the boys were all close friends.

"Besides, Brielle is too stubborn to accept your help," Lincoln continued.

I'd always wondered if I was capable of murder, one of those weird thoughts that sometimes cross your mind. Now I was quite sure I was capable of killing Lincoln. I had actually been starting to loosen up and not think about the impending angel blood tattoos when he went and ruined it.

"Oh, Noah, I'd love a healing from you. It's Lincoln who makes me shiver just to think of him touching me," I snapped back.

"Ohhhhh." The car burst into frat boy noises of shame at my smug glare. When Lincoln's murderous eyes flicked up to the rearview mirror, I kept mine forward.

Take that, you venomous, judging bastard.

He took another hard right, the SUVs behind us following, and then pulled up to a shoddy-looking tattoo shop with literally no one on the street. It looked like a vacated and half-condemned street block.

"Where are we?" I asked, mystified.

"This street is spelled to look like a shithole, so no one will come down it. We call it Angel Avenue. It's where we do all of our magical shopping." Noah winked.

The boy was an expert winker. I was venturing to guess he did well with the ladies.

Lincoln scanned the street. The other three SUVs had parked, Fallen Army officers spilling out of them. My eyes roamed over their weapons, guns, swords, bows and arrows. They were varied, and totally badass.

"Blake, you get those goblets inside," Lincoln ordered. "We'll protect her." His tone changed with the word "her," like I was a venomous snake.

"Let's move out." The doors popped open then and we rushed out of the vehicle. The second my boots landed on the curb, the tattoo shop door flew open to a woman in her mid-thirties, with tattooed sleeves, and long red hair.

"Linc!" she shouted excitedly.

Blake had just reached her with the goblets when a dark shadow passed overhead, momentarily blotting out the sun.

"Incoming!" Lincoln shouted, wrapping his big arm around my waist and tucking me into his body as his huge, white wings snapped out. He crouched, bringing me to the ground with him while his wings curled around us to shield me. Bullets and shouts rang out as I stayed pinned beneath his body, eyes wide as saucers.

I grew up in Demon City. Demon gangs were the vilest creatures on Earth, and Shea and I'd had our fair share of run-ins with them. I was robbed quarterly, so I knew we were totally getting jumped right now, and I wasn't going to hide beneath this asshole and get killed. He smelled good, and his pecs against my back were making my stomach do somersaults, but he was still an asshole nonetheless.

I must never forget that.

Lincoln pulled his sword and popped up on his knees, keeping his wings curled forward to protect me. Or cage me in, depending on how you were looking at it.

Reaching into my boot, I pulled out my switchblade and prepared myself to throw down. I wasn't going to have any luck against the guns, but I could gut someone if they got within two feet of me. I was good with blades.

"Lincoln, look out!" I recognized Noah's smooth voice.

Lincoln stood to his full height then, his wings snapping back to reveal me, and I came face-to-face with a Monkshood demon.

Shit.

The Monkshood demons were by far one of the creepiest kinds. They didn't have tongues, so they couldn't speak. They wore hooded cloaks to cover their misshapen bodies, but their red, knobby horns stuck out through the top, and they were masters of mental compulsion. The demon's eyes were glowing blue, which I knew meant he was using his gift of compulsion. Lincoln was staring at him dreamily and lowering his sword. They didn't even need to speak to use their gift, that's how powerful they were. They only needed eye contact to get the job done.

I saw a glint of steel underneath the Monkshood's

cloak and acted quickly. As the demon pulled out his sword, I pushed the button on my switchblade, revealing the sharp knife. Reaching under his cloak, I slashed wildly, cutting into his thick ankles. A roar bellowed from under the demon's cloak, and he broke eye contact with Lincoln to look down at me. The Celestial burst into action, his sword glowing a vibrant blue as he cut down the demon before us. I stayed crouched, assessing the situation, and wondering what the hell I should do.

Turning my head, I took stock of the scene. Demons and Dark Mages had rappelled from the roof, the ropes still dangling. There were a dozen of them, at least, one a Beast Shifter in the shape of a cougar, curled brown horns coming off his head. We had them outnumbered, but the Dark Mages were going to town on the Fallen Army.

A swarm of magical bees was spinning around a group of soldiers, while a demon-bound slave shot bullets, seemingly at random but in our direction. I sat there, crouched and in shock as the human with the red crescent tattoo on her forehead cut down the Fallen Army. It shook me to my core to know I had the same mark on my own head, as did my mother. For the first time, I was regretful about taking the mark. *Maybe it would've been best to just let my father go...*

One of the Fallen Army soldiers was a Light Mage, her hands were glowing a golden yellow as she built up a powerful spell between them. With a battle cry, she thrust her palms outward and the light exploded. I flinched, unsure what it would do. The demons and Dark Mages left standing all began to scream and hiss, their skin growing an angry red as it smoked.

With one final attempt, a tiny twelve-inch-tall Snakeroot demon slammed against the door of the tattoo parlor. When it didn't open, he leapt onto Noah's shoulder and took a chunk out of it with his teeth.

"Ahh!" Noah screamed, and threw the Snakeroot demon on the ground. All of the demons were looking pretty uncomfortable—close to being set on fire, more like it—and collectively must've decided to ditch the plan. It might've helped that Lincoln was holding the bloody head of the Monkshood demon and his sword was doing a swirly thing of blue light.

"Go!" Lincoln roared, then chucked the head onto the street as they scattered.

The demons and their cohort scrambled then, shielded from view by a puff of black mist, and then they were just...gone.

Holy hell on wheels, what just happened?

"Noah!" Lincoln leapt to his friend's side.

Noah was holding his bleeding shoulder with a glowing orange hand, and wincing. "I'm fine," he stated in a gruff voice.

Lincoln turned to me then. "Are you okay?" he asked, his eyes roaming over my body for injuries, before stopping on the switchblade in my hand.

I just nodded, which was about all I could manage at the moment.

Lincoln seemed to be gathering himself as well. "All right, take up the perimeter and radio me if they come back. I'll call the academy for backup. I want fifty more guards here within the hour!" he roared.

The warriors spread out, pulling their weapons, and watching the end of the street where the demons had fled with eagle eyes.

The door to the shop popped open again. "Hey, sweet thing. You okay?" the tattooed young woman asked me. I just nodded while her eyes fell to the shank in my hands.

Oops. I retracted the blade and stuffed it back in my boot.

"Dude, she sliced up that Monkshood demon's ankles. That was hard-core!" Darren announced.

Lincoln was looking down at me like he wanted to say something but thought better of it. "Inside," he finally snarled, and then I was being pulled up, and into the building.

If this was everyday events in Angel City, I was going to have to upgrade my switchblade, and work on my fighting skills.

CHAPTER 5

"Whoa." The tattoo shop was not trashy by any means. I'd been expecting crumbling plaster, maybe some mold, but the floors were a shiny travertine and the walls were smooth plaster with various angel-related artwork painted on them. There was a check-out counter, where a balding older man with Coke bottle glasses was reading through a magazine.

"Hey, Mr. Hensley," Noah called out, his glowing hand still on his injured and bleeding shoulder.

Is he healing himself?

The man looked up, squinted at Noah and frowned. "Hello, son. You okay?"

Noah shrugged. "Snakeroot demon bite. I'll be fine by tonight."

The tattooed woman led us back to her desk. A leather massage table lay next to it, and a tattoo gun was on the desk beside the four goblets of blood. My heart started to pound in my chest.

"Four. So gnarly." The woman grinned and looked me up and down.

I rubbed my arms. "Yeah...about that. I'm a bit needle shy. Can I get like one today and the rest next week?" I laughed nervously.

She looked at me with pity. "Hon, this blood won't last a week, and neither will you without these tattoos. Once a Celestial goes through the Awakening, they need their tattoos of light within twenty-four hours or—"

"Let's just begin, shall we? She's demon bound, so we need to get her back to her side of the city by noon." Lincoln cut her off.

Mothereffing prick! I wasn't sure if shooting fire out of my eyes was going to be one of my gifts, but I sure felt like it right then. I wanted to burn him where he stood. I had the freaking red tattoo on my forehead, everyone and their mom knew what it meant. He didn't need to explain it to people.

She looked down at her feet. "Yeah, I heard."

Pity. Great. She felt bad for me. What an awful feeling to have people pity you.

"Can he wait outside?" I asked, flicking my head to Lincoln.

She grinned. "He can get a bit snippy, can't he?"

My shoulders relaxed. "That's putting it mildly."

Lincoln rolled his eyes and patted the massage table. "Come on, clock's ticking."

I groaned and thrust myself forward, sitting on the table, and pinning him with a glare.

Murder. The guy made my blood boil.

She sat down and started preparing her space, pulling out cellophane and little plastic cups of ink. When she was done, she picked up the tattoo gun, dipped it in one of the goblets and looked up at me.

"I'm Marleen, but you can call me Mar."

I smiled. "Brielle, but you can call me Bri."

Lincoln made what sounded like a gagging noise, and I had to refrain from pulling my switchblade back out.

"So here's the thing," Mar continued. "Tattoos of light aren't like regular tattoos. They bind to your soul, and it can be quite painful. Do you pass out easily?" At her words, the room spun.

"Yes, she does," Lincoln answered for me.

I crossed my arms and turned to face him. "Please tell me it'll be part of my training to practice kicking your ass," I said through gritted teeth.

Marleen flicked the gun on and it started buzzing. "I really like her." She smiled at Lincoln.

He sighed. "Noah, I'll handle her healing. You can't heal her with your shoulder injured."

The serial winker seemed to consider Lincoln's words. "Yeah, if that's cool with her?"

I chuckled. "I don't need a healer. Let's do this," I urged Marleen. If these boys thought I needed a healer for a tattoo, they would always treat me like glass. They were my master teachers or whatever, and I wanted them to know I wasn't frail.

Marleen grinned. "Hard-core. Take notes, boys."

I gave her a conspiratorial smirk and extended my left forearm. Marleen took a deep breath and leaned forward with the buzzing gun. Her eyes flashed silver, and it was only in that moment that I realized she was a Light Mage.

"Lux sancta," she whispered, and a white beam shot out of the tattoo gun and into my arm. The needle came down, and a searing pain like I'd never experienced before, slammed into me.

"Mother fuahhhhhh!" I screamed.

It hurt *everywhere*! Every cell in my body was on fire.

Lincoln extended his hand, which began to glow orange, and I whipped my head in his direction. "Don't touch me. I don't want a healing from someone who thinks I'm the scum of the Earth," I spat. I knew the moment the hurt crossed his face that I might have gone too far. What scrap of kindness was left within him for me had vanished.

His jaw clenched and he stood taller, crossing his arms. "I'm going to walk the perimeter," he stated with barely restrained anger.

When the pain ramped up a notch, I considered crying out his name but bit my lip instead. I'd been through worse; I could handle this. Besides, the guy was a total dick to me, and I wasn't going to give him the satisfaction of letting him know I needed him.

An hour later I had my first wave of nausea.

"I'm gonna be sick!" I shouted, and Mar pulled up the tattoo gun just as I lunged forward and puked into the trash can near her desk.

"Call Lincoln," she instructed Darren, who'd been standing near me, trying to chat with me, and keep my mind off things.

"No," I shouted in between heaving into the trash can. We'd only just finished the first tattoo. I had three more to go and I wanted to die, but my pride held on strong.

Marleen handed me a towel and sighed. "Look, babe, I get it. You and Linc have something going on, but you're not going to be able to sit for the other three without his help."

Dammit.

"What if I came back tomorrow?" I asked hopefully.

She shook her head. "Aside from the magic leaving the blood, you wouldn't make it that long without the tats. These tattoos harness your powers so they don't shatter your earthly body as they come alive."

My eyes bugged out. I'd heard a story about a Celestial who ran off after the Awakening, and they didn't find him in time. He exploded into a ball of light. I'd always thought it was just a wild rumor.

Lincoln arrived then, towering over me and looking gorgeous as I wiped the puke from my mouth. His eyes fell on the blue Michael tattoo on my forearm, the same one he had. It was outlined in angry red swelling.

He didn't speak, which was a first, and probably the smartest thing he'd done all day. Instead, he just extended his hand to help me up.

I could refuse it and be an asshole, but I was too tired to tend to my pride anymore. Reaching out with my good arm, I clasped my hand in his. When we touched, an electric jolt ran through me and I almost pulled away. Then his hand glowed orange, and like a balm on my wound, the pain was chased away.

I sighed in pleasure, as I crawled back onto the table. "You're like a Vicodin," I mumbled in exhausted pain.

He didn't say anything, but the corner of his lips twitched. "And you're like a third-degree burn."

I scoffed. "Oh please. I'm not that bad. Second-degree burn. *Maybe*."

The corners of his lips twitched higher and I decided to make it my mission to see him smile. I bet he had a good smile. The gorgeous assholes always did.

The tattoo gun started again and my entire nervous system jumped into action. Tightening my grip on his palm, I flinched as the light and needle hit my skin. The moment the pain tore into me, it was chased away, and a numbing sensation lay over it. The pain was still there, just on the surface, but nothing compared to what it was before. Lincoln's hand gripped mine, and I flicked my eyes up to see his dark brows pulled together. A chunk of hair stuck to his forehead, which was starting to sweat.

Interesting.

After being in such extreme pain for over an hour, this was a welcome relief and was actually making me quite sleepy. Not enough to fall asleep, but enough to where I could lay my head down and close my eyes, rest my frayed nervous system.

Before I knew it, she was done with the second tattoo. "Okay, I've never done more than two, so where are we putting the others?"

"The backs of her calves?" Darren offered.

My eyes sprang open. "Oh my God, *no*. Calf tattoos are for overweight men in biker gangs."

Marleen cracked up.

Lincoln and I realized at the same time that we were still holding hands. He pulled his away and the pain came rushing back. Wiping it on his jeans, he looked at Marleen. "Does the placement matter?"

She shrugged. "Not at all."

My eyes flicked up to a picture on the wall of a girl in a bikini top with a heart tattoo on her rib cage that said 'Mom' inside.

"Rib cage?" I asked.

Her eyes widened a little. "That's a painful spot."

My mouth popped open. "Is that a joke? There are actual spots that are more or less painful? You're shoving a burning needle of light into my skin. I think it's all the same."

She chuckled. "Your call, kiddo."

I laid back and peeled up my tank top, tucking it into the bottom of my bra. Every single pair of male eyes flicked to my abdomen for a brief second, even Lincoln's, and then they turned their backs, a few of them clearing their throats uncomfortably.

"Oh come on, it's just a belly button. Turn back around." They did as told, keeping their eyes on my face this time.

"It's a pretty cute belly button," Darren offered.

That brought a smile to my lips. "I was thinking that when I start school tomorrow, it might be nice to hide some of my freakiness. I have the black wings, and it would be nice not to parade the four tattoos everywhere."

Marleen frowned. "I want to tell you that college is better than high school, and bullying doesn't exist, but I'd be lying. Fallen Academy is like high school on steroids."

Nervousness ripped through me at her comment, but I tried to play it off. "I grew up with a bunch of demons. I'm sure I can handle some rich snobs, who think they're better than me."

I'd done it. I'd succeeded in making Lincoln smile,

and damn, he had dimples. The second he caught me looking, he expertly turned his smile into a scowl, trying to cover it up. But I saw it. He thought I was funny.

Score.

Oh wait, no, I hate him. I'd forgotten how mean he was because he'd spent the last hour healing me. It was messing with my mind, playing tricks on my emotions.

The tattoo gun turned on again and I braced myself. My mom was going to have a major hissy fit over the tattoos, but I was hoping the knowledge that I would've exploded without them would ease her pain. Agony flared to life on my side and I muttered a curse word.

"*Why!*" I shouted and gripped the edge of the massage table. "Isn't angel blood holy or something? Couldn't it have Novocain in it?" From my toes, up my tailbone and into my scalp, red-hot needles drilled pain into the very corners of my soul.

Marleen smirked. "You're not the first to ask."

Lincoln's hand slipped over mine again, warm, soft, and gentle. I swallowed hard as heat built in my gut. Orange light covered my palm and then the pain lessened.

Sigh.

Shea wasn't going to believe my day. I wasn't even sure how to describe to her what had happened. The fact that I'd had about five hours of sleep and still had an entire work day ahead of me was starting to hit me. Right after my tattoos, I needed to report to my new boss. My mom's boss. He ran a business of reanimating the dead, and I wasn't a Necro, which meant I would probably be given the shitty jobs at his 'clinic' until I graduated Fallen Academy and learned to use my powers.

Then what? Fight against the Fallen Army? Fly into battle and kill one of the people in this room?

Oh God, what have I gotten myself into?

When Marleen was halfway through my third tattoo, I fainted.

"What's wrong?" Lincoln asked, worried, as I'd regained consciousness.

"It's a lot of power, magic, tying itself to her soul. I've never done four before," Marleen explained.

"Finish. Then food," I'd managed to say.

Lincoln frowned. "Order her a pizza," he barked at Noah, who'd been reading magazines in the corner of the room and regrowing his shoulder flesh the entire time.

Marleen was now drawing the last line of the last tattoo, and Darren was feeding me small bites of pizza.

"It's 11:14 a.m.," Lincoln informed the room, as Marleen finished and pulled the gun away.

The room spun as I sat up too quickly. "I gotta get back. Today's my first day with my mom's boss. He'll make her life hell if I'm not there." I pulled my shirt down and tried to stand, but the room did a somersault and then I was falling.

"Whoa, whoa, whoa." Lincoln caught me. "You can't drive or go to work like this."

My eyes found his. "I have to. Nothing about my life is a choice."

He flinched at my words. "Okay...then let me do one more healing on you before you go. I've had my first officer bring your car out front. There's GPS inside. It'll guide you back."

I nodded. "Okay."

"Be back tomorrow at six. You'll study with the four of us until your first class at eight."

I frowned. "Six is kind of painful. Can we do seven thirty?" I gave him my best sweet girl smile.

"No," he barked with a glare.

I groaned. "Fine."

Lincoln nodded.

Noah had come from his place in the corner of the room and was watching Lincoln keenly. "Are you sure about this last *healing*?"

I was clutching my rib cage and swaying like a drunk chick at prom.

"Yeah, bro, I got it," Lincoln told him.

Suddenly, both of his hands lit up a glowing deep carrot color, and I stared at the light, mesmerized. He took one step closer to me and placed his hands on my head. The moment the light touched my skull, I felt my pain and fatigue lift. A jolt of energy zipped through my body, like I'd just chugged two cups of coffee. Looking up, I saw Lincoln wincing in pain, and sweat bead his brow. His knees suddenly gave out, and he collapsed to the floor as his hands ceased their glowing.

"What's wrong?" I asked frantically, bending down to try and help him.

Noah looked down at Lincoln with an unreadable gaze. "Celestials with Raphael's healing power don't heal wounds on other people. They take the pain into themselves, and then heal it from within. He'll be okay after a day's rest."

Oh God. He...took my pain and now he's feeling it?

"Why would you do that?" I asked Lincoln, perplexed.

He was panting on the floor, holding his rib cage. "Go," was all he said.

Darren gripped my arm and hauled me outside. The last thing I saw was Lincoln sitting on the floor, in pain, and it changed the way I felt about him.

It changed everything.

CHAPTER 6

I WAS IN A MILD STATE OF SHOCK, AND BARELY REMEMbered the drive across the city border to my mom's office at the reanimation clinic. I was seven minutes late and hoping my new boss wouldn't notice. I didn't want to tell Lincoln, but I'd only learned to drive barely three months ago, in my mom's beat-up Volvo, with no power steering. I took the bus everywhere, so I didn't need to learn but my mom had insisted. Now, I was throwing a brand-new, fifty-thousand-dollar SUV into Park, outside of a Necro clinic where I was most likely going to wash dead bodies.

Joy.

As I jogged through the front door, I could feel some mild burning at the site of my tattoos, but nothing as major as it'd been before. Lincoln had taken everything from me so I could get through my shift reanimating the dead.

Why would he do that?

"You're late!" Master Burdock screeched from behind the desk.

I skidded to a stop, clutching my chest. Dude had come out of nowhere, as Brimstone demons often did. I knew better than to offer excuses. "Sorry, sir. It won't happen again."

He peered at me from behind his glowering, black, beady eyes, his horns casting menacing shadows on his face. When he got really pissed, the tips smoked. It was beyond freaky. In the hierarchy of demons, Brimstones were up there. Rumor was, they were almost directly under the Prince of Darkness himself. In his inner circle.

"Did you learn anything at your fancy school?" He leered at the tattoos on my arms.

I wasn't sure what answer would please him, so I offered the truth. "Not really, sir."

He nodded and stepped out from behind his desk, careening to his full seven-foot height. "My source says you'll learn enough to control your powers in the first year. After that, you'll be with me full time."

Terror flushed through me. "Oh, but it's a four-year course," I mumbled.

He stepped closer and crouched down. The ends of his horns started to smoke, and I nearly pissed myself at the smell of sulfur. My mom said he could breathe fire when really mad. I hoped I wasn't going to experience that firsthand.

"You're *mine*. Don't forget that. You think I'm going to allow them to initiate you into the Fallen Army and have you working against me? Not on your life, child. One year, that's all you get."

I swallowed hard. "Yes, sir."

He nodded again, and the smoke began to dissipate. "For now, you'll assist your mother, wash the bodies, mix her potions. Once you're trained, I'll have bigger assignments for you—things that can change this war in our favor. So, learn to fly, and whatever else it is you Celestials do, because I'm counting on you to be powerful, and make me a lot of money lending out your services."

Shit.

"Yes, sir," I said, eyes on the floor. Lincoln was right to hate me. I'd been naïve in thinking I could be a demon slave and not really have to hurt anyone.

"Well go, get to work! We got six bodies today," he roared.

I took off past the reception desk, and through the double doors. The second I arrived in the back room, the stench of death, formaldehyde, and sage smoke hit me.

Mom.

I'd helped my mom out a few times in the clinic when she was swamped, so I knew my way around the back. She was elbow-deep in a soapy washbasin, scrubbing a fifty-something female's body with a sponge.

She turned to me, her face lighting up. "Bri! How was your first day?" Her eyes fell to my tattooed arms. "Oh, wow...tattoos. Okay..."

I rubbed my arms. "Yeah, I guess they're needed for controlling my powers and stuff. Each one relates to an angel whose power I have or something." I wasn't sure I fully understood it.

Her brow furrowed. "How many are there?"

I winced. "Four." I whispered.

She dropped the sponge. "Four! Is that normal?"

My eyes widened. "Mom, is that really what you want to ask your daughter with black wings after her first day? If I'm normal?"

She winced. "Okay, true. Well, it is what it is. Can you finish cleaning up Mrs. Culpo? I've got to get the potions ready for Mr. Denner."

Ugh. Double freaking ugh.

I guess it was better than being a Gristle. So far. Now that I was looking down at my tattoos, I noticed the angry red lines were already healing.

I'd heard about Celestials having self-healing powers, but now that I thought of myself having something like that, it freaked me out. It made me feel less human.

My shift at the clinic was from noon to four, and then I was free to go home, do homework or whatever. My mom didn't get off until five, so I told her I'd pick up Shea from work and start dinner. After her shock wore off that I was now the proud owner of a brand-new car, she let me leave.

Mr. Burdock wasn't at the front desk when I left, which was a relief. Climbing into the SUV, I booked it to the strip club to pick up Shea. She was doing half days at Tainted Academy to learn her Mage craft, and then half days at the club to earn a living, her day ending at four thirty.

I pulled into the parking lot a minute early, and when I saw Shea come out the front door, I laid on the horn. Her eyes flicked up to my car and then she squinted. When she realized it was me, her mouth hung open in shock, which quickly gave way to a grin.

"Shut the front door! Please tell me this is ours," she shouted, after yanking the door open.

"If by ours you mean mine, yes, it's ours."

"Eeeeek!" she squealed, flapping her hands. Her eyes then shot to my tattooed arms. "Holy tatted-up hottie, tell me everything."

I laughed. "Other than the new car, it was actually an awful day. My new Celestial teachers are insanely hot, but the main guy is a total dick. I spent five hours straight in literal torturous pain, and then I spent the last four hours scrubbing dead bodies. Wanna smell my hands?"

She gagged. "I'll take your word for it."

I put the car in reverse and pulled out onto the main road to head back to our apartment. "How was your day? Is Tainted Academy really haunted? Are the teachers really Abrus demons?"

Our schooling in Demon City, thus far, had been taught by humans, a contract the fallen had drawn up for us. Anyone under eighteen received a free, somewhat normal education—math, science, and all that crap, with a few magical classes for added flair. Yet, I heard that at Tainted Academy, all bets were off. Demons taught the classes, and the fallen angels had nothing to do with it.

Shea sighed. "I don't really want to talk about it."

I froze. Pulling the car over in front of a demon-horn trade shop, I shifted into Park. "Shea…shit, was it that bad?"

Shea never wanted to 'not talk' about anything, I couldn't shut her up if I tried. Sure, she had her moments, but she always wanted to gossip. She was hands down the toughest person I knew, inside and out.

Unfolding her arms, she extended one to me. There, on her forearm, was a big black skull tattoo with a green snake head coming out of the eye.

Holy shit. A Dark Mage mark. "W-why do you have that? I mean…isn't it soon to do that?" I thought only advanced Dark Mages got one of those. After schooling, once they'd pledged their magic to the dark side until death. Or maybe that was just a story my mother told me to help me sleep at night.

"I imagine it's the same reason why you got your tattoos so soon. To claim us for their side. Whatever, it is what it is." She crossed her arms and stared out the window as it started to rain.

No.

"Shea, I have a car. Say the word and I'll drive us out of here. We'll go to Canada and live in the woods or something." I'd promised her I wouldn't let her go dark, and I'd meant it.

Her eyes filled with tears as she faced me. "The tattoo is also a magical tracker. Just take me home."

As the tear slid down her face, I tried not to fall apart. I could count the number of times I'd seen Shea cry on one hand. This was bad, so very bad.

"We're going to figure this out together, okay?" It was a total lie, I knew it the second it left my lips, but I had to say something.

"Okay," she said in a flat tone. It broke my heart, because I would forever remember that as the moment she'd lost hope.

We ate dinner in silence. My little brother's eyes kept jumping from my tattoos to Shea's, but when he tried to ask about them, my mom kicked him under the table.

Now, Shea and I lay in our beds in our shared room while staring at the ceiling. We hadn't really talked since the car. I sensed she was in a bit of a depression and wanted some time alone.

"You awake?" she suddenly asked.

"Yeah." I turned over and looked across the room at her curly hair spilling onto the pillow.

"So you said your new teachers were hot. Like how hot?"

I grinned and sat up as she sat up too. This was the Shea I was used to. "It's weird how hot they are. It's also like they get cockier and ruder the hotter they are."

She nodded. "That makes sense, actually."

I grinned. "You'd like Noah. Total sweet-talker, loves to wink."

She grabbed her chest. "I love a sexy winker." I laughed. "Are the girls total bitches, acting all better than you?" she asked.

I shrugged. "I have no idea. I start classes tomorrow. Today was all about the tattoos."

She nodded. "The girls at Tainted Academy are total vaginas. They were already trying to mess with me."

She lifted her arm to show bruising where someone had grabbed her. Shea was a feminist, so calling women assholes or dicks didn't suit her. She thought they should be called vaginas or bitches. I just ran with it.

Anger flared inside of me at her bruising. "What happened?"

She shrugged. "One tried to start shit for no reason, so I took out her front teeth with brass knuckles."

My mouth popped open. "Shea! Where did you get brass knuckles?" Shea had always been scrappy—she owned switchblades, baseball bats, and mace cans—but brass knuckles! That was right under a gun, wasn't it?

She looked at a corner of our room. "From my new Mage master. Weapons and fighting are encouraged at Tainted Academy. She said after my schooling, my contract will probably be bought for seven figures, and I'll get a hefty percentage of that in the deal. Dark Mages are rare, apparently."

"Oh." Someone could buy your contract? Was that what Burdock was going to do with me? "Burdock told me he would only allow me to study one year at Fallen Academy. Then he's probably selling my contract too."

Shea stared at the floor. "I'm tired. Night, Bri." She lay down quickly and faced the wall.

A chill broke out on my skin. "Yeah, night."

Our childhoods were dead and slaughtered. Tomorrow was the start of a sinister adulthood for the both of us. But I couldn't deny that it seemed like I had it a bit better off than Shea did.

I guess tomorrow will tell.

I woke up the next morning to a five o'clock alarm from hell—no pun intended. It was actually 5:07 a.m.

Shea threw a shoe at my face, which alerted me that the alarm must've been buzzing for seven minutes.

"Sorry," I groaned, and turned it off.

I took a quick shower, glad to not have to deal with my wings, and noticed my tattoos were fully healed. No flaking skin, no redness, nothing. It was both eerie and awesome.

After dressing, I grabbed a bagel for myself, and then whipped up a quick PB&J for Bernie. Mom said as long as we had the means to feed him, she didn't mind the extra grocery bill, so I tried to make sure he had at least two meals a day. Once a week, mom lets him take a shower in her bathroom and enjoy a hot cup of tea. I'd known Bernie for as long as we'd lived in Demon City. No drug problem or anything like that. Just a guy down on his luck who couldn't find work. He was also a human. Menial human jobs like accounting and food service got snatched up quickly, and the government fell to shit after the war, so there was no such thing as food stamps or financial assistance.

We took care of each other. That's how we survived.

I pulled on some skinny jeans and a T-shirt. After grabbing a hoodie and my messenger bag, I was ready to go. Walking down the hall with my car keys felt a bit surreal. I had a car, four tattoos, and I was going to Fallen Academy. Was this a dream?

My phone pinged with an email, and nerves rushed through me when I saw it was from a Lincoln Grey.

From: LincolnGrey@FallenAcademy.com
Subject: Your schedule.

Brielle Atwater

<u>Celestial Master Studies</u> 6–8 a.m.
30 mins each master teacher.
(Training Hall 304)

<u>Fallen History</u> 8:05 a.m.–9 a.m.
(Room 506, Mrs. Delacourt)

<u>Battle Class</u> 9:05 a.m.–10 a.m.
(Room 511, Master Bradstone)

<u>Weapons</u> 10:05 a.m.–11 a.m.
(Outside track field, Mr. Claymore)

<u>Lunch</u> 11:05 a.m.–11:30 a.m.
(Dining hall)

You better be awake and on your way here by now.

Lincoln

I scowled at the comment about being awake, then scanned through the schedule four times. *Battle class? Weapons? Yikes.* Then my lovely day ended by eleven thirty so I could wash dead bodies with my mom until four.

I hit Reply.

I've been up for two hours doing yoga and feeding the homeless. See you soon.

Then I hit Send. Let him chew on that. It was partially true.

Opening the door to the street, I saw Bernie was still asleep. Maximus wagged his tail, and I popped an apple slice in his mouth before leaving the bag with the PB&J at Bernie's feet. It was such an ungodly hour that even homeless people were still asleep.

Jogging to my car on the curb, I was relieved to see it hadn't been stolen or jacked of its wheels.

I made it to the campus parking lot by 5:56 a.m., finding a grand total of three cars there, plus a silver Airstream trailer with a motorcycle leaning against it. Probably Lincoln, Noah, Darren and Blake; no one else wanted to be up that early.

Exiting my car with my bag, I stared at the large stone steps that led to the main campus.

Sitting there, in a black hoodie, was Lincoln.

With a sigh, I picked up my pace, the lack of sleep

already pulling at my limbs. When I got within two feet of him, he flicked his eyes up to mine. "Hatha or Kundalini?"

I frowned. "I only speak English," I enlightened him.

He smirked. "I was wondering which was your favorite kind of yoga. I'm a fan of kundalini myself."

Oh. Shit.

"Yeah, that one's cool," I told him, then started walking up the stairs.

"Do you know where you're going?" he asked, making no effort to move.

I growled. "Not really, but I'm guessing you're sitting out here waiting for me so you can show me."

He stood and shrugged. "I was going to, but I'm not a fan of the attitude I'm sensing."

Oh my God, I'm going to kill him. "I'm sorry. Pretty please with a cherry on top, show me where to go." I made sure to lay the sarcasm on *thick*.

He grinned, showing those dimples. "There, was that so hard?"

I nodded. "It was. It *really* was."

He started to walk through the brick entryway, and I craned my neck to see two huge angel statues adorning the gates. "When does school start for the others?"

"Eight." He took a right down a hallway that led to a small brick building.

I traced one of my tattoos with my fingers. "Are you...feeling better from yesterday?" I hadn't exactly thanked him for taking my pain at the tattoo shop. I'd been planning on it, but then he was a jerk right off the bat with the kundalini thing.

"I'm fine."

He reached for the door of the small brick building, and I placed a hand on his outstretched arm. Again, there was that little zap when we touched, but it subsided quickly.

"Hey, um, I just wanted to thank you for…ya know. I wasn't feeling good yesterday, and yeah…thanks for the healing." *Oh. My. God. When did I forget how to speak?*

He nodded. "It's my job."

Then he threw the doors open, leaving me wondering why he hadn't just said, "You're welcome." *Ugh! This guy is a world-class jerk.*

"Is this her?" I heard a female voice ask from inside.

Stepping into the room, I saw a short woman in her fifties with long, red hair. She was a human from the looks and smell of her—don't ask me how I could smell a human, I just could. Ever since I was five. She was buried in layers and layers of black and silver fabric.

"Hi, dear. I'm Rose," she introduced herself.

"Brielle." I waved.

Her eyes roamed over my body, lingering on my hips. "She's curvier than you described. I'll need her measurements, but this should do for today." She threw a black and silver jumpsuit at Lincoln, who caught it and handed it to me.

I grinned, looking at him. "You described my body? That must've been fun for you."

He clenched his teeth, which made his strong jaw pop, and it was actually kind of sexy. "The highlight of my day. Just what I wanted to be doing after my long day at work." The woman beckoned me over then, and Lincoln waved a piece of paper in my face. "Here's a map. When you're done here, meet us in the training hall." Then he left.

I looked at the redheaded woman. "Not the friendliest person in the world," I commented.

She smiled sadly. "Well, tragedy changes people. He was a very sunny boy his first few years here."

And just like that my heart stopped. Lincoln had been through a tragedy. I wanted to ask more about it. I wanted to know so badly, that it was burning a hole through my tongue, but I also didn't want to know. I didn't want to look at him differently, feel pity, or I don't know, hear something so intimate from a stranger behind his back. So, I kept my mouth shut as she measured me.

In a daze, I headed to the dressing room she had in the back, changing into a skintight, black jumpsuit with the Fallen Academy silver wing insignia. It wasn't so tight that I was afraid it would rip, but tight enough that someone could probably bounce a quarter on my ass.

As I followed the map to the training hall, I decided

to try and forget what I'd heard about Lincoln having been through a tragedy. It was better if I just wiped that from my memory.

The moment I stepped into the large gym, Noah did a catcall whistle. I snorted, as Lincoln smacked him on the back of the head.

"She's our student," he scolded.

Noah shrugged. "No rules against it, my brother. She's eighteen."

I dropped my messenger bag on the floor. "Don't worry, he's not my type, anyway," I shouted across the space.

Darren and Blake did the, "ohhhh snap" thing, but Lincoln's eyes just burned into me with an expression I couldn't read.

Noah frowned. "What are you talking about? I'm everyone's type." He flexed his biceps and kissed it.

"You're too pretty," I told him honestly. I could never date a guy with better-groomed eyebrows than my own.

Noah grinned. "Thank you."

I rolled my eyes. "So, where do we start? Want me to show you my moves? I grew up with demons, so I'm probably more advanced than your average student." I pulled my switchblade from my boot and gave it a twirl.

"She's adorable," Darren told the room.

"I'm not adorable. Kittens are adorable. I'm badass.

Look, there's still crusted blood on here from yesterday." I showed them the blade.

Lincoln stepped forward and sighed. "Put that away before you hurt yourself."

Party pooper. I retracted the blade and slipped it back into my boot.

Lincoln looked me up and down. "Pull out your wings. We'll start with flying."

My eyes bugged out of my head. *Flying? I don't know why that didn't even cross my mind.*

"Come on, Miss Yoga." He snapped his fingers as the boys started pulling huge, two-foot-thick pads onto the ground.

Oh my God, those are to break my fall.

I looked behind me and twitched my shoulders. Nothing happened. Swallowing hard, I jumped into the air a little and hoped they would pop out upon landing.

No luck.

The back of the suit had two twelve-inch slits for them to come out of, so I knew it wasn't my shirt keeping them in.

"Umm, how exactly do I get my wings out?" God, it was so embarrassing.

I was sure Lincoln was about to say something jerkish when Blake stepped forward.

"I struggled with it too at first. It's like learning to walk as a baby. You need to think about raising them, like you would your arms, and they'll come out. They'll also appear when you're in danger." He was the sweet one, I had decided.

Okay...my eyes closed and I took a deep breath. I imagined my shoulder blades rising, and even arched my back. After an agonizing second, I felt a pop and then a heaviness on my right side. Falling over to my right, I forced my eyes open. All four of them were holding in their laughter.

"*What!*" I roared. Peering behind me, I saw that I'd only managed to get one wing out.

Kill me now.

Lincoln was the first to be able to control his laughter. He walked over and reached behind me, stroking my exposed left shoulder blade through the slit in my jumpsuit, with one delicate finger. Chills broke out on my arms as the heat from his skin trailed down my back with the sensual touch. My wing popped out, as I was kneeling there breathlessly, staring at the beautiful asshole who'd been through a tragedy, and then he stepped back.

"Okay, first rule of flying. Don't die."

I shook off his sensual touch, and my eyebrows hit my hairline. "Ha. Ha. What are the real rules?"

Noah shrugged. "Our master teachers said the same thing—just don't die. You're basically immortal now unless killed, but you can snap your neck if you land wrong."

I'd been meaning to ask about the immortal rumor, but wow, there it was.

Lincoln pointed to a ladder. "Climb up to the top. Let's see if we can get one good hover before our time is done. You'll get your weapon in class today, and we'll start working with it tomorrow."

"Is now a bad time to mention I'm afraid of heights?"

Lincoln groaned. "Wasting time, Miss Yoga."

Ugh. I never should've said that yoga thing. Maybe I should start doing yoga for real in case he keeps quizzing me.

As I climbed the ladder, I was sure of two things.

1. All four of them were totally staring at my ass.
2. I was going to break my neck and die.

CHAPTER 7

After mastering a two-second hover where I'd smacked Lincoln in the face with my wing—on complete accident, of course—I'd sat through an hour of history class. Much to my dismay, everyone knew who I was, and stared or pointed at me most of the period. I'd even seen a few of them mouth, "Demon lover."

Awesome.

I wondered if I should cut bangs to cover my demon slave tattoo, or maybe get some heavy makeup, but what was the point? It's who I was, and I couldn't change my future. I might as well live with it.

Now, I was standing in a large gym type of room with walls and walls of every kind of weapon I could think of, nestled in cages with golden locks on them. Our professor, Mr. Claymore, was a Light Mage and looked the part, wearing a long, black velvet robe with a silver spiral Light

Mage insignia over the breast. His eyes kept flashing silvery gray as he looked each of us in the eye, his gaze lingering on me. I started to squirm as he pinned me with his stare, a heavy feeling pressing on my skin. Then he looked away, and the trance was broken, the feeling fading.

That was intense.

Seeing him all Maged out made me think of Shea. I wondered what she was doing at her delinquent school, wishing she could be with me instead.

"Today is one of the most important days of your life. You'll find your infinity weapon and be bound to it for eternity." His voice boomed around the room, coming at us from all angles.

Say what? Eternity? Bound?

A prissy girl, by the name of Tiffany—who I'd learned from history class was a Light Mage in training—raised her hand. "Is it true that your infinity weapon will speak to you after you're bonded?"

Either she was high or I hadn't heard her right. Maybe *I* was high, because this girl had just asked if our weapons were going to *talk* to us.

Mr. Claymore shrugged. "It's different for everyone. A talking infinity weapon is very rare, but each weapon does have a soul, so you'll feel its personality even if you can't hear it."

Everyone is high.

I cleared my throat and raised my hand. "I'm sorry, but how can a weapon have a soul?"

He looked down at his roster, and then at my forehead. "Brielle, right?"

Damn this tattoo. I was totally cutting bangs. I nodded.

"In Angel City, we learn all about this in high school, so I'll forgive you for being unprepared. Infinity weapons were given to us by The Powers. Archangels are humanity's protectors, and The Powers are the angels of defense, the warriors of Heaven."

Whoa.

"Right. Cool," I said. Tiffany released an annoying laugh, causing her flock to laugh with her.

I cut her with a glare, but before I could think more on it, the professor clapped and all of the locks on the cages clicked open, falling to the floor. With another clap, the cages sprung wide open, and we all let out a collective "Ahhh."

Magic was cool, I'd give him that.

"Now, finding your infinity weapon can be a challenge. Be patient. It'll call to you—you'll feel a kindred attraction toward it. A love for it. It'll feel *right*, like you've been waiting for it your whole life," he explained.

"If that's it, then coffee is my infinity weapon," I muttered softly, making a few students near me giggle.

The professor gestured to the cases. "These weapons will carry you through every battle for the rest of your life, so take your time."

A few students started walking toward the cases while I hung back, firmly in the "do not want to pick first" group. Next to me, a gorgeous young guy with overly tweezed eyebrows and black hair gave me a hip bump. "I'm Luke," he whispered.

I chuckled at his overfriendly hip bump. "Bri." My gaydar was going off pretty hard, so I wasn't worried that he was hitting on me, or anything sleazy.

He nodded. "Let's just get this out there." He gestured to my forehead. "My aunt is demon bound, she has that whole forehead thing going on, so I understand, and I'm totally cool with it."

I smiled. Genuinely. "Good to know." I glanced at the insignia on the breast of his jumpsuit indicating he was a Beast Shifter. Demon gifted.

I think I just made my first friend. "Shall we?" I gestured to the cages.

He looked apprehensively at Tiffany, who'd just picked up a large sword that was glowing quite brightly in her hands.

"Ladies first." He winked.

Great.

Taking a deep breath, I walked slowly past one cage, feeling for something that made me want to love it as much as I did coffee, but I came up with nothing. I passed to the second cage, filled with a bunch of bows and arrows. Luke was lingering behind me and stopped to gasp a little at the cage holding the bows. I went still, pivoting to look at him as he reached for a solid gold bow. As his hand moved closer, the bow started to glow a faint blue.

"Ah, the arrows of truth. A very fine weapon, young man. You should be honored," Mr. Claymore stated.

When Luke's hand curled around the bow, his lips popped open in surprise. One by one, the students found their glowy weapons; upon retrieving them, they went to the back of the room to wait.

There were only three of us left now, and I had passed by nearly every cage. My heart started beating crazily in my chest. *What if I don't have an infinity weapon? Should I just grab one and fake it?* But if I did that, it probably wouldn't light up.

The last two students found their weapons, and then all eyes were on me. Luke was the only one giving me a look of pity; everyone else seemed…annoyed, like, God why do we have to wait for her?

"This is not a process we rush. Take your time, Brielle," the professor announced, making me even more mortified.

As I stepped over to the last case, I felt something stir within me. My stomach churned with excitement, and it felt like I was standing near open electricity. I scanned the rows of daggers, my heart pounding wildly in my chest.

'*Over here, winged one,*' a small, female voice said inside my head, making me leap backward two feet.

Now the class was really staring at me, but not as

hard as the professor. He stepped closer, gaping at me like I was topless or something.

'*Second row, third one over. Come on, love, let's get this over with. I've been waiting a long time for this,*' the tiny voice spoke again.

Holy mother of all things.

'You're...talking to me?' I said, wondering if I'd finally lost my mind. I was overdue.

She gave a little groan. '*Second row, third one over. Come on, hon. You can do it.*'

Now I was taking far too long and looking far too stupid. In a rush, I charged the case and grabbed the silver dagger that was in the second row, third one over. When I wrapped my fingers around it, a blinding light shot out, at the same time that a great energy ripped through me. It was hard to describe—it was pleasure, the kind I would feel if I got to see my dad again, but mixed with a tremendous power, like I could rip a steel door in half. My wings popped out of my back, causing the entire class to gasp, and I was brought to my knees as the power continued to swirl around me, the breeze lifting my hair.

'*I'm Sera,*' the dagger told me. I felt her, like she was a person, an old friend. It was the weirdest and yet most comforting thing I'd ever experienced.

'*Brielle, but you can call me Bri.*' I felt stupid introducing myself to a knife, but hey, there were weirder things in the world.

"Incredible," the professor breathed.

The wind had died down, and although my legs were shaky, I was able to stand. All I could do was stare at the dagger in my hands. It was about nine inches long, most of that the blade, with a short, golden hilt that was engraved and encrusted with shimmery pearl-like stones.

"A seraph blade. I didn't even know we had one in there," Mr. Claymore gushed.

He walked over to the case I'd retrieved it from, grabbed a black leather scabbard and handed it to me. It looked only big enough to attach around my thigh, so that's where I buckled it.

"Has anyone learned of seraph blades in history class?" he asked.

My eyes widened. *Oh my God, he's going to make a lesson out of this.*

A short, brown-haired girl with freckles raised her hand. "Doesn't it somehow magnify the user's inner light or something?"

Tiffany laughed, pointing at my wings. "That might be a problem in this case."

Luke growled at her, an honest animal growl, and she shut up. He was totally my new friend.

Mr. Claymore nodded. "Partly right, but that is only one feature. If she were fighting to save someone she loved, the light would be extremely bright. If she were protecting herself or other acquaintances, it would be less harmful. The light of true love, coming through a seraph blade, is said to eviscerate a demon without making a single cut."

And by the mercy of God, the bell rang then. With a relieved sigh, I turned to follow Luke outside so we could make our way to our final class before lunch—battle class.

"Stop!" the professor roared.

The entire class froze.

He held out his hands. "You must give your weapon a taste of your blood, to bind to it for eternity."

I was glad to see my eyes weren't the only ones that bugged out. Tiffany was the first to pierce her hand with her giant sword, as if the idea of feeding a weapon her blood didn't bother her. Then everyone followed suit. Luke looked at me and shrugged, poking his palm with one of his arrows.

Pulling Sera out, I made a small slice across my palm. I wasn't even sure I'd cut myself until the blood bubbled up. It didn't even hurt, just felt weird, like I'd put a piece of cold ice on my palm. A blue light shot out of the hilt, and swirled around my torso, making gooseflesh break out on my arms.

That earned me a dozen more stares, including the professor.

"All right, go in peace," he said to the group.

When I looked up, he was watching me with glowing silver eyes.

As Luke and I walked to battle class together, I tried

to get my wings to go back in, but they weren't cooperating. At one point my wing accidentally brushed against Tiffany—who I now lovingly referred to as Bitchany—and she shrieked, asking for holy water. When everyone laughed, I kept my chin up. I wasn't going to let her get me down.

The Nightbloods had to travel the school in underground tunnels because they couldn't be exposed to the sunlight, so they were waiting for us inside the gymnasium first. The same one I'd learned to fly in that morning.

The hour passed quickly with basic weapon holding positions. Before I knew it, I was eating lunch with Luke and his demon-gifted friends on the right half of the cafeteria. The left half was unofficially for the angel blessed. Arguably, I was angel blessed since I was a Celestial, but the red crescent moon on my forehead and black wings spoke otherwise. Besides, I wanted to get to know Luke better.

Luke had an older sister, Angela, who was a Necromancer and two grades above us. "Oh, man, I still remember the day I got my infinity weapon." She was grinning, looking at Luke's bow and arrow. "Mom will be real proud."

He nodded. "And Dad?"

Her face fell. "Yeah, I meant Mom and Dad."

Luke rolled his eyes. "Don't bother, I know what you meant."

I kept my eyeballs on my mashed potatoes.

"My mom and dad are both angel blessed," he explained.

"Ah." Some families had a weird thing where they wanted their kids to be like them. My mom had wanted me to be a Necromancer so we could work together, but we'd ended up working together anyway.

"No issue with my being gay, but he threw a fit when he found out I was a Beast and demon gifted," he said to his broccoli.

Angela chewed her lip. She had long, inky black hair and was quite pretty with green eyes and high cheekbones. "He'll get over it."

Then her eyes flicked up behind me, and her back went ramrod straight. "Oh my God, Lincoln Grey is walking over here."

I froze, swallowing my mashed potatoes quickly, and turned my head just as he said my name.

"What's with the wings?" he asked. Most of the Celestials kept them away unless fighting or showing off.

I rolled my eyes. "Is that what you came to ask me?" God, he was infuriating. *Way to embarrass me, jackass.*

He assessed me, then smirked. "They're stuck again, aren't they?"

Oh my God. I'm going to lie awake tonight and fantasize not about seeing him naked, but about how many ways I could kill him and hide the body.

I didn't answer, and he snaked a hand out and

stroked the top of my wings in one suave move. My wings snapped into my back, as warmth ran down my spine. Not gonna lie, my body liked his touch, but I could barely stand him. Sure, he may have been through some tragedy, but he was just...irritating. On *all* levels.

"You have to leave, right? I'll walk you out," he asked, looking at my friends.

Okay, that was a not-so-subtle way to kill my lunch. "Yeah, okay." I grabbed my messenger bag and turned to my new friends. "See you tomorrow."

Luke frowned. "You only have half days?"

I chewed my lip and pointed to my forehead. "Yeah."

Angela kicked him under the table, and they both put on fake, plastic smiles. "Cool, see you tomorrow Bri," she offered in an extra-chipper tone.

Bless her heart.

Lincoln tugged on my bag. "I need to speak with you."

Ugh. This tall drink of water is nice to look at but becoming a major thorn in my side.

We were making our way through the throngs of students, when Tiffany bolted into a standing position, blocking Lincoln's way. "Hey, Linc."

Linc. That must be something they all call him after they've slept with him.

"Hey, Tiffany." Was that annoyance in his tone? He totally knew her!

"Sucks that Raphael has you babysitting the archdemon," she spat, glowering at me.

Anger boiled throughout my entire body. How freaking dare she! I moved forward to do something impulsive, like rip her face off, when Lincoln's hand came out to stop me.

"Don't be a bully, Tiff. It's unattractive." He blasted past her with a firm grip on my upper arm.

The last thing I saw when leaving the cafeteria was Tiffany's curled lip and a flame of jealousy in her gaze.

Ha. Take that.

The moment we were outside, he released my arm.

"You're going to need a thicker skin if you want to survive here, or anywhere, for that matter. You can't go fighting every person who name-calls you," he said in a fatherly tone.

"Yeah, thanks, Dad, but I'm aware of that. She's been at my throat all day," I huffed.

Lincoln stopped walking halfway to the parking lot and faced me. "Are you ever pleasant?"

I raised one eyebrow. "Are *you*?"

He rolled his eyes and kept walking, forcing me to run after him like an idiot.

"How do you know her, anyway? Ex-girlfriend?"

He made a disgusted face. "Ew, no. She's a…family friend." He didn't sound too convincing.

"Well what did you need to talk to me about?" I needed to get going. Master Burdock would have my hide if I was late a second day in a row.

Lincoln spun and pointed to Sera on my right thigh. "That. That's what I came to talk to you about."

I recoiled a little, hurt by his tone. "What's wrong?" I stroked Sera's hilt.

'Do *we* like him, or not? I can't tell,' she asked me.

I internally groaned. *'I'm still trying to figure that out myself.'*

"The problem is you can't bring a seraph blade into Demon City. It'll be sold or destroyed. Raphael has tasked *me* with fixing the issue!" He did not sound happy about that at all.

I wasn't sure what to say, so for once in my life, I kept quiet.

Lincoln pulled a key from his jeans pocket. "This is a key to my trailer." He pointed across the parking lot to the edge of the trees, where the cute, little silver Airstream sat among the wildflowers. "Each morning you arrive, I'll have the blade for you. Each day you leave, you'll drop it off inside my trailer and lock my door. Do not snoop. Do not use my bathroom or eat my food. Do you understand?"

I grinned. "Aw, sweetie, you're giving me a key to your place already? Gosh, we just met." I snatched the key from his hand greedily.

"Don't lose that," he barked.

I rolled my eyes, fixing it on my key ring. "Relax, I'm not a baby."

"I can be gone for weeks at a time if things progress

with the war, so I'm hoping you won't set my place on fire or anything," he added.

"What's your problem with me? Honestly. Let's get this all out there." I'd decided that now, as I was running late to wash dead bodies, was as good a time as any to have a long, drawn-out argument.

He took a step closer to me, eating up the distance between us, and my breath hitched. He touched my forehead with his index finger. "*That* is my problem. I don't trust you. I never will. One word from your master and you might strap a bomb to your chest and kill us all."

I gasped as tears filled my eyes, unprepared for such a hateful answer. His face fell as my bottom lip quivered, but I wasn't going to give the prick the satisfaction of seeing me cry.

Ripping Sera from my leg sheath, I handed it to him, and took off running through the parking lot. He called something out, but it was too low and muffled for me to hear it.

———•———

By the time I made it to the reanimation clinic, I'd cried off all my mascara, but I was five minutes early, so there was that.

I put the car into Park and then stepped out, but instead of heading for the doors like I normally would, I froze as a strong scent of sulfur and oil hit me. A demon was close, one I didn't recognize by smell.

I swallowed hard, taking wide steps across the parking lot. Just before I reached the double doors, an honest-to-God Abrus demon jumped out from behind the pillar, making my heart lurch into my throat, and my wings snap out in defense. Abrus demons were second to Lucifer himself. They looked mostly human, with only two small, red horns on their forehead, and searing yellow eyes. They were all insanely gorgeous males as well, seductive and dangerous. I'd only met one before in my lifetime.

"Brielle, I presume?" he asked, in a smooth whisky-coated voice, his eyes gazing lustily at my wings.

"Yeah. I gotta get to work or Master Burdock will kill me." I giggled nervously and tried to pass him.

"Oh, I don't think he'll mind. I've been waiting for you to arrive." He grinned, showing every single one of his pearl-white, straight teeth. He looked hungry, and I felt like the main course.

"Waiting for me?" I ran a nervous hand through my hair to keep it from shaking.

He nodded, glancing from my tattoos to my messenger bag. "Did you get your infinity weapon today?"

My face must've registered complete shock because he smiled. "You know about that?" I rubbed my arms anxiously.

He nodded and eyed my bag. "Is it with you?"

My heart was hammering so loud, I was pretty sure he could hear it. "No, gotta leave them in Angel City." I hoped to Heaven he wasn't one of those demons who could smell a lie. He didn't seem to, because he nodded.

"What did you choose?" he asked indifferently. His eyes held anything but indifference.

I knew in my gut that I shouldn't say what I really chose, so I told him the first thing that came to mind. "Arrows of truth."

He looked a bit surprised but then seemed pleased. "That could be useful."

I shifted on my feet nervously. "Sir, I, uh, really gotta get to work."

He nodded. "See you at the full moon."

Anyone living in Demon City knew what the current moon cycle was, because it was posted everywhere there was a clock or calendar. The full moon was in six days.

"Oh?" I almost didn't want to ask.

He grinned. Reaching out, he stroked my feathered wing, and sent a repulsive shiver down my spine.

"That's when I'll be buying your contract, and you will then be working for me. Be sure to bring your arrows of truth to the contract signing. You won't be going back to Fallen Academy." His words hung in the air menacingly.

Leaning forward, he brought the pungent stench of sulfur and tar with him. "I know what you are," he whispered in my ear, as I internally revolted. With that, he left.

I know what you are. I know what you are. I know what you are. That sentence replayed in my head over and over. I stood there for a full three minutes trying to talk myself out of panicking.

What am I?

I decided to email Lincoln before going in to start my shift.

To: LincolnGrey@FallenAcademy.com

My master just sold my contract to an Abrus demon. It's final by this full moon. He's taking me out of the academy. Maybe I shouldn't bother coming in the morning.

Sincerely,
Girl you don't trust,
who definitely does yoga all the time.

I didn't see his reply until after my shift.

From: LincolnGrey@FallenAcademy.com

Come tomorrow. 6 a.m. Pack your personal belongings.

Sincerely,
Someone who has actually done yoga.

I was so bent out of shape, I barely remembered eating dinner or talking to Shea.

I know what you are.

Pack your personal belongings.

That night, I laid in bed facing Shea's back. We'd both been pretty silent at dinner, each in our own drama, but when she flipped over and I saw the tears lining her eyes, my gut clenched.

"I can't do this much longer. I'm going dark, I feel it," she confessed, each word sending agony into my heart.

Then she turned back around and faced the wall.

It was a long time before sleep took me.

CHAPTER 8

That morning when I got to school, Lincoln wasn't there, and Noah, Blake, and Darren were acting really weird at my training. Noah brought Sera, and they'd done basic drills with me on how to hold her, lunges, and other things I already knew from growing up in Demon City with a bunch of Hell spawn.

When I'd asked where Lincoln was, they just said an important meeting. Now, I was in weapons class with Mr. Claymore, and he was having Luke and me practice with each other. The Mage came up behind me and I tightened my grip on Sera.

"She speaks to you, doesn't she?" he asked, eyeing the gold and crystalline hilt. I simply nodded as Luke's eyes bugged out of his head. "She'll be a wise teacher if you can learn to open yourself to her."

Right. Open myself to a knife. Shall I take her on a date?

'I've never been fond of human sarcasm,' Sera announced, quite sarcastically.

"And how would I do that?" I asked Mr. Claymore, ignoring her comment.

The professor stepped before me and placed both hands on my shoulders, peering down at me with wise, cloudy, white eyes. "A seraph blade is no regular infinity weapon. It's a soul weapon. Open yourself to her. Show her your fears, hopes, and dreams, and she'll fight for them. She contains extremely rare magic."

Nerves churned in my gut at his words.

'You hear that, Sera? I'm afraid of being an archdemon, and I want to win the lottery. Can you make that happen?' I asked her.

Before she could reply, the professor's voice rose up. "All right now, I want you all to practice protection drills. We'll split off into groups of three. One person is the protector, one is the victim, and one is the attacker. These drills will prepare you for the final test of the year, when you'll go into The gauntlet in an effort to graduate."

The gauntlet. Sounded scary. Good thing I wouldn't be there to go through it.

I didn't have the heart to tell Luke yet. He was fast becoming a good friend, and I didn't want that to end when he heard my time was limited.

The back door opened and Noah stepped in, much

to the pleasure of every female in the class. Tiffany absolutely purred.

"I want this to feel real," the professor stated. "It's the only way to activate your weapons. Don't try to hurt anyone seriously, but if a small cut or something happens, we have a healer on hand." He gestured to Noah, who winked. Of course.

Mr. Claymore rapidly grouped us together, and when I saw who our third wheel was, I tried to hold in my groan.

Bitchany.

"Hey, Archie," she whispered to me. "Archdemon, Archie. Get it?" She grinned.

'We should cut her,' Sera said, making me smile, and causing Tiffany to look at me confused.

'You can't just go around cutting students,' I enlightened my talking blade.

'I'll make it look like an accident.'

I actually laughed out loud at that point. Luke raised an eyebrow, and I tried too late to turn my laugh into a cough. I probably looked like I'd lost my mind.

"Okay, for our first group, let's have Brielle be the protector. I want to see what that seraph blade can do." He told me. "Tiffany, you be the attacker, and Luke will be the victim."

And just like that, my worst-case scenario of how this class could play out came to life. Not only was I chosen first for this little charade, but I was pitted against the class bully. I missed Shea. She would have some foulmouthed, witty comeback for every time Tiffany opened her mouth.

The professor reached into his coat and pulled out a jar of salt. Going around the room, he poured out a big circle.

"If the attacker can get the victim out of the circle, they win," he declared, then gently nudged Luke and me inside it.

Pulling Sera out, I took my defensive stance in front of Luke. To make the odds of her being able to reach Luke even harder, I brought out my wings. Just that morning, with Blake's gentle guidance and help, I'd mastered pulling them out and putting them back in.

Take that, Lincoln.

Tiffany's jaw popped open as my black wings formed a barrier in front of Luke. "Can she do that?" she asked the professor.

He shrugged. "Don't see why not."

With a growl, she unsheathed her blade.

"Please protect me. I'm legit scared of her," Luke confessed loudly behind me, making the entire class burst out laughing.

I just kept my eyes pinned on her face, her arms in my peripheral vision. The boys had told me that morning that I had tons of magic at my disposal, but we would ease into my powers one by one. So, for the time being, my wings and dagger were my magic.

"*Lux,*" Tiffany breathed, and her weapon flared to life, emitting a bright white light.

Mr. Claymore circled us. "Ah, I see someone has been practicing at home with her parents."

Tiffany's cheeks reddened, but when she lunged for me, I was ready. Squinting to avoid being blinded by the light, I dodged her thrust, and smacked her gigantic sword down with my dagger. When the two weapons crashed together, her light went out and mine sent beams of blue lasers into her face. She recoiled, shrieking, her arm flying up to cover her eyes, and I grinned.

'Take that, you bully,' Sera gloated.

Tiffany gave me a death glare and charged with a battle cry. *Shit.* She was going to cut my head off at that speed.

I crouched, placing my dagger between us, but instead of using her weapon as I'd expected, she kicked me in the chin. *Hard.*

I fell to one knee wincing and she pivoted to the side, grabbing Luke's suit by the collar. If she made it out of the circle, I lost.

I am not a loser.

I burst up from my position, and instinctively grabbed her arm. I knew I couldn't really cut her, not like I wanted to, but Sera sent me a mental picture of me pressing the flat part of my blade to her arm. I did just that, and it flared red-hot.

With a shriek, Tiffany released Luke and stumbled back, ripping out of my grasp.

"Okay, that's enough. Well done, both of you. A strong start to learning from your weapons," the teacher called out.

There was an angry red welt on the side of Tiffany's arm and she was glaring at me, imagining removing my head with her big-ass sword no doubt.

"Allow me to help," Noah cooed, sending Tiffany from red-hot murderer, to mushy flirt in a nanosecond.

The professor paired up the next group, as Luke slipped in beside me. "You're my woman crush Wednesday. I'll never in a thousand years forget the sound of her shriek. It was like a thousand dying cats."

I chuckled. "Thanks." But honestly, all the credit went to Sera.

'Thanks for that. You're kind of a badass,' I told her. Having a dagger send you a mental picture was cool. And also slightly terrifying.

'I am an extension of you, child. That makes you a badass too,' she replied.

I wasn't sure how to respond to that, so I just stayed quiet and watched the next fight.

For a small moment there, I felt proud of myself, and got a glimpse of what it might be like to join the Fallen Army and protect the innocent. But that would never happen, and that thought made all of my hopes come crashing down.

I was staring at my lunch, sick to my stomach about going back to Demon City. Lincoln had told me to pack my personal belongings, and for what? He wasn't even there! I'd kind of hoped he'd had Raphael talk to Burdock and they'd work out something, like maybe Raphael would buy my contract instead, and outbid the Abrus demon, or something. It was a stupid, hopeless thought, and now I was staring at a yummy turkey sandwich I didn't have the appetite for anymore.

"Hey. Brielle, right?"

A petite redhead slid in beside me. I'd seen her in a few of my classes, a Nightblood. She wore a cloak over her hair, only one chunk of red popping out. Her hands were gloved as well, even though the windows in the cafeteria were "UV-coated to the extreme"—Luke's wording—so she and other Nightbloods could join us.

"Hey, yeah," I replied awkwardly. Making new friends was my least favorite thing.

She grinned, showcasing her fanged teeth. "I'm Chloe. We all thought what you did to Tiffany in weapons class was badass." She nodded to her friends, who stood behind her. They nodded back with encouraging smiles.

"Oh...thanks." It wasn't really me, just my weapon, but if it made me more friends, I would take the compliment.

"Anyway." She slid a purple flyer across the table. "My dad owns the Third Eye Moon. It's this underground nightclub. He's letting me rent it out for my nineteenth birthday, and I want you to come. Bring any of your friends if you want." She smiled at Luke and Angela.

Wow. I'd never really been invited to a big club party before. My heart sank as I scanned the flyer. It was that Friday night. At ten.

I scratched my neck nervously. "I…uh…don't live here." I pointed to my forehead to drive it home.

She shrugged. "So what? You could get past the border guards by showing your school ID. Say you have night class or something."

I could hide Shea in the back seat. I wanted to go so bad. "All right, I'll try my best," I told her with a smile.

She nodded. "Cool. See you later." Then she left, taking her Nightblood friends with her.

Luke watched her leave and gave me an impressed look. "Chloe Brisbane is like Nightblood royalty. Her entire family are Nightbloods. Rumor has it that two demons crashed into their living room the night of The Falling, so they all got the same magic. Her dad is like the mafia leader of them all or something."

Sounded like a big fat rumor. "But she's cool, right?" I didn't want to get in with the wrong crowd. The bullies and assholes could keep to themselves.

He nodded. "Totally. Her older brother is a senior

officer in the Fallen Army. He's so frickin' hot I can't even breathe around him. He's in Lincoln's brigade."

Lincoln.

I'd almost forgotten about him and the key to his trailer, which was burning a hole in my pocket. I needed to drop my weapon there and then get back to work.

"Cool. I gotta get going. See you tomorrow?" I told Luke, standing up. I wouldn't tell him I was on borrowed time until the last day.

He nodded and then eyed the flyer. "Yeah, see you tomorrow. Hey, what are you doing Friday night?" He gave me big puppy-dog eyes.

I laughed, pulled out my phone and snapped a picture of the flyer so I'd have the address. "You and Angela are totally coming with. I'll bring my best friend Shea, so you can meet her. She's a Mage."

They brightened and gave me enthusiastic nods.

Racing out of the cafeteria, I pulled out my car keys. I was kind of dying to see what Lincoln's house looked like. It probably smelled like sweaty boy and was a mess. He'd said not to snoop, but I was totally going to be tempted.

I was just passing the double doors to Raphael's office when they opened and I smashed into someone's chest.

"Ommph!" The breath came out of me, as strong arms wrapped gently around my biceps to steady me. I looked up to see Lincoln's dark hair messed over his forehead, stormy blue eyes assessing me with great care.

As the door was closing, I peeked inside. All four archangels were standing there, looking at me with unreadable blank gazes.

"Lincoln, I..." I didn't know what to say. I was still smashed against his rock-hard body, which was a teensy bit distracting.

He looked down at me. "Go put your seraph blade away in my house, and I'll meet you at your car, okay?"

I frowned. "What's going on?" He'd previously said all four archangels only got together for special occasions, so why were they all back?

"I'll tell you on the ride to your work," he said, and my mouth popped open.

"You're coming to work with me?" Maybe Raphael *was* going to buy my contract.

He simply nodded.

Why does he look nervous? And why is he looking at me so...differently?

"But—"

"Please, for once in your life, do as I say. This is important."

"Okay." I frowned.

Walking to his trailer, I looked behind me, but he was nowhere to be seen. When I got to the silver Airstream, I eyed the motorcycle next to it. With a bit of nervousness, I put the key in the trailer's lock and popped the door open. A waft of fresh linen, and something spicy and *manlike* hit me. Two small steps led up to an open kitchen and eating area. Everything was clean and modern, with a red-and-black theme. My eyes went to the dining table, an acoustic guitar and a small bowl of picks lay on top.

He plays guitar. He drives a motorcycle.

I never would've guessed that...though I guess I didn't know what to expect from him. An Asshole of the Year award gracing his dining table, maybe. It smelled good in there too, dammit. Again, not what I'd expected.

Bending down to peek out the window, I made sure he wasn't watching me, then walked back to the open bedroom at the very end of the trailer. There was a large bed with a messy, dark blue blanket, a book of classic poetry atop it. I grinned, knowing I was so going to use that against him one day.

Quick strides brought me back to the dining room table and I started to unhook my leg sheath.

'Take me with you. I have a bad feeling about this,' Sera said, spooking me.

'Bad feeling about what? I'm not allowed to take you into Demon City,' I told her.

'Why is he coming with you?' she asked.

With a shrug, I placed her on the table. '*Maybe to buy my demon contract.*'

'*That could be done over the phone, and with a wire transfer. Take. Me. With. You.*'

I frowned. Why exactly was Lincoln going with me to my work? He'd said it pained him to even be in Demon City, after all.

'You need to trust me. I have a feeling. Take me with you,' Sera added, in a voice of finality.

A growl escaped me. If I got caught or she was stolen, Lincoln would have my ass. Sighing, I laid the empty sheath on the table, then slipped Sera into my boot. I'd never forgive myself if something happened and I hadn't heeded her advice.

I left the trailer, locking it behind me, and jogged to my car.

Lincoln was standing next to the passenger side with a large duffel bag. "Can you drive?" he asked.

I scoffed. "As if I would let you drive my brand-new car."

His lips curled into a momentary smile, though it quickly faded, and his face took on a serious look. Unlocking my door, I slipped in and he sat next to me.

"Now, can you tell me what's going on?" I asked, heading off campus, and onto the freeway.

Lincoln pulled his shirt off in one swift move, and my eyes widened. "Okay...I mean, we just met a few days ago, but I wouldn't mind a little show," I joked.

He pulled out a thin chain-mail top and started working it over his head.

My brow furrowed. "What...? Why are you putting on chain mail? Lincoln, talk to me! I'm getting scared." My gut clenched in fear. I hated the unknown.

He sighed, and pulled out a metal breastplate, clipping it over the chain mail. *He's putting on full freaking battle armor. What the hell!*

"Every demon slave contract has wiggle room. I'm going to find yours," he stated.

I was half listening to him and half wondering if he was going to take off his pants next. But then his words registered, jarring me.

"You need full battle armor for that?" He remained silent. "Lincoln," I pressed, as we neared the checkpoint.

He threw a long-sleeved T-shirt over the armor, so it couldn't be seen. "I'm going to fight your boss. Winner gets you." He revealed it like it was no big deal.

My eyes bugged out of my head. "You? You're going to fight Master Burdock?"

He glared at me. "I happen to know a thing or two about fighting."

I hadn't meant it like that.

The border demon stopped us, and I flashed my card, showing my work hours and allotted travel access.

"And him?" the demon asked.

Lincoln pulled out some laminated card. "Fallen Academy business."

The demon furrowed his brow at the card, holding it to the light. A holographic image reflected on it, and he handed it back. "You're not permitted to stay the night."

Lincoln nodded. "Of course not."

The demon slapped the side of the car twice, hard, and I drove through.

"So you fight Burdock and he just, what, lets me go?" I asked him incredulously.

Lincoln winced, as if he were in pain. "Look, I can spend the next ten minutes explaining this whole thing to you, as I grow weaker and weaker, or you can take this time to tell me all about your boss. What kind of demon he is, what his weaknesses are, things like that."

Oh shit. This was real. It was really happening.

"Is this a fight to the death?" I asked him in shock.

Lincoln looked sideways at me. "Yes. Now unless you want it to be mine, start talking."

Oh my God.

"Burdock is a Brimstone demon. He can spew black smoke and fire out of his mouth and horns."

He nodded. "Okay. What else?"

"I've heard that he can create direct portals to Lucifer, and that he's impossible to kill unless you cut off his horns first. They carry some regenerative power or something. But those are all rumors."

"Worth trying."

We were one block away from the clinic. I wanted to circle for a few minutes just to process everything.

"Can't Michael or one of the archangels fight? I mean…why you?" I didn't want him to think I didn't have confidence in him, but…I didn't. I was scared for him. Yeah, he was a Celestial, but he was twenty-two going against a demon who was hundreds of years old.

"The archangels can't intervene in certain human matters. This is one of them. You signed that contract of your own free will."

Damn.

"And I have all the archangels' blessing to do this. They chose me, and I'm honored," he told me defiantly.

Well, okay then.

I pulled into the parking lot of the reanimation clinic, parked the car, took a deep breath, facing him.

"Why are you doing this? I mean, why fight for me?" *He could be killed. This is stupid.* "Just let me be sold to the Abrus demon, and go on about your life," I told him grumpily.

He turned to face me, his piercing blue eyes practically glowing. "Because you're special."

My entire body melted, warmth spreading throughout my gut.

His eyes widened a little. "I mean to the war and to the fallen angels. You're special to them, and I work for them, so that makes you special to me." He cleared his throat and looked anywhere but at me.

"Right," I said, as the fire he'd lit inside of me completely died.

He shrugged. "And I might've read your file today and discovered you may not be as bad as I thought you were. It's really admirable what you and your mom did to try and save your dad."

And just like that the tears threatened to fall, my throat throbbing as I tried to swallow my emotions. "There's a file on me? Where is it, and how do I destroy it?"

He smirked, but then the smile faded. "There's something I want to tell you."

Everything felt so serious, I was scared of what he was going to say. "Okay…"

He swallowed hard. "The reason I hated you when I first saw you is because my parents and little sister were killed in an attack, and you reminded me of it."

It was like all of the air was sucked out of the car and into a black hole. That was the trauma he'd been through. My entire body froze. Why would I remind him of his parents' death?

"We'd gone to a café near the border to celebrate my graduation from the academy. I was running late, goofing off with Noah and the boys," he continued, staring at his hands.

I rested my hand on his arm, and he didn't pull away. My breath was starting to come out in ragged gasps as I fought to keep calm. He'd lost his entire family. I couldn't imagine.

"I was two blocks away when the bomb went off. My mother, father, and little sister were gone, just like that." His voice cracked, and I couldn't hold back the tears before they ran down my face.

"Lincoln...I'm so sorry." I tried to hold my shit together, biting the inside of my cheek.

His piercing blue eyes bored into me. "When we replayed the footage, I expected it to be a demon...but it wasn't. It was a demon slave who waltzed into the café and ruined my life." The anger in his voice could've cut glass.

Oh shit. Is that possible? I didn't really know much about how the slave mark worked, but I'd heard the demons could control our actions with it, if they wanted. It explained everything, why he was so mean to me.

"I would never do that. I'd rather die," I told him passionately.

He shook his head. "You'd have no choice. That's my point. I'm here to give you the choice." With that, he popped open the door, and turned to me. "Come on. I grow weaker and weaker every second I'm in this city."

I just nodded. I was totally going to throw up.

When I went to open the door, Lincoln's hand came out to stop me. "If...something happens to me, make sure my body makes it back to the academy. I don't want to be reanimated."

Oh. My. God. The severity of the task at hand came crashing down on me. I could only nod once again.

This gorgeous man, who apparently played guitar, and was still definitely Asshole of the Year, was going to fight a Brimstone demon for me. If he weren't being asked by the fallen, I might've even said it was romantic. And now that he'd shared his parents' story with me, I was seeing him in a whole new light. I'd be an asshole too if a demon slave blew up my family.

Please don't die. You're nice to look at.

And that was the last thought I had before all hell broke loose.

Pun intended.

CHAPTER 9

The moment Lincoln threw open the doors to the clinic, a dark feeling descended. Burdock appeared suddenly, smoke coming from his horns.

"What are *you* doing here?" he growled, pointing to Lincoln.

I just froze, flattening myself against the wall.

Lincoln pulled his sword free and pointed it at Burdock's chest. "I challenge you to a fight to the death. If I win, Brielle Atwater is absolved of her slave contract, and becomes a free soul."

It felt like time had stopped. There was a kind of charged electricity hanging in the air, nobody moving.

Burdock tipped his head back and roared in laughter, black smoke coming out of every orifice, and settling on the ground. My eyes flicked to movement at the back. My mother was watching everything from the open back room door, mouth agape.

"Nothing you can offer me is more valuable than her. Trust me. No deal." He pulled a mace from his belt. "But I will kill you for trespassing."

Lincoln didn't look fazed as he reached behind his back and produced another weapon. That one was extraordinarily larger and shinier. It radiated a certain power, and when Burdock's smoke neared it, it fled, as if in fear.

"I present Archangel Michael's sword. Freely given to the winner of this fight." He laid the sword on the ground, the black smoke chasing away from it.

Burdock stood there, in absolute shock, eyeing the weapon with the greediest gaze I'd ever seen. "So, I kill you, and I get the sword and the girl?"

Lincoln nodded, holding out a glowing scroll of parchment paper.

"Signed with the blessing of the fallen angels themselves. All four of them." Lincoln tossed the scroll on the ground.

Burdock grinned, then clapped, a red, glowing scroll appearing in his hand. "I accept." He tossed it to the center, where the sword and other scroll lay.

Lincoln nodded. "Brielle is my witness. Call yours."

Burdock chortled, showing his razor-sharp, blackened teeth. "He's on his way. Outside. I'll draw the perimeter."

Add mental communication to his powers. Oh God.
Lincoln backed through the doors without ever

turning his back to Burdock. I did the same. Michael's sword and the two parchments remained on the floor of the reanimation clinic.

"Kate, watch the collateral. If anything happens to it, I'll kill you," he told my mother.

She nodded and scurried forward, picking up the three items.

My mother and I shared a look through the glass door. A look that said everything. She wanted this for me. *I* wanted this for me. I didn't know what it meant for her and Mikey though, and that had me apprehensive.

Turning to face Burdock, I saw his witness had indeed arrived. He'd called Shea's boss, Master Grim. And Shea was in the driver seat next to him. Lincoln was sweating a little, clearly weakening with each moment he spent in the city.

The second Shea's boss exited the car, Burdock pointed to him.

"You are witness. If I die, this young man gets to leave with Brielle and the sword, and her contract is absolved."

Grim nodded, looking Lincoln up and down like he was a meal. Then he spat on the ground, the sidewalk steaming where the spittle hit it.

"If I kill him, which I will, I get Archangel Michael's sword, and get to keep Brielle and her contract. Is that correct, boy?" he asked.

Lincoln nodded and stepped into the parking lot. "Let's do this."

Burdock grinned. "Gladly."

Moving forward, he then bent over, spewing black fire onto the concrete. It chased along the parking lot, drawing a perimeter in a perfect circle around Lincoln and himself. The flames danced about two feet high, and reeked of brimstone, the acidic sulfur burning my nostrils.

Holy end of days. Lincoln's going to die.

"That's hellfire, son, so unless you want to meet the Prince of Darkness, I suggest you don't touch it," Burdock growled.

My eyes widened. *The fire is a portal to Lucifer?*

Lincoln glared at Burdock and flexed, popping out his glorious, white wings. They stretched out close to a fifteen-foot span, and he flapped them up and down really hard, blowing out half of the hellfire circle.

"You don't scare me, old man," Lincoln spat.

Oh shit.

Burdock was a blur of motion. Like a freaking vampire, he was there one second and then standing before Lincoln the next. He swung his mace out and connected with Lincoln's chest, knocking into his armor and tearing his shirt.

The breath rushed out of Lincoln, but he held steady and used the proximity to lunge at Burdock with his sword. The Celestial was able to nick his arm before the demon moved away.

I'd forgotten to tell him Burdock was superfast. *Oops.*

Burdock swung out with his right arm, intending to clip Lincoln in the face, but the Celestial pumped his wings and shot up into the air, hovering above the demon, out of his grasp. That enraged Burdock, who spewed orange flames from his mouth, without warning, catching the tips of Lincoln's wings. Lincoln panicked, flying higher into the sky, flapping his wings faster and faster in an effort to douse the flames. I chewed my nails as I watched everything go down, wondering how the hell all of this had happened so fast.

The fire sputtered out and then Lincoln suddenly let go. He tucked his wings in, right above Burdock, so he dropped like a hundred and fifty-pound weight, fast and hard. He landed on top of the tall demon, taking him to the ground, and with one hard slash of the sword, hacked Burdock's left horn off.

"Kill this fool!" Shea's boss roared.

Black smoke burst from the gaping hole where the horn was, and Lincoln started to cough. The smoke covered their bodies, hiding them from view, until all I could hear was grunting, and the clanging of metal against metal.

My startled gaze found Shea across the lot, looking completely shocked and confused. Her slack jaw and death mark tattoo had a thought forming in my mind. A wild thought. A thought that could get me killed.

Suddenly, a bright blue light rose above the black smoke, and then Lincoln was flying out of it with Burdock in his arms. My master was hornless, bleeding, and freaking enraged. He shouted in anger as Lincoln flew them higher and higher.

Then he dropped Master Burdock.

From fifty feet up.

The demon screamed the entire way down, spewing fire and smoke as he fell. When he crashed into the parking lot, the pavement caved in like a crater, and chipped up at the edges. His legs had to have been broken, but he didn't seem to care. He pulled a dagger from his boot, and as Lincoln sped toward him, sword outstretched, the demon flung the dagger straight at him. I screamed, but it was no use. It sailed through the space between them and sank into Lincoln's thigh. With a painful roar, the Celestial dropped clumsily the last few feet and landed awkwardly, snapping his ankle. I could hear the crack of bone from where I stood.

I winced, stepping forward to help in some way, when my mom pulled me back. "No interference or it voids the whole thing. He's got this."

I wanted to protest, to run in there and help, but she was right. It was probably against the rules, and he was so close. It looked like he really had a chance.

I could be free.

Lincoln and Burdock were staring at each other, both bleeding and broken. Lincoln took a calming breath and then opened his eyes. They were an eerie blue, and *glowing*.

"Back to Hell with you, demon!" he roared and then swung his sword. Burdock swung his mace in circles around his head, and then, just as Lincoln got close, he let go, intending for the mace to smack Lincoln in the face. Lincoln raised his sword, and a blinding blue light shot out, sending the mace to the ground, and shattering it into a hundred pieces.

Whoa.

You could see it on Burdock's face, the moment when he knew he had lost. He opened his mouth to speak, but Lincoln came down sideways with his sword, and took the demon's head clean off before he could utter a word.

Holy freaking shit. Burdock's dead.

The glowing red contract in my mom's hands puffed to ash, and we both gasped.

I was free. I was a free soul.

Tears slid down my mom's face, and I wanted to enjoy the moment with her. It was everything I'd wanted, to be free of this shithole, everything my mother wanted for my life as well, but I couldn't enjoy it. Not with my best friend standing across the way, death mark on her arm, dark circles around her eyes and bruises on her face. Tainted Academy was going to break her. Her strong, beautiful spirit was fading day by day, and I'd made a promise to never let that happen. I wouldn't let her go dark.

"Your slave mark is gone," my mom said, mystified.

I rubbed my forehead in shock.

Lincoln is so going to kill me.

I reached out and took Michael's sword from her. "I love you, Mom," I told her, then advanced into the circle, stepping over Burdock's severed head.

I pulled my dagger from my boot and it flared to life, emitting a golden-yellow, buttery light. I pointed the tip of the blade at Shea's master.

"Grim, I challenge you in a fight to the death. If I win, Shea's contract is absolved, and she's a free soul."

Chaos erupted. My mother, Shea, and Lincoln all screamed in protest. If Lincoln hadn't just killed my mom's boss, I would have fought him to free her but seeing as though he was dead, there was no way to get my mom's contract. I had to fight for Shea while I had the chance. I knew my mother would understand. Eventually. Assuming I survived.

Master Grim just smirked, his eyes flashing red. "And if I win?" He took off his jacket, revealing a hairy, scarred chest with leathery skin.

I threw Michael's sword at his feet. "The sword of Archangel Michael. Freely given." I tried to remember the wording Lincoln had used.

More like freely stolen but I was hoping that wouldn't matter.

He grinned. "And you. If I win, I want the sword and you. And I change the terms from fight to the death to forfeit. If one of us forfeits, we may keep our life."

"Fine!" I replied through gritted teeth, before my nerves got the best of me.

"Absolutely not!" Lincoln burst forward, limping. The knife still stuck out of his leg, the tips of his wings were burned, and his hands looked bloody and battered. He hooked a hand under my armpit and started to drag me toward my car. "Have you lost your mind?" Blood-tinged spittle flew from his mouth in rage.

'*We can do this,*' Sera egged me on. '*Shea is family.*'

I clenched my jaw and pointed to Shea, standing with my mother at the edge of the circle in shock.

"The girl right there is my sister," I told him.

He furrowed his brow as he looked from my pale skin to her brown tones.

"And I know you don't trust me, or know me that well yet, but one thing you will learn is that I'm loyal as fuck, and I'm not leaving her behind. I'd rather die!"

He looked defeated, weak, and tired. "Then you might just get your wish." Lincoln collapsed onto the back of my car, blood leaking from his leg.

Does that mean he's allowing it? I didn't wait to find out. Turning, I faced the Grimlock demon. "I accept your terms."

He sneered and clapped, producing Shea's contract and handing it to my mother.

"My witness will be here any moment," he stated.

Lincoln was mumbling something, reaching for me. *Shit*. He was getting worse by the minute. I opened the back of the car and helped him inside.

"Are you going to be okay?" I asked. "Should I call for help?"

He shook his head. "No one can help me in here. Just make this quick. The longer you draw it out, the better chance you have of losing."

Thanks for the confidence.

I turned and came face-to-face with Shea, tears pouring down her cheeks. "What the hell are you doing? Call it off!"

I shook my head. "I'm not leaving without you. You'll go dark, we'll stop talking, and my mom will cry all the time. So *no*."

She barked a laugh through her tears and threw herself at me for a bone-crunching hug. "He has an old left knee injury, pains him all the time. His throat skin is the thinnest. Everywhere else is like rubber," she whispered, then pulled back.

It hit me then that I was about to kill a man, or at least attempt to. The thought was horrifying. Demon or not, I was about to become a killer. Looking across the parking lot, I saw his witness was the Abrus demon that was going to buy my contract.

Great.

I moved to walk into the circle, when Lincoln snaked an arm out, and grabbed my wrist. "If she's really your family, then there's nothing that can stop your seraph blade from defending her."

Whatever I was going to do, I needed to hurry. The back of my SUV was overflowing with crimson blood.

It started to rain, as it often did in Demon City, mercifully snuffing the black portal fire.

'When he advances, kick his left knee out and then go for his throat,' Sera told me.

It was like having my own personal battle instructor in my head.

Taking a deep breath, I popped out my wings. I didn't exactly know how to fly yet, but I could at least hover, which could be useful in a bad situation.

The demon grinned, black, leathery, bat-like wings erupting from his back.

Oh shit. What have I done?

Without ceremony, he charged for me, holding a big-ass, flaming, red, serrated sword, flapping his wings to hover and advance his height.

'Plan B!' Sera shouted. *'Slide under him and cut his groin!'*

My eyes bugged out. *'What?'* But I didn't have time to protest; he would be on me in a second.

Here goes nothing.

I used his momentum and dropped to my knees. As he sailed over me, I arched back and thrust Sera into his groin. I connected with something, but I wasn't sure how much damage I'd inflicted. He didn't even scream, and the dagger pulled away clean.

Popping up into a standing position, I flapped my wings twice and hovered. Grim was coming at me *fast*.

This is for Shea.

The only thing standing between us being free souls together was him. There was no way in hell that I was letting that happen.

He flew at me, his long flaming sword outstretched. We were going to collide, and there was nothing I could do. With no shield or armor, that sword would gut me like a fish.

'*Stick out your leg!*' Sera urged.

I did, connecting with his chest as he sliced into my outer thigh with his sword. Searing pain tore through my leg, and a wail ripped from my throat. The bastard had cut me, but at least my guts were still firmly inside my body.

He grinned and then flew backward to get better momentum, but I didn't give him a chance. With a battle cry, I flapped my wings harder than ever before, and rushed him, intending to cut into his neck. As I lunged for him, he moved down and my dagger went into his eye instead.

Good enough.

'*Keep it in there!*' Sera shouted.

The dagger lit up a searing hot blue color, and Grim's high-pitched wails filled the air. He started to lash out blindly, attempting to slice me. I had to let go and leave the dagger in his eye to avoid being cut again, abandoning my only weapon. Beams of white light shot out of his ears as he continued screaming.

'*Shea is family*,' Sera declared in a vicious voice. '*She's ours, not his.*'

Holy shit, my weapon's gone postal.

I dropped to the pavement as he fell in front of me, trying to pull the dagger out of his eye. The hilt kept burning his hand, so he had to let go, unable to keep a strong enough grip to remove it.

Now that he was on the ground before me, and I was weaponless, I wasn't sure what to do.

I took too long to think about it, and he grabbed me by the neck, throwing me across the lot. I didn't have time to pump my wings as I sailed across the space quickly, so I landed hard on my ass, pain exploding in my tailbone. I got the sense from his drunken walk, and tearing vision, that he couldn't see well out of his remaining eye, or else he would've already cut me open easily with his scary-ass sword. He still managed to stalk toward me, at an alarming speed, ripping across the pavement with a growl.

'*Get up and kick out his knee!*' Sera instructed.

Oh yeah, the knee injury.

I shot up, moaning when the pain tore into me. My lower back and leg were jacked up for sure. My left outer thigh was cut and bleeding, so I used my right leg to support my weight as I lifted my left into the air and sent all of my power into the kick. Just as he reached me, my booted foot connected with his kneecap and a snapping sound rang out across the parking lot.

"Kick his ass!" Shea shouted in a throaty scream. That was the Shea I knew, the fiery spirit who'd been broken down lately.

"Finish it!" my mother added, encouraging me.

He dropped his sword, and as the demon went down, Sera sent me a bunch of mental images, flashes through my mind of things she wanted me to do. I didn't have the luxury of stopping to think about them or question them. I also didn't want him to have the time to forfeit and live. I threw myself over him, grabbing the knife. The hilt cool to the touch for me. Pulling it out of his eye with a nasty sucking sound, I went to slam it into his throat.

"I forfeit!" he screamed.

Screw that. I brought my arm down hard, but an unseen power wrapped around my wrist, suspending it an inch from his throat. My eyes flicked up to the Abrus demon. He had one of his hands in the air, playing me like a puppet. He raised his arm and suddenly my body was lifting off the Grimlock demon. Then his power left me, and my feet slammed to the ground, pain shooting up my thigh.

"You've won," he reminded in a smooth voice. "Run along. Don't worry, we'll be seeing each other again very shortly." His eyes rested on Sera. "Nice seraph blade."

I swallowed hard, and then glanced at Shea in shock.

Her forehead was free of the crescent moon tattoo.

Her contract in ashes on the ground.

Holy shit.

I looked at my mom as she rushed over, head bent low, submissive. Handing me the Michael sword, she pulled me in for a hug. "I'm very proud of you. Call me later, but don't ever come back here again."

Her words shocked the absolute shit out of me. Tears swam in my vision, making it blurry. "Mom, what about you and Mikey?"

I was starting to feel dizzy. *How much blood have I lost?*

"We'll be fine. Go," she said more firmly, then turned her back on me to walk back inside the clinic.

What will happen to her? Why is her mark still there if Lincoln killed our boss? I had a hundred questions, but a wave of dizziness took me again. When I looked down, I saw I was standing in a puddle of my blood.

Shit.

Everything was starting to blur at the edges. Shea hooked a hand under my armpit, hauling me into the back of the SUV and pushing me lightly so my body interlocked with Lincoln's. Two bloody, half-dead people spooning in the back of my SUV.

"Get us...to the...academy," Lincoln told her

weakly. She slammed the back door and ran to the driver side.

My back was against Lincoln's chest, his warm breath coming out in short rasps against my neck. "You're…the wildest…girl…I've ever…met." He reached out to me with a glowing orange hand. With a jolt, the car peeled out, and I remembered Shea didn't have a license.

Too weak to care, I just stared at the glowing, orange hand as he laid it on my bleeding thigh. He was trying to heal me. He was bleeding to death, weak as shit, and *still* trying to heal me.

"You're the hottest guy I've ever met," I said stupidly. The blood loss had obviously made me loopy, let my inhibitions down.

A low laugh erupted out of me, and then a black wall slammed into me as I lost consciousness.

CHAPTER 10

MY CONSCIOUSNESS RETURNED IN BOUTS. I remembered Noah standing over me screaming, then there was a bright golden light, and Raphael appeared. I remembered Lincoln's terrified face hovering over me, and Shea crying.

It all came in snippets, like a dream.

Now, I could feel bedsheets underneath me, my rib cage, thigh, and tailbone were throbbing. I tried to speak, but only croaked. Opening my eyes, I winced against the bright light.

Shea's face swam into view. "You wild bitch! Don't ever do that again," she scolded, sticking a finger in my face for good measure.

I tried to smile, but my face hurt. "I can promise you that." Shakily lifting a hand, my thumb brushed across her clear forehead.

She burst into tears then and threw her arms around me. "Thank you!" she sobbed in my ear. "*Mi familia.*"

"You're welcome, *mi vida loca.*" I didn't really know Spanish, but I threw out what I did randomly because it always made her laugh.

I was rewarded with that laugh now.

Peering around for the first time, I noticed I was in some type of medical room, with only a chair next to my bed. The door was propped open, leading out to a tiled hallway.

"You're in the healing clinic at Fallen Academy," she told me.

I nodded. "Am I expelled? In deep shit?"

We were free souls, but without jobs we wouldn't be able to live in Angel City, and now we were banned from Demon City. We were basically homeless if they wouldn't take us.

She shrugged. "I don't think so. I mean, there was a lot of yelling, but I heard the words 'brave idiot' tossed around a lot. Seems like the old dude likes you."

I smiled. *Raphael.*

"Is Lincoln okay?" I asked, eyeing the open door.

This time it was her turn to smile. "You mean the hottie who fought for your freedom? Yeah, his injuries were pretty minor. Being in Demon City was just zapping his energy, or whatever. Once we got over the border, he perked right up. Moderate blood loss and some stitches, I heard them say."

I sighed in relief. "Is he pissed at me?"

She grinned again. "*So* pissed. *Unnaturally* pissed. He punched the wall." She pointed to a hole in the plaster. I grimaced. Her hand rested on my shoulder. "You almost died, Bri. You can't go fighting demons, like you're some badass."

I'd nearly killed a demon, so I was arguably a badass, but I wasn't going to say a word. Shea would go all Puerto Rican on me, start cussing in Spanish, and wave her angry hands in my face. So I just nodded, glancing at the pile of my clothes on the chair, and noticed for the first time that I was wearing a thin, white cotton gown, and nothing else.

"Where's Sera?" I asked, eyeing the gown.

Shea frowned. "Who?"

"My dagger."

Dawning shone on her face. "Ah yes. In the middle of his rant, Lincoln ripped it off you, and said you weren't allowed to have it outside of weapons and battle training."

That motherfu—

"Brielle. You're awake." Raphael's voice came from the open doorway.

I sat up, nervously clutching the sheet around my body. Raphael was with Mr. Claymore, both looking at Shea.

"Come in," I told them. *Please don't kick us out.*

"What you did was *very* dangerous," Raphael chastised me.

I frowned. "I know, but—"

"But also admirable. I'm very taken with the story. To save your sister from a lifetime of slavery like that. It's touching."

Shea raised one eyebrow at me.

"Sister?" I asked. I mean, yeah, I considered her my sister, but…

"Lincoln said you two were family," Raphael stated, seemingly oblivious to the fact that Shea's hair and skin were about ten shades darker than mine.

Lincoln told them that? Hmm. Maybe they would only let her stay if she was related to me.

I grasped Shea's hand. "We are, and if you kick me out, we'll have nowhere to live. But…no pressure."

Both gentlemen laughed and exchanged smiles. For a man in his early forties, Mr. Claymore was quite handsome, his short, brown hair woven through with silver streaks over kind eyes.

"We're not kicking you out," Raphael reassured. "I brought Mr. Claymore to see if it was possible to erase Shea's death mark. Assuming that's what she wants. That way she could become a student here. Room and board is included, of course."

I wanted to act tough but I couldn't, tears leaked from my eyes.

Shea shot out of her chair. "*Yes!* That's all I've ever wanted. I took the mark against my will. They pinned me down, and—" Her voice broke before she could continue.

Mr. Claymore frowned, stepping forward. "If that's true, if you took the mark against your will, then I can easily remove it. It'll take a day or two for me to brew the potion, but it'll fall away as if it were never there."

Shea's chest was rising and falling, clearly trying to hold her shit in.

Raphael clapped once. "Then that's that! I suppose you two would like to room together? I'll have the groundskeeper make up your room so you can get settled. Were you able to bring any belongings?"

Shea and I shared a look. *Yeah right. We ran like a bat out of Hell. Pun intended.* I'd packed a bag like Lincoln told me to, but it had one pair of clothes and one pair of underwear with my toothbrush. Nothing to last me...forever.

"No, and I'm worried about my mom and my brother," I confessed to him.

He nodded, his glossy hair falling around his shoulders. "I spoke with your mother an hour ago when she called to inquire about your health. She said she's fine and has been permitted by her new...employer to visit you once a month. She can bring your belongings then. In the meantime, we have an overflowing lost and found pile that I'll have Mrs. Greely bring in for you to go through."

I barely heard the rest of it, glad my mom was okay. I was curious who her new master was though. I was kind of hoping that when Lincoln killed Burdock, she would be free.

"One more thing." Raphael held up a finger. "School, room, and board is free here, but if you want extra cash, you'll need to get part-time jobs. I happen to know that the clinic is looking for someone, Brielle, and with your healing abilities, you'd be hired on the spot."

My healing abilities, I know nothing about.

I nodded. "Thank you, sir. I'll look into it."

Mr. Claymore looked to Shea. "And I could always use a Mage student to keep my supplies organized. Crush my powders, help with the potions."

Shea, eyes wide, just nodded.

They were letting us stay. They gave us jobs.

Holy shit, Angel City is Heaven on Earth.

We were finally free of the darkness that had lurked over us most of our lives. We were slaves to no one. We were free souls, and it felt good.

Raphael went to leave the room, but I sat up straighter. "Sir, one more thing."

He turned.

"Umm, Lincoln took Sera, my seraph blade. Can I get it back?" Surely he thought it was preposterous that Lincoln was treating me like a five-year-old.

He frowned. "I've put Lincoln in charge of your training. If he feels you shouldn't have the blade outside of classes, then there's nothing I can do."

With a bow, they both left.

Grrr. Lincoln was lording his power over me, but

dammit, he'd given me my freedom, so I was going to have to do whatever he said.

Oh God.

A memory came back to me then. He'd called me wild and I'd called him hot. I hid my face in my hands, mortified, praying he'd forget. When I looked up, I saw Shea staring at a blank spot on the wall, her face a mask of complete shock.

"What's wrong?" I asked her. "Aren't you happy?"

She nodded. "I'm so happy. But it feels weird. I'd forgotten what happy felt like."

I smiled and reached for her hand. "Promised you I wasn't going to let you go dark."

She nodded. "And I promise not to let you get through your first year without kissing Lincoln."

My eyes widened. "Shea, stop. He's my teacher, kind of. *And* an asshole, kind of. Anyway, not happening."

She grinned. "That was a lot of kind-ofs."

I punched her arm and she laughed.

There was a knock on the door then, and a short, brunette woman in her early-forties came in, holding a huge basket of clothes. I even saw a backpack and water bottle poking out. She also held a pair of crutches.

"How are you feeling, dear?" she asked, setting the basket and crutches at the end of my bed. I recognized the Raphael tattoo on her forearm.

"A little sore, but I'm okay."

She nodded. "I'm Mrs. Greely. I'm in charge of the

healing clinic here at the academy. Raphael tells me you're looking for some part-time work? I'd love to hire you."

I nodded. "Yes, ma'am. That would be wonderful."

She smiled and handed me a packet. "Fill this out and bring it by tomorrow. Then we can go over the schedule."

I grabbed the packet, clutching it to my chest. "I will." I'd traded up, from washing dead bodies at the reanimation clinic, to this.

"You girls are free to leave. Housekeeping is putting linens on your beds. Here's a map with your room designation. Come back if you feel any worsening pain and take anything you like from the lost and found." She indicated the basket of clothes she'd set down.

I nodded. "We will. Thank you so much."

She smiled and then left the room quietly.

Shea glanced at the map. "Dude, this place is huge. Way bigger than Tainted Academy."

I still couldn't believe I'd gotten her out of there. That I was out of there. I rubbed my forehead in disbelief at the slave mark being gone.

Swinging my leg gently over the bed, I gestured to the pile. "Help me find some clothes." There was no way I could put that torn and bloody jumpsuit back on.

Shea rummaged through and found a pair of large, smelly sweatpants, and a too-tight tank top. After I shimmied into them, we both looked at my clothes and burst out laughing. "It's going to be a rough two weeks until we get paid," Shea admitted, once she'd calmed a bit.

I winced. "Maybe my mom can send Mikey with some underwear."

Shea nodded, hopeful. "Please God, yes. I don't want to free-ball it unless I absolutely have to."

After we filled the backpack with a water bottle, headphones, a hoodie, two gym shirts, and an umbrella, we checked out of the clinic, and searched the grounds for our room. We quickly got lost and realized Shea had been reading the map upside down.

Once I took over, we found Bright Hall. The common room was bustling with students, the female-only Bright Hall sharing the room with the all-male Stone Hall. I was thrilled when I saw Luke and Angela, introducing Shea before giving them a brief rundown of what had happened. After their shock subsided, they were super enthusiastic that we'd both be attending the academy full-time.

"Oh my God, girl, now I have someone to freak out over the gauntlet with," Luke squealed.

"The gauntlet?" Shea asked warily.

Angela leaned in. "It's the end-of-year test to graduate you," she whispered. "If you fail, you go home, and good luck getting a magical job. You'll end up with some shitty human job, maybe private security for a rich human family. If you pass, you're admitted into the second year here."

My eyes widened. I'd imagined a written test, maybe a few sword moves, but *the gauntlet*? "Well, you're a third year. Can you tell us how hard it was?"

She shook her head. "We've all been spelled not to. But trust me, you'll need every advantage you can get, so study hard. That's all I can say."

The lights suddenly flickered, and we were told we needed to go to our rooms for lights out. Once we bid Angela and Luke good night, we made our way down the hall to room 11.

Leaning against the doorframe was Tiffany.

When her eyes landed on me, they narrowed, jumping from my outfit to Shea's death mark, and then to my crutches. Finally, they rested on my forehead.

"What happened to your slave mark, Archie?" she crooned, still blocking our door.

I glanced at Shea, who looked absolutely feral, then shrugged. "It must've rubbed off on Lincoln's chest while we were in the back of my car."

Her whole face flared red, anger boiling out of every pore. "Enjoy the room. It used to be mine, and now I have to share." She blasted past me, knocking into my shoulder.

Pain shot up from my tailbone at the jostling.

"I can make her hair fall out. I learned how at Tainted Academy," Shea growled.

I waved my hand. "She's not worth it. She's obsessed with Lincoln, so I'm pretty sure I just ruined her night."

Shea grinned. "That was a really good line, I must say."

With a laugh, I opened the door. The room was small but cozy and clean. It had a window in the middle of the back wall, and a twin bed with drawers underneath on each side of the space. Typical dorm style. There was shelving high above the beds, about two feet from the ceiling, that wrapped around the room, containing books and other magical items. I spotted jars of weird-looking things, like frog legs on Shea's side, and on mine were books on the angelic realm and other Celestial-related things.

"Whoa. At Tainted we had to pay for all our books." She stepped up on the powder-blue bedspread and started rummaging through the volumes. At the end of each bed was a desk, and mine held a new class schedule.

"Hey, we got new schedules. Check yours," I told her.

When my eyes fell on my new start time of 8:00 a.m., I nearly wept. Reading more, I started to laugh. Lincoln had clearly made my schedule.

Brielle Atwater

<u>Fallen History</u>   8 a.m.–9 a.m.
                (Room 506, Mrs. Delacourt)

*You may retrieve your dagger from
Lincoln's trailer at 9:01 a.m.*

163

<u>Battle Class</u>	9:05 a.m.–10 a.m. (Room 511, Master Bradstone)
<u>Weapons</u>	10:05 a.m.–11 a.m. (Room 405, Mr. Claymore)
<u>Lunch</u>	11:05 a.m.–11:55 a.m. (Dining hall)
<u>Celestial Master Studies</u>	12 p.m.–2 p.m. 30 mins each master teacher. (Training Hall 304)
<u>Studies of Light</u>	2:05 p.m.–3 p.m. (Room 401, Mr. Rincor)

3:01 PM RETURN YOUR DAGGER TO LINCOLN'S TRAILER OR ELSE.

He was so grumpy.

After comparing our schedules, I was sad to see I only had two classes with Shea, battle class and weapons, but it was getting late, and I felt like I'd been hit by a truck. Pulling my dead phone out of my messenger bag, I groaned. It was useless without the charger that was right next to my bed back home. I'd have to borrow someone's phone tomorrow and call my mom, make sure she and Mikey were okay, and that she would continue to take care of Bernie and Maximus without me there.

I didn't bother showering, just crawled into bed. "I'm glad we're in this together," I mumbled to Shea.

She peered at me. "Me too. And if you want blondie's hair to fall out, just say the word."

I fell asleep with a smile on my face.

CHAPTER 11

Shea and I were relieved to hear that three meals and two snacks a day were included in the free tuition here, so it looked like we just needed to earn enough money to pay for personal items.

I was so nervous to see Lincoln after everything that had happened, that I nearly threw up that morning during breakfast. I'd eaten two bites of my oatmeal, and then my stomach threatened to upheave it, so I pushed it away. I'd awoken to find that I no longer needed my crutches, and other than some slight throbbing pain when I walked and itching around my stitches, I was healed. It would take a while to get used to that.

Shea said she wasn't nervous, but I knew she was. We'd both gone to the seamstress to get new jumpsuits early that morning, but Rose didn't have any more long-sleeved ones. That meant Shea's death mark was on full display.

"It'll be gone in a few days," I reminded her.

She just nodded, keeping her arm tucked across her chest. When the bell sounded, both of us jumped a little.

"Okay...I'll see you in battle class," I told her.

She nodded again.

I sat through history trying not to doze off. Everyone had heard the story. Lucifer rose from Hell to wreak havoc on Earth, a war broke out in Heaven, the archangels fell to fight Lucifer, yada yada. Then we all got powers, and now we were screwed. But when Professor Delacourt, a centaur, started talking about Raphael, my attention snapped back to the lesson.

"Lucifer unleashed his creatures onto the Earth, intending to build a bridge to the angelic realms so they could climb, and then wipe out all of the Creator's most blessed creatures. But it was Raphael who decided to lead the fight and come to Earth, meeting them head on before they could go through with their plan, and kill the angels."

They didn't teach that in Demon City.

She continued pointing to a poster with drawings of the different angels in a form of hierarchy. "Up here at the very top we have the seraphim, the guardians of the Creator's throne."

I was practically hanging off my seat with interest now. The seraphim were who were rumored to have made my dagger.

"Then the Cherubim, angels of harmony and

wisdom. The Thrones, angels of will and justice. The Dominions, who are the angels of intuition and guide the lower angels on their paths."

Her hand lifted, pointing to a picture of an angel holding a scale. "The Virtues, angels of choice. The Powers, who are my personal favorite," she crooned. "They're the warrior angels."

Whoa. I had no idea there were so many kinds. I raised my hand and she pointed to me. "Brielle?"

"So, is Michael a warrior angel?"

She shook her head. "He is one of the lowest, and yet most noble angels. An archangel, which are the protectors of mankind."

I didn't know why I was emotional over her words, but I was. A war broke out and the lowest rung of angels, the archangels, left the realm and fell to help humanity?

"Why didn't The Powers or whatever do anything?" I asked.

She sighed. "I don't know, but a war broke out in the angelic realm over it. There are a lot of rules, and Raphael and the other archangels broke some of them to come here."

They broke the rules. Whoa. Did they get in trouble? Before I could ask, the bell rang.

I had four minutes to get to Lincoln's trailer and retrieve Sera, then go to battle class.

Snatching my bag, I took off, limping through the

quad. I still had stitches in my thigh, so I had to be careful. The angelic healing had worked wonders, but a little bit of man's medicine was needed as well. I tore across the parking lot as quickly as I could and hobbled up the steps to his trailer. Whipping out my key, I thrust it into the lock, and flung the door open.

Lincoln was sitting at the dining room table, eating scrambled eggs and an apple. My dagger was on the bench next to him.

"Geez! Do you have to bust in here like a cop? Feel free to knock next time, and see if I'm home," he groaned.

I was panting like a wild animal, my mouth dry from breathing openmouthed on my way here. I hadn't expected Lincoln to be there. I didn't know what to say to him. He was acting totally normal, like we hadn't almost died together. Like I hadn't called him hot.

"I didn't think you'd be home," I said between gasps.

He nodded. "Took the day off to finish healing."

Healing. He was hurt.

I swallowed hard, trying to find saliva so I didn't look like a horse with my lips stuck to my teeth. "Hey, about yesterday…thank you so much for what you did."

He nodded. "And?" He pinned me with a blue-eyed glare.

A frown scrunched my brows. "And…I'm sorry?" I winced.

"And." He added with a nod.

I growled. "I'm sorry I almost got us killed, but Shea's my family! I couldn't leave her."

"*And?*" His eyes opened wide, questioning me.

I crossed my arms. "And what?" The asshat was going to make me late.

"And you will never, *ever* do anything like that again." His hands balled into fists.

I rolled my eyes. "Obviously. I'm not *that* stupid." Of course I wasn't going to make a habit out of fighting higher-level demons and almost dying.

He grinned. "Are you sure?"

I stepped forward, snatching the dagger off the seat with one hand, and his apple with the other, taking a bite to wet my mouth. "Later." I slammed the apple down on the table, sans one bite, and left.

Lincoln Grey lit a fire within me. I wasn't sure if it was a good one or a bad one, but I was engulfed in the heat nonetheless.

The rest of the week passed rather quickly.

Shea had her death mark removed, but not before everyone saw it. Tiffany was now referring to us as Archie and Demon Lover respectively. Shea didn't take too well to the nickname and had "accidentally" tripped in the lunchroom and spilled scalding-hot soup all over

Tiffany's chest. It was the highlight of my week. Shea would normally have rearranged her face, but we had a good thing going at the school, so she wasn't going to mess it up, and get kicked out over name-calling. At least not yet. Tiffany hadn't called her Demon Lover since then, so I think it worked.

Mikey had dropped off two huge duffel bags of our stuff, including homemade cookies, and a sweet note from my mom. Now that I had my phone charger, I was able to call and text her. Her new boss was Grim, the demon I'd almost killed to free Shea. *Whoops.* He and Master Burdock had an agreement that if he was killed, Master Grim would inherit his clinic and contracts. I guess because Lincoln had cut off Burdock's horns, he couldn't be reanimated. Thank God for that. My mom mentioned that Master Grim was so busy with his strip clubs, that he let her run the clinic, so she was actually alone most of the time there, and happier for it.

"Dude, when was the last time we went to a club?" Shea asked, eyeing the flyer for Chloe's birthday party at her dad's club that night.

"Like a year," I told her, rummaging through my clothes. "God, Mikey and my mom packed all practical clothes. Nothing cute," I griped.

Angela and Luke were in our room. Luke was doing Angela's makeup, carefully applying black, thick winged eyeliner. He paused from reaching for her false eyelashes and she nodded at me. "You guys can raid my closet. You're a bit taller, Bri, but otherwise we're about the same size."

Shea and I shared a conspiratorial look.

"You sure?" Shea asked.

She'd spent like six hours after class the night before rolling her curly hair into twists, then slept on a silk pillowcase. Now the curls hung chin high, like perfect little wrapped locks. She was clearly more excited for the party than I was. She'd met my Celestial master teachers and was crushing on Noah hard.

I'd started work at the healing clinic, where Mrs. Greely informed me that Noah was in charge, second to her, and assured me my healing lessons would start there with the smaller cases. Other than hovering, doing basic karate and blocking, I hadn't learned to do any of my Celestial magic yet.

"I'm sure. I have a hot, red silk jumper that would look great with your skin tone, Shea," Angela encouraged.

You didn't have to tell us twice. We tore down the hall laughing, then spent the next thirty minutes making a mess of her closet. Shea had indeed decided on the red jumper. The pants were straight-legged and tight in the butt while the top was sleeveless. We'd have to duct-tape Shea's big boobs because apparently my mom didn't think a strapless bra was a necessity.

After much deliberating, I'd decided on royal blue silk shorts with a lace hem, and a black silk corset top.

It was more revealing than I normally wore, but Shea assured me I looked totally boneable—her words, not mine. Considering I'd only 'boned' one guy, and it was the most awkward thirty seconds of my life—*thank you, junior prom*—I wasn't looking to do so with anyone that night.

Shea had picked her infinity weapon in class, a small, fist-size circular blade that you could grasp like wolverine claws. She tucked that blade into her purse now. Even Angela was bringing a weapon.

"Should I get Sera?" I asked them.

Angela nodded. "We're Fallen Academy students in the middle of a war. It's rare, but attacks inside Angel City do happen."

I wondered if Lincoln was home. I was wearing my trusty boots, so I could just slip it inside and no one would know.

Lincoln hadn't said anything about taking my car back now that I lived in Angel City, so I was just going to keep driving it until he did. I pulled off my key and handed it to Angela. "Meet you at my car in five," I told her, then took off running with Lincoln's trailer key in my hand.

He had been very short and businesslike in our time together during trainings, only showing up for his thirty-minute slot, and keeping the social talk to a minimum unless he was making fun of me, at which time he proceeded to talk to no end. I had no idea what he did at nine thirty on a Friday night, but I was hoping he wasn't home, so I wouldn't have to deal with that twice in one day.

As I jogged across the parking lot, I saw the lights were on in the trailer, but his motorcycle was gone.

Hmm…

Jumping up the first few steps, I knocked hard. If he answered, I would just play dumb, and tell him I was coming to 'ask permission' to take my dagger to a club. Said club could get dangerous, etc.

I stood there an entire minute and knocked again.

Nothing.

Using my key, I popped open the door and crept inside, feeling like a burglar as I looked left and right. *No one home. Whew.* I shut the door behind me, and tiptoed across the space to grab the dagger that sat atop the kitchen table where I'd left it that afternoon.

Just as I was spinning to leave, the bathroom door popped open and Lincoln stepped out, dripping wet, waist covered in a towel.

Good Lord, what a body. I froze with my mouth open, just staring at his chiseled chest. When a bead of water dripped from his neck and down his six-pack into his V—*oh God, he has a V*—I exhaled louder than I should have. Okay, I moaned. I freaking *moaned*.

Kill me now.

"Brielle!" His eyes roamed across my bare shoulders, down my exposed legs, and then back up to my face.

"I...knocked. Twice." I couldn't form words. *What's my name? Where am I?*

His gaze landed on my dagger in hand and his eyes narrowed. "What are you doing?"

"Uhhh, well." I ran a hand through my long, blond hair, loosening the curls with the nervous gesture. "There's a party tonight at a club, and Angela said attacks can happen, and I thought—"

"You're going to Chloe's party?" He sounded surprised.

I put a hand on my hip. "Yes. I have friends, you know." Kind of. Four of them.

He swallowed, seeming to finally grasp that he was standing there half-naked and wet, and I was just staring at him like I wanted to lick the water off his chest.

'*We like him. I've decided,*' Sera said. I chose to ignore her comment.

"Fine, take it. Don't do anything stupid though."

I rolled my eyes. "I'll try, but no promises." Turning to grasp the door handle, I paused and spun to look at him once more. "Are you going too?" I asked. He sounded like he knew of Chloe's party.

He nodded. "If you would finally leave, so I can get dressed."

My eyes sharpened and I reached out, snagging a pear from the counter before slamming the door behind me.

"Stop stealing my food, woman!" he roared out the window.

I just grinned. Every time he pissed me off, I was stealing a piece of fruit. By the time the year was over, I'd have a whole orchard.

CHAPTER 12

"Brielle!" Chloe shrieked as we stepped into the club. She was greeting people at the entrance, literally just a blue door, and then two flights downstairs led us underground.

I smiled, giving her a hug, and introduced Shea. She was super welcoming, hugging Shea and Angela, and Luke as well. We gave her our gift, a potion to change her hair color for a month, which Angela had made. Chloe loved it and gave us tickets to the VIP booth before shooing us inside.

The moment we stepped into the space, I was assaulted with music, lights, and warm bodies pressed against mine. There was a stage with a live singer who had purple hair, and over her head hung the club's logo, a moon with the third eye inside of it. Under that a sign read "Happy Birthday, Chloe."

"Can I have my next birthday here?" Shea begged, linking her arm with mine.

I laughed. "Sure, just don't expect me to rent out the VIP lounge." I smacked the VIP tickets on her arm and she grinned.

"All right, I'm broke as hell, so let's get some guys to buy us drinks." Shea shook her cleavage to drive the point home.

This was an eighteen-and-up club, but I was pretty sure they carded at the bar. "And what will you be drinking, missy?" I asked her, trying to scream over the music.

She rolled her eyes and snatched the tickets from my hand. "Don't mom out on me," she growled. "They have Mage drinks here. Similar to the donuts. Bliss drinks, etc." She walked toward the red roped-off entrance of the VIP section.

Ugh, I wasn't momming out. I was…okay, I was momming out.

Screw it. I need to relax, dance, and let go of this week.

After getting past the big Nightblood at the VIP entrance, we stepped into an open, less-crowded space.

Noah, Darren, and Blake were all leaning against the bar. When we walked in, Blake caught my eye and waved me over.

"OhmygodNoah'shere," Shea rushed out.

I nodded. "Be careful, he seems like a player."

She shrugged, looking him up and down. "I don't mind getting played."

I rolled my eyes. She said that now, but when she was crying herself to sleep because he cheated on her, I'd hear a different story. We reached the boys, and I introduced everyone again, as Luke and Shea had only met the boys once.

"Who wants a drink?" Noah asked, eyes on Shea.

"Bri and I will take a bliss bomb," she told him with a sugary smile.

He nodded, looking seductively at her, and then took Luke's and Angela's orders next—a mellow margarita for Luke, and a water for Angela.

"Boring!" Shea shouted at her.

She laughed. "Someone has to watch over you kids."

"Ha! You're like barely older," Luke snapped.

She sucked her finger and stuck it in his ear, making him squeal. They were so cute. Nothing like Mikey and me, who were always at each other's throats. My mom said it was the shock of her life to find out she was pregnant with Mikey when I was ten weeks old. I couldn't believe that just next year Mikey would be at school with me.

The drinks came, and after a few sips, I started to laugh. They were *just* like the donuts.

"Let's dance!" I shouted, chugging the rest of my drink and dragging Shea, Blake, and the entire crew to the private VIP dance floor.

I quickly learned that Darren was the joker of the group, challenging us to a dance-off, and battling with some pretty hilarious moves. Shea grinded all over him, making him go rigid and wide-eyed, then finished with a butt slap that had Luke and me in peals of laughter. Shea didn't give a shit. *Ever.* And I loved her for it.

The music changed to something more sensual, and I started to grind my hips in the air to the beat, my arms above my head.

I love this drink. I love life. I love love.

Spinning around quickly, I slammed right into a familiar chest. It was his scent that hit me first, earthy and…yummy. God, he was so tall. I wanted to just climb him like a tree.

"Drunk already?" Lincoln scowled down at me.

My hips continued to move, still dancing. *Screw him, I love dancing.* I shook my head. "No. Bliss bomb. You should have one. Maybe that stick will fall out of your ass."

"Ha-ha," he yelled, bending down so I could smell him more.

"Dance with me!" I shouted, grabbing his arm and holding it above my head. I twirled underneath it like a ballerina.

Lincoln glared at Noah. "Did you do this?" He pointed to me, keeping his body stiff, just letting me dance with his one floppy arm.

Noah grinned. "Come on, man. Lighten up, just for one night."

Lincoln just glared at his friend and slipped his hand from me, taking his warmth to the edge of the bar where he sipped on a bottle of something clear that looked suspiciously like water.

During the next four songs, we continued to battle and dance as Lincoln drank his water, watching me from across the dance floor. His long sword hung from his hip. Chloe had joined us and was dancing with Darren. When I broke into the running man, Blake was sent into fits of laughter, but the bliss bomb was wearing off, and I was becoming acutely aware of those blue eyes watching me from across the bar.

"Be right back!" I told Shea, who was grinding on a happy Noah. My chest and forehead were glistening with sweat, and I was dying for some water. I sank into the seat next to Lincoln and got the bartender's attention. "Can I have a glass of water?" I asked.

He shook his head. "Bottles only. They're four dollars. You can get free glasses of water outside the VIP section."

Oh. My face fell. "Okay, never min—"

Lincoln slid a five-dollar bill across to the bartender without a word. The man grabbed it and gave him the water bottle. Lincoln handed it to me.

What's happening? Is the world ending? Did Lincoln Grey just do something nice for me?

Our fingers brushed for a moment as I took the bottle. "Thank you for the water, but are you feeling all right?" I joked.

He chuckled. "Shut up and hydrate yourself, so you can go back out there and keep dancing like an idiot. I'm getting some really good videos to blackmail you with later."

My mouth popped open. "You'd better be joking. Let me see your phone!" I reached for his pocket but he grabbed my wrist.

"You'll never know." He winked.

Oh. My. God. Lincoln winking was nothing like when Noah did it. Noah was an abusive cheesy winker, doling them out all the time. Lincoln had never winked at me before, and now that he had, I felt like my heart was going to jump out of my chest.

Oh shit. I totally like him. How the hell did that happen?

I was standing there, just stupidly staring at him, when people started screaming. Looking out into the main area of the bar, I could see black smoke filling the air.

"What's that?" I asked, panicked. Lincoln stood, pulled out his sword, and stepped in front of me just as the music came to a grinding halt.

"Demon attack!" someone yelled.

A flash-bang grenade went off right at the entrance of the VIP area, and I was blinded by a bright light; the bang was deafening. For the few seconds before the lights had gone off, I'd seen two Brimstone demons in the crowd, and another demon that gave me the chills—that

Abrus demon who was set to buy my contract. Terror flooded my system. *Why is he here?*

Lincoln yanked me to the ground, pinning me under the bar where the stools were.

"Shea!" I started screaming. I couldn't see anything but huge, white circles, my ears still ringing.

"*Shea!*" I screamed, going hoarse. There was no use, she was probably momentarily deaf as well. My vision started to return quickly, thanks to my Celestial healing, and along with it, my hearing.

Lincoln was caught in some kind of scuffle with the Brimstone demon. They were clanging swords as people ran screaming for the exit. Reaching into my boot, I pulled Sera out.

'*Help,*' I said, unsure what we could do from the ground.

Lincoln's wings were out now, and Darren had jumped to his side as the second Brimstone demon tried to attack him. Of all the places in the bar to go, they attacked this spot. I was just mulling it over when a strong hand reached down and grabbed me by the hair, pulling me up. Pain shot up my scalp and I screamed, holding on to my attacker's arm to lessen the strain on my scalp.

"There you are, princess," The smooth-talking Abrus demon cooed in my ear.

Fear ripped through me at the realization that he seemed to be there for me.

"Brielle!" Lincoln shouted. He was cutting down the Brimstone demon, but not fast enough. The Abrus demon yanked me backward and started dragging me toward the exit. I slashed out with my dagger, but with him behind me, dragging me with an iron grip, I had no stability. I decided then to pull out my wings and see if that would help me pry myself from his grasp but when I tried to extend them, there was a painful popping between my shoulder blades and they stayed in. He had some kind of magic that was keeping them in or something. *Oh God.*

A blur of red to my left pulled my attention to Shea. She was crouched about five feet away, farther up where the Abrus demon was walking backward, holding her sharp-bladed disc in one hand.

Oh God. What is she going to—

She sprang from her stance and chucked the weapon at the demon.

My eyes widened as it hurtled through the air and, from the sound of it, sank into the demon's back.

"Not so fast, asswipe!" Shea roared.

With a roar, the Abrus demon dropped me and I fell onto my bruised tailbone, but he was still holding onto my hair. He flung a hand out, shooting a purplish-black ball of smoke at Shea, which had her gasping on the ground and screaming in seconds.

'*Sera!*' I shouted in my head, holding my useless dagger.

'Hold me up and close your eyes.'

I did as she asked. We were a few feet from the exit door, and I didn't fancy being kidnapped.

The second my eyelids closed, a bright light shot out and the Abrus demon screamed, releasing my hair. I fell farther backward, with no way to steady myself, and cracked my head on the ground. Wasting no time, I rolled to my side, eyesight blotchy but intact, and thrust Sera into the demon's calf muscle, halfway to the hilt. His scream was so high-pitched, that I nearly dropped my blade to cover my ears. It sounded like screeching bats, which was absolutely terrifying.

'Ew, he tastes awful,' she whined.

I didn't want to know what that even meant. *'Umm, sorry?'*

Lincoln leapt into view then, Darren by his side. Both were covered in inky demon blood, and holding their swords up, ready to fight.

The Abrus demon was holding Lincoln's gaze, but one of the Dark Mages he'd come in with yanked his arm and pulled him out the door. I held onto Sera as she was ripped from his calf and then he was gone. The squeal of tires announced their exit.

What just happened?

Two strong hands wrapped around me, one under my neck and one under my legs, and then I was being pulled into Lincoln's arms. His eyes roamed over every inch of me.

"Are you hurt?" he asked.

If I say no, will he put me down?

"I hit my head." It wasn't a lie.

"Bring the car around!" Lincoln barked to Blake, who started jogging out the front door.

"Shea!" I shouted, craning my neck. Then I remembered she'd been hit with some smoke spell.

Noah kneeled over her, hands glowing orange. "She'll be fine," he told me.

Her eyes were tearing from coughing so hard, but she met my gaze and nodded.

"Can you walk?" Lincoln asked me.

No. "Yes."

He set me down and I felt like pouting. It was kind of nice being in those strong arms for a minute.

"Were they here for her?" he asked Darren, who stood at his side.

Darren frowned. "It looked like it."

Now they were all staring at me. I shrugged. "That's the guy who was supposed to buy my contract. Maybe he wanted to sell me or something?"

Lincoln's jaw tightened. "You're not for sale."

Holy winker, I really like him. What's happening to me?

A loud knock came on the other side of the exit door from the VIP lounge and Lincoln ripped it open. Blake was standing there with his car backed up to the doorframe. Another guy was standing with him, tall, broad-shouldered with light brown hair.

"Brisbane! Can you get me the video surveillance from tonight? I want to know how they got in, and what their plan was," Lincoln barked. He was in warrior mode now, and it was totally hot.

The guy nodded. "On it." He burst through the entryway and ran down into the lower level. It seemed like he knew where he was going, and since his last name was Brisbane, I guessed he was Chloe's brother. The one Luke had a crush on.

Luke and Angela appeared with Shea linked between their arms and walked over to me. My best friend's eyes were tearing, and it looked like she'd been maced. I had no freaking clue what kind of magic Abrus demons had, but from what I'd seen over the past few days, it was scary-as-hell magic.

Lincoln looked me up and down once more. "You're not hurt?" he asked again.

My head was throbbing from where I cracked it, but it wasn't bleeding, I pushed a little at my wings and felt them slide out a ways before retracting. Whatever spell he'd had over them was gone. I shook my head to Lincoln. "I'll be fine."

"Okay. Get back to school and stay there. No more leaving the grounds. And keep that blade on you at all times." His eyes flicked to Sera.

'He's a sensible chap,' she noted.

Talk about a sudden change of heart.

It was stupid, but I took the time to wonder if he'd

take my key to his trailer away now that I had no reason to go there. That meant no more walking in on him half-naked, which bummed me out.

As Darren was guiding me to the waiting vehicle, Lincoln called out my name. "Three nights a week, from seven to eight o'clock, I want you to take extra battle training with me. This might happen again. Until we know why they want you, we need to be prepared."

My stomach flipped. Extra training with Lincoln? Just the two of us? I knew he was only doing it because it was his job to keep me alive, but part of me wondered if he liked spending time with me.

I was totally falling for the resident asshole. Except maybe he wasn't an asshole.

Maybe he never was.

CHAPTER 13

It had been six weeks since the night club. I was officially employed and loving my job at the healing clinic, which consisted mostly of goofing off with Noah, and sometimes actually helping heal a patient.

Healing people sucked. It hurt. *Literally.* I healed a cut on Shea's leg for practice and it hurt *my* leg. Healers had to be super selfless, which was surprising considering how self-absorbed Noah seemed.

My private training sessions with Lincoln were torture in so many ways. The sexual tension was so thick, I could cut it with a knife. Of course, I had zero clue if he was feeling it too, since he was always barking orders at me, and scowling when I held a weapon wrong. I, on the other hand, was finding ways to touch him—an arm graze here, a bump into him there. I had it bad, and it was pathetic. He'd taken my key to his trailer back and seemed completely uninterested in me sexually. Meanwhile, I was thinking about the way those water droplets had rolled down his V on a daily basis.

"Miss Atwater?"

My eyes snapped to the front where Mr. Rincor, a Celestial with Gabriel's power, was shooting glowing sparks out of his hands.

The issue with my studies of light class was there were only two students, a senior named Fred, who had Gabriel powers, and me. Mr. Rincor was his master teacher. With only two students in the class, it was easy for him to tell that I wasn't paying attention.

"Yep?" I tried to act like I was super *extra* paying attention. Eyes wide and alert, I pinned them on the professor.

He motioned to my hands. "Give it a try."

I sighed. I was a serious badass in weapons and battle class—growing up around demons meant Shea and I were the scrappiest, dirtiest fighters in the class—I'd also come to love fallen history, but this class? I sucked. It was awful. For a girl who carried powers from not one, but *four* archangels inside of her, I sure as hell didn't have an ounce of light in me. I tried not to think that it was because there was some darkness inside of me eating up the light.

I went to grab Sera and he shook his head. "With your hands."

I growled, earning a smile from Fred. He could shoot

the freaking Fourth of July from his hands, stunning anyone who got in his way, and momentarily blinding them if he wanted. Me? I could make my hands glow about the same as a two-watt light bulb, before they petered out to nothing.

I stared at my hands, flexing every muscle in my body and pushing.

Fred laughed. "You look constipated."

I picked up my pencil and chucked it at him, which he caught in midair. *Show-off.*

Mr. Rincor walked over and sat next to me. "Your tattoos have created a channel for the power that's already inside of you. You just need to let it flow. Don't try so hard."

If looks could kill, mine would cut through Mr. Rincor. Nothing he said made sense. *Ever.*

"Ohhhhh, I gotcha," I said sarcastically.

The bell rang then. Thank God.

The Celestial stood, looking down at me. "I hear you're good with weapons. That's all fine until your weapons are taken away, and all you have are your bare hands." Then he walked away.

Debbie Downer.

I didn't let his comment bother me. Since I didn't have work at the clinic that day, Lincoln had asked me to meet him for our private training early. There was something we needed daylight to do, apparently.

I bolted from the classroom and went into the

bathroom to apply some lip gloss and brush my teeth—ya know, on the off chance he wanted to kiss me.

I'm hopeless.

After primping and feeling pretty lame for doing said primping, I met Lincoln out on the field. He was standing there, arms crossed, scowl in place. "You're late."

I put a hand on my hip. "So I'm not allowed bathroom breaks, then?"

He rolled his eyes and started to circle me like a shark. I was pretty sure he couldn't stand me, and I was totally falling for him. What a horrible combination. I tried to push all thoughts of a relationship aside.

"The winter ball is coming up," he said, looking me up and down.

Oh. My. God. He's in love with me. He's going to ask me to the dance. Breathe. Breathe. Water down the V.

"Yeah?" I croaked. The winter ball was some charity thing Raphael put on. The students got to be wined and dined by the rich benefactors, and there were silent auctions throughout the night.

He nodded. "I don't normally work the event, but since it's off campus, and could lure potential kidnappers, I've decided to work security. So just let me know what time you and your date are leaving, and I'll have a security detail on you at all times."

Crash. Burn. Blood. Guts. End of world.

"Gotcha," was about the only intelligible thing I could think to say at the moment.

"Now, I hear you're doing amazing in battle class, taking your opponents to the ground, and winning in one-on-one drills."

I breathed on my nails and buffed them on my shirt. "One might even call me a badass."

His lips quirked but no smile. "And I'm quite impressed with your swordsmanship and weapons control. You're an amazing shot with the bow, and if there were fencing tournaments for scrappy girls with no proper form, you would probably win."

I grinned. "Gosh, you're really doling out the compliments. What did I do to deserve such stellar treatment?"

That time he did smile, but it was sadistic and full of teeth. "*But* you. Still. Can't. Fly." He drilled the words into me one by one.

I rolled my eyes. "This again? You and Mr. Rincor should party together. You'd have a lot to talk about."

He crossed his arms, making his biceps flex. "Don't get me started on your failure at studies of light."

Failure. Ouch. That word stung.

"Brielle, in seven months, there is an end-of-year test. If you fail that test, you're cast out from the school. Considering you can't go back to live with your mom, and demons are trying to kidnap you, that would be a bad idea."

Gosh. He had to lay on the reality check?

"Okay, I'll try harder."

I didn't want to leave school. Shea and I had it

pretty good here. I made enough with my part-time job for all the expensive luxuries in life, like tampons and chocolate, and I got to share a room with my best friend. Bonus, they hadn't asked for the car back. Not that I was allowed to drive it anywhere but circling the campus, of course.

He placed a hand on each of my shoulders, sending a warm heat to my navel. "It's time for some tough love."

Love. He said love.

His wings snapped out then, and his grip on my shoulders tightened. Suddenly, I was being hauled into the air.

"Lincoln!" I shouted as my wings sprang out, my eyes skimming the ground as his hands went from my shoulders to my waist.

We flew higher and higher, me flailing in Lincoln's arms, him with a determined scowl.

"Brielle, as your lead trainer, I will take it as a personal offense if you fail the gauntlet," he told me.

I looked down. Big mistake.

Holy shit! We're like a hundred feet in the air.

"Okay, good, then keep training me!" I shouted at him.

He shook his head. "Me and the boys have gone too soft on you. It's not working. You need a reality check."

"You asshole! Don't you dare drop me!" I seethed.

"You're kinda cute when you're really mad," he confessed.

And then he let go.

He called me cute.

I'm falling.

"Ahhhhh!" My scream echoed, all other thoughts fleeing from my mind. My survival instinct kicked in, and I flapped my black wings like crazy.

Come on, you bastards, hold up my weight! I'd pinched my eyes closed when I started to fall but opened them now, because by my calculations, I should've broken my neck and died by that point.

Lincoln was hovering in front of my face, grinning. "You did it."

"You jerk!" I screamed, reaching out for him, but he flew backward, and took off through the sky.

"Catch me!" he called out.

Oh, I would. I would catch him and pulverize him.

Speeding through the sky after him, I flapped my wings wildly to catch up. "You could've killed me!" I shouted as I got closer.

Turning back to look at me, he smiled. "You're totally flying."

My gaze shifted downward. *Holy crap, I am.* We were almost to the ocean.

"I'm flying!" I shrieked, laughing.

Lincoln grinned, then spun and came at me. I backed my wings up, stopping my advance to hover in midair as he approached me.

"Good. Next practice, we'll fly with weapons."

My eyes widened. "Why?"

He looked at me like I was a five-year-old. "Because there are some demons with wings, remember?"

Oh. Yeah. I shivered thinking of my battle with Shea's master and his bat-like wings.

His hand lifted, gesturing to the horizon. "Outside this city, a war is raging. If you get recruited into the Fallen Army, you'll have a huge advantage with being able to fight while flying. You could save thousands of lives."

Whoa. I never thought about that. Fighting while I flew could help save lives. What would it be like to save thousands of lives? I'd never even saved one.

"Is that what you do?" I asked him. I knew nothing about the war beyond the city.

There were open portals out there, where the demons came up from the underworld, and wreaked havoc on the smaller suburbs and towns. We didn't travel outside the city walls because of it, so it must've been bad. The news barely covered it because reporters said it was too dangerous.

Lincoln's face darkened. "Yes. But I can't save them all. It's a harsh reality that you'll learn the hard way."

There was something else there, something else he wanted to say but didn't.

"All right. Gold star for today, Bri." He winked, and then started to descend.

Ah, the wink. It did funny things to my insides. If he was that sexy of a winker, I wondered what it was like to kiss him. I flew back to the field where we'd started and noticed Shea, Luke, and Angela waiting for us. Shea was clutching some type of paper and bouncing on her heels with excitement.

"What's up? You win the lottery?" I asked my best friend as I landed in front of them.

She laughed. "Close. Noah just invited us to some super-exclusive thing he does every year called 'the beach games.' Winner gets a cheesy autographed photo of him, but it's supposed to be super fun."

Angela nodded. "I wasn't invited last year but I hear it's a blast. Goes all day and night, bonfire and all that jazz."

Lincoln was scowling. "Noah invited you guys to the beach games?" He said it like it was the Emmys.

Shea thrust the invitation in his face and put one hand on her hip. "Well gee, I've only been reading since I was five, but yeah, I think that's what it says."

I grinned. Shea was the best at a verbal bitch slap.

Lincoln chuckled, handing her the flyer. "Good luck. My team's won four years in a row." Then he turned and walked away.

I ripped the flyer from Shea's hand. There was nothing more I wanted in life than to beat Lincoln at something, and lord it over him for the rest of my life.

The Beach Games

<u>When:</u> This Friday

<u>Where:</u> Santa Monica Pier

<u>What:</u> Volleyball, tug-of-war, sandcastle competition, and more! Come with a team of four. Using powers is allowed.

<u>Dress:</u> Beach wear (Ladies, feel free to wear a bikini.)

Winner gets a signed copy of a hunky photo of Noah and bragging rights.

Oh, that flyer had Noah all over it, the little slimebag, but it sounded awesome. I looked up at my friends. "Okay, this is in three days. It's time to practice."

I assumed it would be some weird magical game thing, but normal beach games…I was all over it. My competitive side was ready to throw down.

CHAPTER 14

The beach games were tomorrow after school, and I was so nervous and excited that I could barely sleep last night. My sandcastle game was tight. I'd borrowed cake-decorating supplies from Angela's mom, and I had a design mapped out in my mind. To top that off, with Angela's Necromancy skills, she was going to add something to my design that I was sure was going to win us that round.

We'd asked around and found out there were five rounds, each worth a certain amount of points: beach volleyball, sand castle design, tug-of-war, swim race, and one random new one Noah picked every year. We'd been practicing sand volleyball each night, and I'd already made and crushed my sandcastle, so I was feeling super prepared. The tug-of-war and swim race competitions were just going to have to be an in-the-moment thing, but I figured we could pull it off.

"So, we get paid tomorrow morning. I say we ditch our last hour, cash our checks, and get new bikinis," Shea offered as we walked into the gym locker room to change for battle class.

Bikini. The word that sent every girl screaming internally. No matter how in shape I felt my body was, it scared the shit out of me. Wearing a bathing suit in front of Lincoln made me want to die.

"Okay. Yeah…" I feigned enthusiasm.

Shea rolled her eyes. "Whatever. The beach games aren't going to know what hit them when we show up."

A locker door slammed, making me jump, and then suddenly I was staring at Tiffany. "You got invited to the beach games?" She looked horrified.

I grinned. "Yeah, didn't you?"

Her face recovered and then she was cool, calm, and collected. "Of course. Can't make it though. Besides, I heard they were deviating from their 'angel blessed only' rule and inviting the riffraff. Now that I see it's true, I'm glad I'm not going." She spun on her heel and left.

"That bitch!" Shea roared, charging after her, but I caught her arm.

"Throwing her in the healing clinic will only get you detention, and we need you on the team. She's lying anyway. Noah doesn't have some elitist 'angel blessed only' rule."

Right?

Shea shot a death glare at the door Tiffany had gone through, then nodded. "The day we graduate, I'm going to beat her ass within an inch of her life."

My eyes widened. *You can take the girl out of the hood...*

"Come on, killer. Let's just get through this class, and then before you know it, we'll be bikini shopping."

She nodded. "Noah texted me that he likes the color red on me."

I laughed as we walked out to the gym. Noah and Shea were making out in the parking lot every Wednesday night, after his clinic shift and her shift with Mr. Claymore. They'd already had the "we're just having fun, no exclusivity" talk, so I was no longer worried about her getting her heart broken.

"Then you should totally get a red bikini," I agreed.

She leaned in close to me. "He also said sky blue is Lincoln's favorite color."

The color drained from my face. "Shea, you better not be telling Noah I like him," I whisper-screamed.

Her mischievous laugh rang around us. "Oh please. He knows. It's so obvious you both like each other."

Shea pulled out her phone and showed me the text. Noah had offered his two cents without her even mentioning it.

Oh good, I won't have to kill her. "Trust me. It's

unrequited," I informed her, thinking of the hundreds of times he'd scowled at me.

"I don't think so." She added with a frown.

A loud whistle rang out, and Mr. Bradstone raised his voice. "No weapons today. Hand-to-hand combat, and for the first time, we'll use our magic. Pair up with the names I've arranged on the board and begin."

Shit. No weapons. I looked at my useless hands. I'd maybe gotten up to a four-watt lightbulb, but nothing that was going to hurt anyone.

"Ugh. Sucks to be you," Shea whispered.

My eyes snapped up to the board to see I was paired with Tiffany.

Freaking perfect.

Tiffany waltzed into one of the battle rings, a ten-foot circle of blue tape, then squatted into a wrestling position, grinning wildly. Shea had nearly every class with her and said she was an advanced Mage for her age. Her mother was a Light Mage and her father a Celestial. They helped her outside of school, so she was 100 percent about to kick my ass with some light magic. When I had Sera, or any other weapon, I was definitely on equal playing ground, but using just our magic?

I was so screwed.

"Come on, Archie. We don't have all day," She crooned.

Shea caught my arm, and I turned to meet her eyes. "This might be the only opportunity any one of us has to kick her ass without getting into trouble." Then she winked.

Ha. I would try my best, but I'd seen Tiffany's magic at work. It was pretty incredible.

I stepped into the ring and squatted to her level. We'd been learning jujitsu that month, and I was good with takedowns. But so was she. Mr. Bradstone usually let us pick our sparring partner, so I always chose Shea or Luke. Now I was stuck with my nemesis. Lincoln's "family friend."

We started to circle each other, hands outstretched, gazes locked.

"You know, Lincoln practically spent all of last summer at my house," she purred.

Jealousy flared inside of me, but I didn't let it show. Instead, I swiped my leg out, trying to take her down, but she jumped over it.

"Why in God's name would he do that?" I gave her the stanky-est face I could muster.

She growled, lunging for me, and yanked me down to the ground. *Dammit!* With some fast and hard footwork, she had me pinned underneath her.

"Because my parents were best friends with his parents. I've known him my whole life, and he'll be mine one day, so back. The. Fuck. Off." Spittle flew from her mouth onto my face. She was legit losing her mind. Her hands were wrapped tightly around my wrists, emitting a warm glow that burned my skin.

"Let me go, Tiffany," I warned her.

My skin grew hotter.

I jerked my pelvis up hard, trying to buck her off in the way Mr. Bradstone taught us, but to no avail. She was in her zone. She'd probably been planning this since the day she met me.

"You're *seriously* hurting me!" I shouted in her face.

She grinned.

Bitch! Anger boiled inside of me like heartburn, starting in my chest and working its way up my throat. When I screamed in her face once again, an inky black smoke flew from my mouth, and wrapped around her throat.

Shock ripped through the both of us and she fell backward off me, clutching her throat and trying to breathe. A thick, black magical band was strangling her.

Oh frick.

"Mr. Bradstone!" I screamed.

Tiffany's face was turning blue, the black smoke an iron vise around her neck.

Mr. Bradstone took one look at her on the ground, then at me, and flew into action. Running to the cabinet on the wall, he produced a bottle of holy water and his infinity weapon, a glowing orange blade. Dousing the blade with the holy water, he laid the flat part across her neck. The second the cool steel touched her, the blackness broke apart, and disappeared.

With a huge gasping breath, Tiffany looked at me, terrified. "Archdemon!" she shouted in a raspy voice.

Oh my God. What have I done?

"That was some *Exorcist* shit," someone from the class commented. That's when I ran. Turning around, I bolted out the door, ignoring Shea and Mr. Bradstone's calls after me.

I was evil.

Something dark and evil *flew* out of my mouth, and wrapped around Tiffany's throat, nearly killing her. My legs pumped harder as I burst onto the field, tears streaming down my face. I wanted to run away, hide in shame.

Maybe I *was* an archdemon.

"*I know what you are,*" that Abrus demon had said.

My wings burst from my back, and I took to the skies. This was only my third time flying, but it came back like muscle memory. I pumped higher and higher as I flew away from the school. The night of The Falling, when the archangels fell from Heaven and warred with the demons, power had lashed out at random. Monsters had been created, and I was one of them.

"*I know what you are.*"

I flew harder, heading for the ocean.

"Brielle!" The wind carried Lincoln's voice to me, and I soared faster. He was the last person I wanted to see right then, the last person I wanted to know what I'd done, what I was.

When I hit the beach, my legs crash-landed, and I sort of fell onto the sand. The moment I righted myself,

I started running for the pier. I wanted to hide, to crawl into a hole and be alone.

"Brielle!" he shouted again, closer that time.

I didn't dare look back when I reached the pier. Slinking down against one of the pillars, I pulled my knees up, wrapped my arms around my legs, and buried my face between my knees. Sobs racked my chest as I curled inside of myself and hid from the world.

I stayed there for a full minute, listening to the crashing of waves, and letting the emotions crash through me. Then he found me.

"Brielle." His voice was so warm, so understanding, it made more tears spill out onto my knees.

"Please go away. I want to be alone." My voice was muffled, hiding against my legs.

I could feel his body heat against my left side and then his hand on my back. "Shea told me what happened. It's going to be okay. Just come back to school where it's safe. *Please*."

My head snapped up. "*Nothing* about this is going to be okay."

I'd never seen him look so...caring.

"So you have demon-gifted powers. We guessed that with your black wings." He tried to sound nonchalant and failed.

I shook my head. "No, Lincoln. I nearly killed Tiffany with black magic that flew from my throat. Those are not demon-gifted powers. That's some other kind of next-level evil shit." I turned away from him, looking out to the ocean.

He gripped my chin and forced me to face him. "Brielle, nothing about you is evil. Trust me."

My breath caught in my throat. His hand on my chin was sending warm tingles down my back, and he wasn't pulling away. My tears suddenly dried up, and I swallowed hard. "How do you know? Maybe I am an archdemon," I told him, holding his gaze.

He didn't waver. "Because the worst thing you've done since I've known you, is save your best friend and steal fruit from me. You're harmless."

I laughed, and his hand slid from my chin to my neck.

"You're also way too beautiful to be an archdemon," he added, eyeing my lips.

Beautiful. Lincoln Grey called me beautiful.

Maybe it was the sound of the waves, or his hand on my neck. Maybe it was the way he was looking at my lips like he wanted to taste them, but I grew bold then. Wrapping my hand around his biceps, I leaned in and kissed him. The second my lips hit his, he parted them, deepening the kiss. Pleasure filtered out into my body, and butterflies danced in my belly. As his warm tongue stroked against mine, his hand trailed from my neck, down my arm and settled firmly at my waist.

I'm kissing Lincoln Grey.

I moaned in pleasure, and in one swift move, he leaned back onto the sand, pulling me on top of him.

Straddling his waist, I kissed him with a hungry passion; it felt like I'd been waiting to unleash it my entire life. I reached up into the sand and stroked the back of his neck just as his hands slipped into the back of my shirt and he grasped my rib cage. Heat traveled in a downward expressway to my groin.

The kiss was epic, all-consuming—and gone all too soon. He seemed to realize what we were doing, and abruptly stopped, using his strength to pull me off him and sit up.

"*Shit*. Bri, I shouldn't have done that." He stood, sand falling off him.

I touched my swollen lips, still warm from our kiss. "Why?" *I want to do that all day, every day.*

"You're my student, and you're too young," he said to the sand, unable to meet my eyes.

I stood, all talk of archdemons forgotten. "I'm nineteen in like two months, and you teach me thirty minutes a day." Was I pathetically arguing to reinstate the kissing? Yes. Yes I was.

That time he did meet my eyes. "It was a mistake. Let's get back to the school, or I'll have to call Raphael and send the army."

I wasn't sure which hurt more, the word 'mistake' in relation to that life-altering kiss, or the threat to send the Fallen Army to make me go home.

I stepped closer to him and he flinched, like I was going to kiss him again, and the thought scared him.

"Kissing you will never be a mistake," I declared. Then my wings sprung out, and I burst from the sand, airborne.

Shea better be buying two tubs of chocolate peanut butter ice cream, because I have a feeling I'm going to cry myself to sleep for many, many reasons.

CHAPTER 15

I did cry myself to sleep. Luke, Angela, and Shea tried to reassure me that I wasn't an archdemon, and that Lincoln would come around. It did nothing to help. The worst part? Shea and I were broke, so I'd had no ice cream to drown my sorrows in.

Now it was Friday. The beach games were imminent, and I was trying to think of a hundred reasons to back out. I didn't want to see anyone, couldn't bear the archdemon whispers that had sprung up at breakfast that morning.

"This paycheck is burning a hole in my pocket," Shea said.

We'd both gotten paid that morning, the checks left in the mailbox on our door.

I nodded. "I can't bear to see Lincoln at my Celestial master studies class, or Noah, or any of them. I need time."

Shea shrugged. "So cancel. Tell them you feel sick."

"Great idea," I agreed with a nod. "And I'll cancel the beach games too."

"Whoa, girl." Luke shot his hand out to stop me. "Don't take it that far."

My voice mixed with a groan. "I don't want to go." Shea rolled her eyes and snatched my phone. "Hey, give that back!" I shouted, but she got up and circled the table, texting away wildly as she walked. "Shea, I will kill you if you embarrass me."

"There, done. Now, let's ditch and go shopping," she declared.

Luke laughed. "This is college, so it's not really ditching."

Shea glared at him. "Don't take away my fun."

"What did you do with my phone?" I asked her.

She set it down in front of me, and I hurried to read the email.

To: Lincoln, Noah, Blake, Darren

Hey guys,

Let's cancel Celestial studies today. I just realized my boobs have grown so big since last summer that I need a new bikini before the beach games.

Cheers,
Bri

"Oh. My. God. You're dead," I growled. *Has she lost her damn mind?*

Luke and Angela busted up laughing, and I realized they'd been reading over my shoulder.

My phone buzzed with a reply.

From: Noah
Totally understandable.;)
See you later.

It buzzed again.

From: Blake
Girls.

Another buzz.

From: Darren
Whatever. Cool.

Just as I was setting the phone down, it buzzed with Lincoln's reply.

From: Lincoln
Nice try. Your boobs are tiny. See you at the beach.

"Ahh!" I screamed, earning some stares from people around me. He was back to being an asshole. "My boobs

212

aren't *tiny*, they're petite," I told the table, slamming my fist down.

Luke grinned. "You know what this means?"

I wanted to die. "What?"

"Lincoln's totally been checking out your boobs."

Well, I guess that's the silver lining.

Wait, did Luke just confirm they're tiny?

———•·•———

Three hours. That's how long it took Shea and me to pick out our suits. We'd gone to a shop within a few blocks of school and taken one of the Fallen Academy school guards with us, since I wasn't supposed to leave campus without a security detail now. Luke and Angela left after an hour, dying of boredom. Now I was wearing a powder-blue string bikini that Shea promised me looked killer, and a pair of tiny, cutoff jean shorts over it. We'd had no issue at the shops, so I was thinking the kidnapping plot was behind me.

We'd just pulled up to Santa Monica Pier, the same pier where I'd kissed Lincoln.

"Oh my God, this looks awesome!" Shea squealed, doing a mini shake in her seat to invisible music.

There were two huge, white tents set up with open sides.

"This is catered?" Angela asked, peeking her head into the front seat.

Two caterers in formal attire were serving a spread of different foods in one tent. Looking farther out onto the beach, I saw two volleyball games going on and some other things set up.

"Oh my God, Chloe's brother is here." Luke breathed from the back seat. "I should've worn the red shorts. Angela, move. I can get in twenty more sit-ups."

I burst out laughing. "Come on, y'all. Enough pining over these asshats. Let's just let loose and have some fun."

Angela tapped my shoulder. "I like your style."

"Did you just say 'y'all'?" Shea gave me the stank eye.

I ignored her because something hit me then. "Wait, Chloe's brother is a Nightblood. How is he in the sun?"

Angela pointed to a tall, brunette female. "She's a super powerful Light Mage in the Fallen Army and can do temporary sun protection spells."

Cool.

I turned off the car and jumped out. I'd spent nearly half my paycheck on the bikini, so Lincoln had better freaking notice. Slipping my bag over my shoulder, I locked my car and we all started to walk to the beach. I didn't bother wearing a shirt; I had one in my bag for later, but I wanted to get a decent tan, and make Lincoln hopefully lust after my *tiny* boobs.

As we walked up, I noticed my dark-haired hottie right away. He was dishing out a plate of corn on the cob, BBQ ribs, and a few other items I couldn't see from my vantage point.

"Ladies! And Luke," Noah said, coming over to shake the Beast Shifter's hand.

"Thanks for inviting us," I told him.

He nodded. "Of course." He turned to Shea and popped a kiss on her cheek. "You look killer." He winked at her.

She grinned.

Noah's wink was a dime a dozen.

Lincoln looked over then, his eyes running a quick up and down my body before coming back to my face.

"Bri!" a familiar voice shouted.

Snapping my attention to the right, I saw Fred, from my studies of light class, making his way over to me.

"Fred? Hey, I didn't know you were going to be here." I reached up and gave him a quick hug.

"Yeah, Darren is my good friend. Sweet rib cage tats. I always wondered where you were hiding the other two." He glanced at my abdomen.

I brushed my fingers across them and looked past Fred to see Lincoln standing just behind him, dishing more food on his plate but totally listening in on my conversation.

"Yeah, I forget they're there sometimes," I told him honestly.

"Hey, listen, I wanted to ask you today but you weren't in class. Are you going to the winter ball?" No shame, no fear. He just asked me in front of everyone.

I liked a take-charge guy like that.

"I was thinking about it," I said, watching Lincoln for any sign of distress. None so far, except about ten pounds of food on his bowing plate.

He smiled. "I'd love to take you. Assuming you don't have anyone?"

My eyes flicked up, to find Lincoln craning toward our conversation.

"You're dazzled with my light magic, aren't you? That's why," I joked.

Fred grinned. "What can I say, those little four-watt bulbs really do it for me."

Genuine laughter erupted from me. Fred was funny and sweet, and he wanted me. Even with all the rumors swirling that I was an archdemon, he still wanted me. "I'd love to go. That sounds fun."

He smiled, and it was handsome. He wasn't sexy, but he was still cute. "Cool. You're in Bright Hall, right? I'll pick you up at seven."

I nodded, but before I could answer, Lincoln spun around and placed a hand on Fred's shoulder. "Ever since Chloe's birthday, we've had to be extra careful about where Brielle goes and who she is with, so if you're taking her to the dance, you'll have to be escorted by her security detail."

Lincoln's eyes were burning holes into me. He cared. He totally cared.

Fred shrugged the hand off. "No problem with me. Tell her *security detail* to be at Bright Hall at seven."

"Fred, you're up!" someone yelled from the sand, where some game was happening.

Fred squeezed my upper arm lightly. "See ya." Then he ran off.

Lincoln and I just stood there staring at each other. It was then that I noticed Shea and everyone had left me.

I took a step closer to Lincoln, lowering my voice to keep it private. "You know, I can cancel with Fred if *you* want to take me to the dance."

There, I said it. Maybe Fred asking me out had flipped a switch in him, and he'd changed his mind about our age gap, or whatever it was that bothered him.

He looked like I'd given him a cow dung cookie, his lip curling. "Don't be ridiculous."

My face fell, and I swallowed down the tears that threatened. Lincoln Grey was a heartbreaker, and I wasn't going to have *anything* to do with that.

Unhooking the button, I peeled off my shorts, holding his gaze the entire time. Then I broke eye contact and threw my shorts on top of my bag before storming out of the tent. I'd been told many a time that my ass was my best physical feature. Best to throw it in his face so he'd know what he'd be missing.

I am done with Lincoln Grey.

———•·•———

We won two of the four games. My wedding cake

sandcastle was lit and helped us win that round, Angela used her Necromancy gift to make live roses grow out of the top tier. We lost the swim relay race, and also our round of beach volleyball. There was some huge, complicated scoreboard that I didn't understand, and about ten different teams, but I didn't really care. I was having a blast. I'd even managed to put Lincoln and my *Exorcist* magic from my mind and focus on the fun.

"All right, partygoers. One final game, then the winning team will be announced, and the bonfire party will begin!" Noah shouted through a bullhorn.

He walked over to a small bucket of water and threw a single red apple inside. "This year's mystery game is the apple run. One member from two opposing teams will compete against each other. Your hands will be tied behind your back and you'll run, try to get the apple into your mouth, and then make it across the finish line with it. Anything goes—tripping, shoving, whatever. Just get that apple!"

The teams roared in excitement. Most of them were drunk, so I was pretty sure we had an advantage.

"Each team will pick a member to represent them, and put their name in the basket," Noah shouted, pointing to an old Easter basket sitting on the table.

Shea immediately turned to me. "Oh, girl, you got this! You're the best at bobbing for apples on Halloween."

It was true. Our apartment always had a wicked

Halloween party, and I'd had lots of practice. I looked at Angela and Luke. "You cool with that?"

They nodded, and excitement thrummed through me. If we won that round, did we win the whole thing? Maybe not, since we lost our swim heat. I wasn't sure how the point system worked. I'd make a horrible mermaid, but our team was currently in third place on the board, so I didn't know.

After tossing my name in the bucket, I stretched out my legs and prepared for the run. I just needed to get the apple first and dash like hell, hoping the person didn't chase after me, and knock me over. We'd lost our volleyball game because people more advanced than us kept using magic to win. I didn't have any magic to help me, except maybe flying across the finish line once I got the apple.

"All right," Noah screamed in his bullhorn. "The first pair of competitors are..." He pulled two pieces of paper out of the bucket and then grinned, looking at me. "Brielle and Lincoln!"

Shit. Does the universe hate me? I was trying to get over the guy and now I was right next to him. Ugh.

Shea gave me a sympathetic smile as I walked over to where the judges were to have my hands tied behind my back. Looking over, I saw Lincoln watching me closely, an unreadable gaze as always.

Screw you, you gorgeous asshole.

"You two clear on the rules? There's one apple. First one to get that apple across the finish line wins," Noah told us with a slight slur. He was only wearing low-slung beach shorts, showing off his chiseled chest and abs, and was definitely drunk.

I nodded, then turned to catch Lincoln's gaze. "Careful. I can play dirty." I winked.

There, you sexy winker. Take that!

Lincoln pursed his lips. "I have no doubt."

With a zipping sound, the plastic tie went tightly around my wrists, and everyone lined up along the edge of the run to cheer us on.

Noah grinned. "All right, on your marks, get set...go!"

I took off like my ass was on fire, but running in the sand was hard, and my hands were tied behind my back. Lincoln was fast as hell, reaching the bucket first and leaning over. I came in next and hip-checked him, sending him falling to the sand with a grunt.

The crowd roared.

Bending over, I dunked my face into the bucket, but Lincoln's was next to mine within seconds. Dammit, he was quick. I pressed the apple to the side of the bucket with my cheek, trying to get my teeth into it, when Lincoln bumped me, pushing me. He didn't do it hard enough to knock me over, but I still lost my grip on the apple. He jerked his neck toward the apple and I plunged my face into the water again, trying to wrestle it away from him. Cold water hit my skin, but I was too determined to let it slow me down. Our faces were inches from each other, but due to my awkward standing position since he'd hip-checked me out of the way, Lincoln had better ground. I was just coming up for air when I saw his teeth clamp around the apple. Then he took off running.

I was a really sore loser, so I tried to make a habit of not losing. Especially not to him. Not today.

I took off after him, hair and face dripping wet, legs pumping in the sand. When I caught up, I decided it was time to play dirty. I swiped my leg out, tripping him and sending him to the ground.

The crowd exploded into cheers.

Lincoln hit the sand hard but immediately recovered, and rolled onto his back, the apple still in his mouth. Before he could try to sit up, I leapt forward, swung one leg over him and plopped down, pinning him to the ground with my hips. I had straddled him. His eyes widened, just as mine did. The only thing between our bodies were two very thin pieces of fabric, and I *felt* him. Every second I sat there, I felt him more and more.

Desire flared to life between my legs, but I pushed all that out of my mind. I was there to win, not grind on some guy who didn't like me.

Leaning forward and sticking my ass into the air, I pressed my chest on his bare pecs. I had no hands to hold myself up with, so my *tiny* boobs were acting as my stabilizer. Opening my mouth, I leaned over and bit into the apple.

He grinned—the motherfricker *grinned*—letting me take it.

Whatever.

The crowd went wild.

I launched into a standing position as the crowd roared my name, then tore across the finish line.

Noah was beaming, bullhorn in hand. "Is it hot out here, or is it just these two?"

Lincoln was sitting up in the sand, glaring at Noah.

"Holy shit, girl, that was awesome." Shea told me as she worked to cut the zip tie.

I smiled. "Yeah." Except it did nothing but confuse me where Lincoln was concerned.

The rest of the day passed in a blur, but I couldn't get out of my head and enjoy it. We'd won second place, partied till two in the morning, and I still wasn't any closer to figuring out the Lincoln issue.

In the end, I decided to just focus on my studies. The gauntlet was months away, but I needed to put my nose to the grindstone if I wanted to pass.

CHAPTER 16

"Aw, you look so beautiful!" Shea squealed.

I smiled, giving my friend a once-over. She was wearing a blue princess ball gown and looked amazing. "So do you."

Shea was going to the winter ball with Luke. Just as friends, of course.

"Red looks amazing on you," she told me.

I'd spent a shitload of money on that dress, hoping it would improve my recent morose mood. Fred was awesome, but to be honest, I only felt friendly toward him. He made me laugh and smile, but that heat, and that passion, just wasn't there.

"I'll see you at the dance?" I kissed her cheek.

She nodded. "Have fun with Fred. He's sweet."

He was sweet, the exact opposite of Lincoln. Ever since the beach games, Lincoln had doubled down on his professional demeanor.

I did the same with my schooling. I was acing all my classes, except studies of light. No matter what I did, I couldn't get my hands to shoot out white light, and after two times of having black smoke come out of them, Mr. Rincor told me to stop trying. I felt like a failure.

Raphael and Mr. Rincor had a meeting with me and told me they thought what I'd done to Tiffany was just a demon-gifted power, which a lot of students had, and they weren't going to encourage developing it. So, I basically just listened to the lectures, and when it came to practical application, I watched Fred light up the room. It was depressing, but Fred was cool about it, and hadn't told anyone. I still heard the archdemon whispers a few times a week though.

I walked out of my dorm room to find Fred waiting in the lobby. He looked handsome, wearing a black suit and blue button-up shirt with a tie, but it was my security detail that held my gaze. Noah, Blake, Darren, and Lincoln stood just behind Fred, all dressed in suits and looking incredibly handsome.

Lincoln's gaze ran down my dress and I blushed. My heart throbbed at the sight of him, his dark hair slicked back, cleanly shaven, and dressed in a black suit.

"You look beautiful," Fred stated, pulling my attention from the man who held my devotion to the man who should.

I smiled. "Thanks. You look nice too."

He gave me a hug and I tried to feel something romantic, but the friend vibes were strong.

Friendzone Fred. Poor guy.

"Shea and Luke will meet us there," I told him.

He nodded, sticking out his arm for me to link with it. "I borrowed my dad's Porsche." He waggled his eyebrows.

I grinned. "Does he ever let you drive it?"

Fred shook his head vigorously. "No way. I had to convince him I was taking the prettiest girl in school out."

Aw. He was a total sweetie. "My dad loved cars. Before the fall, my mom said he'd spend hours in the garage fixing up old beaters."

Fred gave me an easy smile as we reached the parking lot. Sure enough, there was a white Porsche waiting. "Your chariot, my lady."

Lincoln stepped forward. "Please go straight to the venue and use valet."

Fred gave him a sharp look but didn't respond, just opened my door.

Awkward.

I slipped in and Fred closed the door, then walked around the car to slide in next to me. My eyes flicked to the rearview mirror to see the boys piling into an SUV with the school's logo on the side.

"So, is there something I should know about you and Lincoln?" Fred mused as the SUV followed us out of the parking lot.

Oh God.

"Not really," I hedged.

He looked sideways at me. "So you don't like him?"

Dammit, I couldn't lie. "I want to not like him, but…" I played with the hem of my dress.

He nodded, shifting gears. "But you do."

I couldn't bear to look at his face as a frown pulled at my lips. "Yeah. It's complicated."

"That's cool. I can do friends. I mean, I wanted more, but…"

My heart pinched. This was *not* the way to start a date. "I'm so sorry. You're such a nice guy."

"Ouch. Nice guy." He feigned a painful look.

I laughed. "Hey, nothing wrong with being the nice guy."

He chuckled. "But the dark, broody asshole always gets the girl."

Yeah, I guess that's true in this case. "We're still going to have an awesome night," I declared.

He gave me an easygoing smile, looking sideways at me. "Yes we are, because I'm an amazing dancer."

I held my hands out. "Whoa. That's a bold statement. I'm going to need some proof."

He nodded. "You just wait. They don't call me Footloose Fred for nothing."

I laughed again. Fred was funny and always lighthearted; there wasn't a serious cloud over every conversation like there was with Lincoln. Why couldn't I like him? Maybe in time I could… My mom always said the best relationships came from friendships.

Before I knew it, we were pulling up to the Beverly Hills hotel. He rolled up to the valet and then whipped his phone out. "Selfie for my dad? Proof there was a hot girl in his car with me?" He held it up, the camera facing us.

With a grin, I leaned in and kissed his cheek. He'd already declared we were friends, so I figured it was harmless.

After snapping the pic, he smiled. "Thanks. He'll get a kick out of that."

My door opened suddenly, and Lincoln was there, glaring down at me. "Let's get inside. This area isn't secure."

"My date can get my door, Lincoln," I snapped.

"Your *date's* too busy ogling you," he just sort of growled.

Lincoln Grey is jealous.

"You don't get to do that. You don't get to play hot and cold. *Nope.*" I gave him a death glare.

Mofo better not mess with me like that.

Fred cleared his throat near the big double doors, and I blasted past my "security detail," leaving Lincoln with his jaw tight and fire in his eyes.

Shea, Luke, Angela, Chloe, and everyone else arrived shortly after us. The winter ball was like an amazing catered wedding, except with no ceremony. It was a fundraiser for helping underprivileged families transfer from outside the war zones to inside the safety of Angel City. I guessed the tickets were pricey—Fred had paid for both of us.

They were also having a silent auction. Shea and I bid on bestie pedicures. I doubted we'd get it, since our highest bid was twenty-five dollars and the retail amount was sixty, but a girl had to dream.

Lincoln was watching me like a hawk all night. Anywhere I went, his eyes moved. It was unnerving, to say the least. Darren, Blake, and Noah were a little more relaxed. Noah took breaks to dance with Shea, as Darren stuffed his face at the chocolate fountain. A man after my own heart. Blake, whom I'd dubbed the sweet one, was standing near Lincoln, and doing whatever he said. The sides of the large ballroom were sprinkled with Fallen Army guards.

Shea took a sip of her water, and then pointed to a fellow student—Ryce, a super-hot centaur. It was weird to call him hot since he was half animal, but his upper half had it going on.

"If I slept with him, would that be considered bestiality?" she asked the table.

"Eww, Shea! Is this the shit you think about on a daily basis?" I asked her, shivering from the mental images.

She nodded seriously.

Fred chuckled. "The Centaurs stick together when mating, for obvious reasons."

Shea seemed sad about that, sitting back in her chair.

"Let's dance!" I declared and grabbed Fred's hand. I wasn't going to sit there and talk about Shea's weird thoughts anymore. Plus, I looked three months pregnant after eating so much amazing food. It would be good to burn some of that off.

Fred laughed and followed me to the dance floor. We danced for an hour, and he was indeed good. He popped, locked, moonwalked, and all of that, and not in the cheesy way. Michael Jackson was totally his spirit animal.

"Damn, boy. You've got moves!" I gushed.

He grinned. "My mom always wanted a daughter but got three sons instead. So she put me in hip-hop lessons when I was three."

I nodded, impressed. "You should do that professionally or something," I shouted over the music.

"Maybe in another life," he added with a shrug.

Yeah, pursuing our artistic passions wasn't really at the top of the agenda for any of us right now.

"I gotta pee. Be right back," I told him.

Fred nodded, doing circles around Shea, who was pulling off a very impressive Beyoncé number. For as long as I'd known Shea, we had loved dancing. It was our thing, our stress reliever, and we danced without a care of who was watching.

"Where are you going?" Lincoln's deep voice called behind me. I stopped in my quest for the restroom and threw a death glare over my shoulder. I'd forgotten he was there.

"I'm going to the bathroom. Is that okay?" I crossed my arms over my chest.

He nodded, placing one hand on his sword. "Lead the way."

I rolled my eyes. "You're not coming. I'll be fine."

Lincoln simply stared at me and stood there, waiting for me to start walking again.

'*He has no idea what we're capable of,*' Sera said from inside my boot. She sounded as offended as I felt.

'*I know. He thinks I'm a baby.*'

When I didn't budge, Lincoln sighed, gripped my arm lightly, and pulled me to the edge of the room. I could now clearly see a sign that said 'Bathroom' hung overhead, and at the end of the long hallway were two doors.

"Listen, I know you think I'm being overly cautious, but trust me. I have it on very good intel that there could be an attack at this party. That's why I'm so jumpy," he murmured.

My whole body went rigid. "An attack? Why didn't you say something earlier? Call off the event." Now, it made sense that there were so many of the Fallen Army stationed at the doors.

He sighed, running a hand through his hair. "Raphael doesn't trust my intel, said it wasn't enough for him to call off an event that brings in thousands for charity, so we compromised by beefing up security."

I rubbed my arms, itching to pull out my dagger. I had to pee really bad, but I wanted to know more. "Why would they attack a charity event?" I realized the second it left my mouth that it was a naïve and stupid question.

"They'll always try to take out Fallen Academy students. Less people to serve in the army that destroys them," he explained.

I rubbed my arms again, doing the pee dance. "Sometimes I forget we're at war."

Lincoln looked haunted. "I'll never forget." I squirmed again. "Go pee, woman!" he shouted, pointing down the hall.

"Now I'm scared," I told him, eyeing the dark hallway. He'd just told me there was probably going to be an attack. A bathroom stall, or a dark hallway, was the best place to jump someone.

He chuckled, his blue eyes twinkling. "I'll watch your back. Go."

Why is he so gorgeous? Why does he kiss so good? Why am I staring at his lips?

Not wanting Lincoln to think I was a total wuss, I took off down the hall, my eyes darting all over the place as I sniffed for sulfur, vinegar, or any weird demon smell. Coming up with nothing, I opened the bathroom door, and peeked my head inside.

"Hello?" No response. "Demon-friendly girl coming in," I said nervously.

I bent down and checked under the stalls, a sigh of

relief escaping when I saw I was alone. I peed quickly and then washed my hands, but when I was reaching for a paper towel, I heard a muffled scream.

My eyes widened, and I reached for Sera. Maybe I was just in a jumpy mood and the scream was a shout of joy, but now that I was focused, it sounded like the music had stopped.

More screams.

I peeked out the door and stared down the dark hallway.

Oh shit.

I had to squint to see, but it looked like Lincoln was fighting someone. His sword arm was outstretched, and I could see people beyond him running and screaming.

Shea.

I took off down the hall, holding Sera ready. When I reached Lincoln, I came face-to-face with that same damn Abrus demon. Lincoln thrust out his left hand and shot a bolt of white light into the demon's face. He shrank back but recovered quickly, standing to glare at me.

"Why are you after me?" I screamed. I couldn't take it anymore, not knowing. "What am I?"

Lincoln backed into the hallway, blocking me with his body.

"You're one of us. You belong with me. I can train you to control your dark magic," he said in a smooth, beckoning voice.

Dark magic. He knew about my dark magic. Maybe I wasn't a Celestial, or I wasn't *just* that, at least. Maybe my wings were black because I was half Brimstone demon. Those black bat wings mixed with white angel wings could make mine. Maybe.

"Never!" Lincoln roared, then burst forward while the Abrus demon was distracted, slipping his sword into the demon's rib cage.

The Abrus demon's eyes bugged out, and then his entire face turned sinister.

With a roar, his mouth opened and bees flew out. Honest-to-God *bees* flew from his mouth and attacked Lincoln. He started batting at the air and moved left to right in his spot, but didn't get out of the way, not allowing there to be a space between the demon and me. While Lincoln was busy with the bees, I saw the demon pull out a sleek black sword.

"No!" I shouted, then rammed my shoulder into Lincoln, pushing him into the wall and out of harm's way. I thrust my hand forward with all the anger I could muster, the black magic I'd tried so hard to keep hidden flying from my palm and wrapping around the Abrus demon's neck.

Surprise filled his face, and then he grinned. He had a sword in his stomach, was being choked out by black magic, and was grinning.

Freaking weirdo.

'*I can take care of those bees,*' Sera said.

Shit, I'd forgotten about Lincoln. He was on the ground now, getting stung from the looks of it.

While the Abrus demon was wrestling with his new necktie, I held Sera against Lincoln's back, the flat of the blade touching his shirt. A burst of white light shot out, and I jerked my head to the side, closing my eyes against the brightness. The blade heated up but didn't burn me, and then the light died down. Opening my eyes, I saw every bee had been turned to ash.

'*You're seriously badass,*' I told my partner in crime.

'*Thanks, love. Now run before he gets that off!*'

Oh yeah. The Abrus demon was still wrestling with my dark magic choker.

Hooking my arm under Lincoln's armpit, I hauled him up to a standing position. His skin was covered in red welts, but I could see his hands were glowing orange and he was already working on healing them. He pulled his sword out of the demon and tucked the other arm around me. The winter ball was in utter mayhem, people running around like crazy.

"Shea!" I shouted.

"Over here!" my best friend replied somewhere to the right.

My head snapped in her direction, and I saw she was holding the back door open for people. Noah and Blake were with her, ushering everyone outside.

Lincoln and I took off running just as the Abrus demon lunged for us. Lincoln threw his hand out behind him, and another brilliant white light shot from his palms, smacking the demon in the face.

Whoa. He definitely aced his studies of light class.

Once we'd made it safely across the ballroom, Darren popped up in front of us. "We've got an Abrus demon, two Brimstones, and a handful of Castor demons," he reported to Lincoln.

Lincoln nodded to Darren, then grabbed the back of my neck gently, turning me to face him. He ran his thumb along my jawline softly, looking my body up and down, seemingly admiring my dress. "You clean up nice. I'm sorry your date got ruined." He said 'date' like it was the plague.

He totally liked me. *The bastard.*

I grinned. "Thanks. It's all the yoga I do."

He chuckled, but then a scream tore his gaze from me, and he looked strained. "Go back to school with Blake and Noah, and text me the second you're safe. Sit in Raphael's office and wait for me."

My brow furrowed. "No *way*. Come with me."

He looked behind him. The Abrus demon had dissolved the necktie and was grinning wickedly at us.

Lincoln turned back to me. "I don't run from demons, Brielle. Go. I need to know you're safe."

I don't run from demons. That was both the cockiest and hottest thing he'd ever said.

"I can help," I told him, holding Sera up to him.

He shook his head. "Take her," he whispered to

someone behind me, and then I was being forcefully dragged away.

"No! Lincoln!" Whoever held me had a firm grip; I bucked and thrashed to no avail, ultimately giving in, and looking back in Lincoln's direction.

With me forgotten, he swung around and thrust his sword in the air. Blue shards of light burst from the tip and the two Brimstone demons were brought to their knees. Just as I was sucked out the back door, the Abrus demon charged for him.

"Lincoln!"

I didn't realize tears were streaming down my face, until whoever held me eased their hold, and wiped them.

"I'm sorry. Forgive me," Fred apologized.

Then he shoved me into the open door of Noah's SUV and closed it. His melancholy face was the last thing I saw that night as the SUV peeled out of the parking lot.

CHAPTER 17

I screamed for Noah to turn the car around the entire drive to Fallen Academy, but he insisted he was following orders, that the Fallen Army was inbound, and Lincoln would be okay.

I'd numbly texted Lincoln when we arrived, and then was ushered to Raphael's office, though he wasn't there. Noah instructed me to wait on the couch, that it was the safest place for me, and he would guard the door from outside. Shea wasn't permitted to wait with me, so she ran back to the dorm to hide, and we texted back and forth for over an hour, until, by some miracle, sleep finally took me.

It was the early hours of the morning, still dark out, when the murmured voices woke me.

"What is she? They want her because she has demon powers, but so do a lot of kids at this school," Lincoln whispered.

"She's awake," Raphael informed him.

Dammit. Freaking psychic archangel!

I peeled my eyes open and sat up quickly, taking in Lincoln's disheveled appearance. He hadn't slept, that much was clear, and I could see by the fresh dressing on his shoulder, and the full sling, that he'd been to the healing clinic.

"Are you okay?" I bolted to a standing position, the last remnants of sleep fading.

Patches of his skin were still welted from the beestings.

"I'll recover." His blue eyes roamed over my body as if checking *me* for injuries.

I was on the verge of a nervous breakdown. I could feel my sanity dancing in a chicken hat at the edges of my mind, threatening to jump off the cliff.

"You have to tell me everything you know. I can't live like this. Why do they want me? Why are my wings black? *What am I?*" I shouted the last part and ran a shaky hand through my hair. Raphael had answers, and I needed them, or I was going to lose my mind. The unknown was more terrifying to me.

The archangel sighed, shared a long look with a confused Lincoln, and then walked toward me. With each step, his presence pressed in on me like a balm to a burning wound. My energy settled as he reached for my shoulder, resting a calming hand there.

"When you took the angelic blood test, it showed

some demonic powers." His words came like a punch in the gut. Every. Single. One. I mean, I'd guessed that I'd been demon gifted with the black wings, but I'd been in complete denial until right then.

I wasn't angel blessed. I wasn't like the other Celestials.

I shrugged out of his touch and crossed my arms, facing the wall for a moment to compose myself.

"So what? Her own mother is a Necromancer. Half this school has some form of demon power in them. Why do they want her?" Lincoln was trying to downplay it, which made me fall for him even harder in that moment.

Raphael cleared his throat. "Because of the prophecy. Because of *whose* powers she has."

My whole body went rigid as I tried to remind myself to breathe. I slowly turned around, my eyes snapping to the archangel's face. "What did you just say?"

Prophecies were never good. I'd never heard of a prophecy where someone forecasted peace on Earth, or that starting in a certain year, everyone would be happy.

Raphael sighed again, seemingly resigned. "Right after the war, when we'd realized what it had cost the humans, we found our first Sighted. She was an older woman, about sixty years in age, and she told of a prophecy that each Sighted after her has repeated verbatim, despite never being told about it."

No.

My thoughts immediately went to James and those

few minutes before the Awakening ceremony. He'd told me to be careful, and what else? I couldn't remember, and we'd been interrupted before he could tell me more. I hadn't seen or spoken to him since. Now that I thought of it, I hadn't even heard about him. *What happened to him after the Awakening?* I'd have to ask Shea if she saw him at Tainted Academy. The Sighted received the rarest of the powers; I didn't think I'd even met one at this school.

"What's the prophecy?" I asked, wishing I had Teddy, my stuffed bear with one eye and a split neck from when Mikey tried to kill him with a bow and arrow. He was somewhere in a landfill right now, but I desperately wanted him back.

Raphael looked to Lincoln, who was just glaring at him with barely contained anger.

"Prophecies are fickle. If I tell you that you'll trip and break your leg, and you do, then did you break your leg because you were meant to, or because I planted the seed in your mind?" Raphael asked.

"Sir." Lincoln bit out that one word, and it was enough to set the tone.

Tell us or we'll unleash the full rage of two people who don't like being kept in the dark.

Raphael nodded. "The prophecy states that a young girl with black wings will go into the underworld, and kill Lucifer, ending the war."

This isn't happening. I'm still sleeping.

I laughed then. An "I'm losing my mind" laugh. Lincoln was staring at me with worry, eyebrows furrowed, mouth dipping in a slight frown.

"That doesn't mean it's you, or that the prophecy will come to pass. The future is always changing—"

"Why do I have black wings? What am I?" I'd asked many times, and he'd always danced around it, conveniently leaving that part out.

Raphael took on the face of a father then, one who was about to tell a child their cat had been run over. "You're a beautiful soul who was empowered with gifts from me, Michael, Uriel, Gabriel and..."

He paused and I leaned forward, though I wasn't sure I really wanted to know.

"Lucifer."

He actually said it, spoke my worst nightmare out loud. Not that I could conceive of such an awful thing, but pretty much the worst thing that could ever happen to a human—being endowed with powers from Lucifer himself—had happened to me. *Hooray...*

I shook my head vigorously. "No. No, you're mistaken." Bile rose in my throat.

Denial. I would fly into the sky and live there forever, because there was no way I was accepting that as truth.

My eyes flicked over to Lincoln, who stood there slack-jawed, staring at me like I'd sprouted an extra head.

Raphael moved closer to me, and I took a step

back. "I don't want comfort. I want the truth!" I shouted at him.

He frowned. "Of course." Then he walked over to the desk and produced the box and knife from my blood ceremony. "Lucifer's emblem, the snake, lit up when I tested you."

Shock ripped through me at such concrete proof, my eyes filling with tears as denial turned to shame.

"That's not fair!" I yelled as the tears overflowed and trailed down my cheek. "I didn't ask for this. You love talking about free will, well I didn't *will* any of this. I was an innocent five-year-old girl when *you*"—I jabbed my finger at him as the rage built within me—"and the rest of the angels started a war, infecting *my* people. Innocent humans were turned to freaks because of *you*!" I shouted.

Hurt crossed Raphael's face. "I know. I'm so sorry."

Lincoln winced. "Brielle."

"No. Leave me alone." I turned and burst out of the door, blasting past Noah, Blake, and Darren, who were stationed on either side.

I was dark. Shea had made me promise I wouldn't let her go dark, and I was the one who did. Not just any dark magic ran through my veins—*his* did. Lucifer's. The Devil. Freaking evil incarnate. I felt sick to my stomach thinking about it.

I ran harder, pumping my legs to take me to the open field where I knew I could be alone. Everyone was still sleeping, the sun just starting to rise. I wanted to fly far away from there, to another country, and never speak of it again. Live an entirely new life.

If I was Lucifer's weird little stepchild, would the demons ever stop coming for me? Especially if they believed in some prophecy where I was going to kill him?

Really? *Me,* an almost nineteen-year-old girl, go into the depths of Hell and kill the Devil? I laughed as more tears streamed down my face.

Footsteps sounded behind me, and I whirled around to Lincoln. I just stood there, chest heaving from running, tears covering my cheeks. I was a hot mess, and I was still wearing my dress from the ball.

"I'm evil," I whimpered. I had to voice my fears out loud to someone—why not him? He was probably there to lock me in my own area of the school, where they could keep an eye on me.

His face contorted in agony. "No. Never."

He pulled me by the shoulders and crushed me into his chest for a bear hug. As those strong arms wrapped around me, his scent washing over me, mixing with the warmth of his tight muscles, I felt so safe, so at home.

Lincoln Grey was hugging me. *Hard.* Like he didn't want to let go.

Maybe I am still sleeping.

"We'll figure this out together," he promised.

What?

I looked up into his eyes as he looked down at me, our lips a mere agonizing inch apart. "Together?"

He nodded. "Yeah. You've grown on me. You're mine now."

"You're mine now."

My brain barely had time to process those delicious words, when his lips claimed mine in a tender kiss. It wasn't heated like the one on the beach; it was soft, exploring, and over all too soon.

When he pulled back, he brushed his fingers through my hair. "When I met you, I was in a dark place, fresh from the loss of my family, but something about you lit me up again, made me care again. I tried to fight it, to look for reasons why this wouldn't work, but I can't anymore." His thumb stroked my jaw, and a pulse of heat shot straight to my gut.

Whoa. I had no words for that announcement.

"Tell no one of this news. Except for Shea." Then he switched to battle mode. "I'm going to double your training. I want you to become a lethal, demon-killing machine by the end of the year. Pass the gauntlet and get accepted into year two. It's the only way to keep you safe," he declared.

My mind was still on that kiss, that declaration that I, Brielle Atwater, lit him up inside. But then reality came crashing down—I was Lucifer's daughter, for all intents and purposes.

"What if I go dark?" Black, throat-choking magic

flung from my mouth, after all. We certainly couldn't ignore that.

He shook his head. "Not possible."

Denial. I used to live there.

"Lincoln, I appreciate your faith in me, but if I go dark—"

Grasping both sides of my face, he cupped my cheeks. "Brielle, you annoy the shit out of me sometimes, you're stubborn as hell, you don't listen, and I'm pretty sure the black magic you choked the Abrus demon with is super-dark stuff, but *you are not* evil. I know your soul."

"I know your soul."

Lincoln must've spent a lot of time with his nose shoved in those poetry books I saw in his trailer. Though I wasn't complaining one bit.

I'd heard rumors of those who went completely dark and ended up committing suicide after being surrounded by such evil all the time. A twenty-three-year-old Dark Mage killed herself in our building just last year.

"Wait, I annoy you?" I asked, confused, and his laugh warmed my stomach, bringing a smile to my face. "You're the biggest asshole I've ever met." I winked, turning the gesture against him for once.

He kissed the tip of my nose. "Well, aren't we quite a pair?"

Lincoln Grey and I are a pair. What alternate universe is this? I'd wanted to kill him when I first met him, but now I wanted to see him dripping wet in his towel again. That V needed its own instant replay.

"Now what?" I asked.

His hands fell from my face, and he gritted his teeth. "Now we train. I'm going to teach you everything I know, above what I should for your first year of schooling."

"I'm already tired just thinking about it."

He nodded. "You should be. I'm no longer going to go easy. It won't do you any favors in the end."

Stepping back, I crossed my arms and glared. "Excuse me? Go easy? I saved your ass back at the dance from those bees, remember?"

He chuckled. "No, Sera did. And if they kidnap you, that's the first thing they'll destroy. You need to become a weapon—your hands, your mind. I'm going to make a weapon out of you, Brielle." He ended the last sentence with a sinister look.

Shit. Sounds scary.

I shrugged. "Couldn't we just go on a date instead? Movies, maybe?"

His face didn't budge and I groaned.

"When do we start?" *I slept on a frickin' couch last night and he's injured, so he better not say—*

"Now. Go change," he commanded.

I groaned even louder as I succumbed to my fate.

The next few months were going to suck.

And suck they did.

Lincoln trained me harder than ever before. I was falling asleep in class because I was so exhausted from the extra workouts, but the past few months had been pretty great otherwise. Fred and I had remained friends, and he actually started dating Angela with my blessing. Lincoln and I were going strong, only verbally abusing each other 60 percent of the time.

"Get up, woman!" he roared.

My boy toy stood over me, sword drawn, the tip pressed into my neck slightly. "If you would allow me a weapon, this would be a fair fight!" I snarled at him.

Our make-out sessions, back in his trailer, were epic after a really good training session of talking shit to each other. I kept trying to go all the way with him, but the age thing freaked him out, even though I'd turned nineteen two months back, in November. I also might've let it slip that I'd only had sex once for thirty seconds. Now he kept calling me a virgin.

"Demons don't do fair fights. Get. *Up*," he growled, the blade tip tight to my neck.

He was definitely a bit unhinged, but his looks more than made up for it. Hadn't we all lost our minds a bit, after all?

"You have a blade to my neck. If I get up, I'll bleed out," I explained.

He shrugged. "Think of something. Use dark magic, bend light, kick me in the balls. Just do *something*."

I wanted those balls to help create my children one day, so that was out. Bend light? Was he drunk? That was some advanced-level shit that Darren was trying to teach me, but I had yet to even be able to *produce* light. And I wasn't using dark magic. No way. Never again. And definitely not on him.

"I'm pregnant and it's yours," I stated calmly.

His eyes widened and his arm relaxed. "*What?*" he roared.

Using the distraction to roll out of the way of his sword, I kicked out with my leg, tripping him. He dropped the sword and went flying on his ass.

I grinned from my place on the floor as he turned to glare at me. "That was a low blow." Then he looked impressed. "But effective."

My body swiftly moved, crawling over to him, and straddling his waist. We were alone in the smaller side gym, and Lincoln was getting less pissy about public displays of affection. He kept threatening to find me a new trainer so there wasn't a conflict of interest, but then he'd say he didn't trust anyone enough.

When I plopped down on his crotch and arched my back, pressing my pelvis into him, he groaned.

"Silly. We haven't had sex, so I can't be pregnant." I bent down and kissed his hot mouth.

He sucked my bottom lip, palm flattening against

my back, and then suddenly I was being spun, until I was underneath him.

"Maybe I need to remedy that situation." He looked me up and down with a half-lidded gaze.

Oh God, yes, please.

I checked a fake watch on my wrist. "Now's good for me."

He grinned, a mischievous glint in his eyes. "I'll tell you what. Pass the gauntlet, and then maybe I'll consider deflowering you."

A groan escaped me. "I'm *not* a virgin! Since when does a girl have to beg for sex?"

He kissed my forehead and rolled off me. "Since now."

The sexual tension between us was so strong, and I knew he was hurting as much as I was. I'd never wanted someone as badly as I wanted him. All of him. We'd been exclusively dating almost three months now. If we used protection, and were both consenting adults, we could totally bring on the sex!

"Pass the gauntlet," he reiterated.

Standing, I peeled off my tank top to reveal my blue sports bra. I hoped my nipples were hard, like two little fingers flipping him off.

His eyes widened. "What are you doing?"

"Nothing," I answered with a shrug. "It's hot in here."

He scowled. "I see what you're doing. Trying to kill me?"

"Is it working?"
He adjusted his pants. "Yes. We're done for today."
I grinned.

CHAPTER 18

That night, I met Luke, Chloe, and Shea in the training room for practice. We'd heard a rumor that in the gauntlet, you were forced to work in teams, so we were practicing team drills and team takedowns. My arms and legs were ripped after lifting weights with Darren every day, and Shea was getting scary good with spell casting. Last week she'd done some illusion thingy to make it look like Lincoln was sleeping in my bed. It was super depressing to roll over and see him disappear.

"Okay, so my dad let slip that the gauntlet isn't just to keep you in this school. It also determines your rank if and when you join the Fallen Army. It's timed, so better time, better rank," Chloe said, her fanged teeth protruding slightly onto her bottom lip.

I shrugged. "Sounds cool, like a magical fitness test."

She nodded. "But my dad says they make it real. He

couldn't say more, but he insinuated that our lives could really be in danger."

That had my eyes widening. "Why would Raphael allow that?"

Shea rolled her eyes. "You put Raphael on this pedestal. Yes, school here is free, but that's only because the archangels are recruiting for their army."

"Their army that protects people from demons," I interjected.

Shea shrugged. "I'm just saying. They want to sort the weak from the strong, and I like my cushy life here, so let's practice."

I grinned. "Are you sure you can miss your Wednesday night date?" Wednesday was her "make out with Noah in the car and leave him with blue balls" day.

"Have you slept with him yet?" Chloe asked.

Shea made a disgusted face. "I would never allow his wee-wee in my va-jay-jay."

I burst out laughing, not just at her verbiage, but also at the look of horror that crossed Luke's face when she said it.

"Did you seriously just say 'wee-wee'? Oh my God, you're such a kindergarten teacher," I teased.

Shea rolled her eyes. "Fine, I don't want his dirty dick near me. He gets around."

Ew, that was vulgar. I almost prefer wee-wee. "Why not break it off?" I asked, setting up practice mats around the gym.

She shrugged. "I have this fantasy that one day he'll stop whoring around, we'll get married, have two-point-five children, and live in the 'burbs."

Now it was Chloe's turn to laugh. "Well, he keeps coming back for more, so you must have something he wants." She winked, and smacked Shea's butt.

Shea blew her a kiss, and then rubbed her hands together. "Check this out. I found an advanced Mage book while I was grading papers in Mr. Claymore's office, and I've been dying to try this spell. It creates a portal between two points. So, let's say the gauntlet is a long run. I can open the portal here and end it at the finish line, bringing us all through to win."

Luke let out a low whistle. "But remember the time you tried that spell to make my horns drip poison and I almost died?"

Oh, ouch. That was pretty scary. Luke's Beast form was frightening, but it was even scarier that his horns could pierce flesh. Shea had the brilliant idea to make them drip poison, but it went all wrong, and he'd ended up in the healing ward for a week.

Shea rolled her eyes. "I've improved a lot since then. This is harmless. No one has to go through right now. I'm just going to start practicing opening the portal."

Chloe shrugged. "Fine, but do it over there so if it blows up, we don't get hurt." She gestured to the corner of the room.

Shea gave her a pissy look but did as she'd asked.

"Okay, Luke, you shift," I instructed, then pointed to the Nightblood. "Chloe, I want to test your strength."

She grinned. "I thought you'd never ask." Her lips puckered as she laid a kiss on her inner arm, which she then lifted and flexed.

I chuckled. I'd somehow become leader of our little practice group. So far no one had died, so I figured I was doing something right.

Luke started shifting, and I knew I'd never get used to the sound of cracking bones. There were varying types of Beast Shifters. Most of them were earthly animals with horns, which was the case with Luke. His bulked-out brown bear form with curled, black horns was pretty terrifying to look at. The only thing that calmed me was knowing that it was my good friend inside it, and that he'd never hurt me.

After Luke was on all fours, letting out a little roar to make sure we wouldn't easily wet our pants during the gauntlet, we were ready.

"All right, Chloe, strength and speed are your main two gifts," I acknowledged.

She put a hand on her hip. "And my devilishly good looks."

I grinned. "And that. So, let's see if you can chuck Luke's bear into that mat across the room."

Luke's big, brown-bear eyes went wide, but Chloe didn't look fazed. She was a daredevil who liked a challenge; it was what I admired most about her.

"You ready, big boy?" Chloe asked, tossing her red hair over one shoulder.

He *hated* being called big boy, so at her words, he spread his paws out, and stood as still as a five-hundred-pound statue, just glaring at her.

Chloe tore across the room blindingly fast and slammed into Luke's rib cage, knocking him on his side. I winced at the impact. She wouldn't go hard enough to hurt him, but that definitely wasn't comfortable. With a grunt, she heaved him six inches into the air before slipping, and then he went plopping down to the ground again.

"Uhhh, guys?" Shea shouted from her corner of the room.

I turned back over my shoulder to look at her, my eyes bugging out of my head. *What am I seeing?*

Shea had created some hole in the ground and a tiny Snakeroot demon was crawling out of it, looking pissed as all hell. She went rigid and slowly started to back up, knowing full well how nasty those little shits could be. It was best not to startle them either, as one spit to the face could leave you blind for life. I had the acid scar on my foot to prove how temperamental the little buggers could be.

Chloe was staring at the demon with abject horror. She'd likely never seen one in her whole life by the shock written on her face. Luke was a bit more relaxed, shifting his weight as if deciding to charge it or not.

"Don't move. They spook easy and spit acid," I told my friends. We'd all taken the course on demonology in history, but I wasn't sure how much of it they'd retained. I didn't want anyone losing an eye or being scarred for life over a careless move.

The Snakeroot demon had fully crawled out of the portal by that point and was looking around the room. Those little creatures loved sugar. Cupcakes, syrup, candy—anything sweet would distract them. But fate wasn't on our side, because we were in the freaking gym without a scrap of food on us.

The demon snapped his head in Shea's direction and hissed.

"Shea, Monkshood illusion," I shouted.

That brought the creature's attention to me, and he puckered his lips and spit in my direction. I leapt out of the way just in time, the acidic goo landing a mere foot away.

"Calm down. We know where the candy is," I told him.

He cocked his head to the side, drool forming in his lizard-like mouth. If he didn't spit acid and act like a total weirdo, he'd actually be cute. At twenty-four inches tall, he was reminiscent of a medium-sized dog, except with scaly skin, and sticky hands and feet that let him climb walls.

"Yes, and cupcakes too."

Shea was working her magic, arcs of purple spell

work spinning through the air. I was hoping she'd gotten my meaning that I wanted her to create an illusion of a Monkshood demon, because Snakeroot demons were terrified of them.

Just when it looked like she was doing exactly that, all hell broke loose.

Loud sirens burst into the night, blaring deafeningly, and sent the Snakeroot demon into a spitting frenzy. He scurried up the wall, his sticky-pad feet holding him there as he continued to spit rapid-fire.

"Take cover!" I shouted, diving behind a huge practice mat. The sirens were so loud, I was surprised I had never noticed them before, but sure enough, on the top of the far wall, there was a red, blinking light and speaker.

"Students, the demon alarm has been activated. Please proceed to a safe place and wait for help," Raphael's booming voice came over the speaker.

Shit. Demon alarm?

"Shea, you tripped the school's demon alarm!" I yelled. She was hiding behind a row of weightlifting medicine balls and probably didn't hear me.

The alarm sound stopped then, but the light kept blaring. My cell phone was in my bag across the room with Sera, so I had no way of calling Lincoln or getting my dagger.

"Oh God!" Chloe shrieked.

My head snapped in the direction she was looking

and my whole body went rigid. Out of the portal, another demon was climbing up and into the gym—a freaking Hellhound.

"*Shea!*" I roared, then heard the sound of spit hitting the mat I was trying to seek safety under. The smell of burning foam wasn't pleasant, and I'd probably need to ditch the mat soon, or suffer the consequences.

"Shit! I'll close it," Shea said, stepping out from behind her medicine ball hideout. The Snakeroot demon saw and took his chance, sending an arc of spit right at her outstretched hand.

"Look out!" I screamed, tearing across the room with my mat as a shield.

It was no use. The acid connected with Shea's arm just as she started her spell, and a wail of pain cut through the air.

"Screw this," Chloe muttered. In a blur, she streaked across the room with something in her hands, and then the Snakeroot demon was flying to the other side of the gym.

Chloe was standing there grinning, holding a wooden bo staff. I'd barely even seen her punt the tiny demon from his perch on the wall.

I used the distraction to get to Sera, chucking the disintegrated mat, and picking up my dagger.

Shea was huddled on the ground, whimpering over her arm, and Chloe seemed to have the Snakeroot demon in check. She was faster than he could spit, so she was dodging his acid attacks, and knocking him across the room with the bo staff like he was a baseball. Luke padded over to my side, both of us staring at the Hellhound.

"Shea, how you doing?" I called out to her, keeping my eyes on the two-headed mutt before me. Hellhounds would rip your throat out in a millisecond and eat your entire carcass in an hour. Bones included.

"I'll be fine. You take care of the Hellhound, and I'll close the portal." Her voice was racked with pain, and I knew how bad she must've been hurting. I'd been there.

One of the Hellhound's heads was glaring at me, the other at Luke. In that moment, both bared their teeth and growled at us simultaneously. I didn't know much about them, except that they were rare, and rumored to be Lucifer's favorite creature. Without a clue on how to kill them, I was at a huge disadvantage.

'Behead them,' Sera shared.

I winced. *Nasty.*

'Are you sure?' I asked. Beheading a wolf dog with red eyes wasn't my idea of a good time.

Sera had no time to respond as the Hellhound lunged for me, probably determining Luke was a greater threat. I dropped to one knee just like Lincoln had taught me, and readied myself for the blow, but the collision never came. As the hound arced through the air, Luke bent his head low and then snapped it up, goring the creature's side. One of his horns pierced through the animal's rib cage, and a shriek ripped out of both mouths.

With a toss of his head, Luke chucked the Hellhound across the room and it hit the wall, sliding down into a slump, and leaving a trail of black blood down the wall.

I did a quick assessment of the situation. Shea was closing the portal, hunched over as she flung magic, cradling her injured arm. A hurried look to the right revealed Chloe had the Snakeroot demon pinned under her boot, its jaw forced closed by the weight of her shoe on its face.

Luke and I needed to finish off the Hellhound.

Just then, the double doors to the gym opened and Lincoln stepped in with no less than twenty Fallen Army soldiers, including Raphael and Mr. Claymore.

Lincoln's eyes widened to saucers. "What the hell is going on here?" he bellowed, striding inside, and pulling two swords—both glowing a ferocious blue.

The Hellhound snapped his heads in Lincoln's direction and growled, trying to get up. There was a puddle of blood at its feet, but it still looked ready to party.

Lincoln advanced, and in two clean swishes through the air, he took the Hellhound's heads right off. Easy-peasy.

"Over here, please," Chloe said. The Snakeroot demon was squirming hard, probably sensing his impending doom. Blake came up behind Lincoln with a flamethrower in hand and lit it.

The Snakeroot demon wiggled harder, and Chloe started to lose balance. With one final pull, he slipped out from under her boot and scrambled up the wall. Lincoln slowly pulled a bag of Skittles from his pocket, opening them with his teeth and scattering them on the floor. The colored candies spread out across the ground, offering a distraction for Chloe to back away gradually, as Blake came around the other side of the demon, flamethrower in front of him.

My eyes flicked to the left, where Raphael was inspecting the now-closed portal with Shea and Mr. Claymore. If we could get the Snakeroot demon under control, everything was going to be okay.

Just when I thought it, I heard the telltale spitting noise. I flicked my head back to see the demon spit in Blake's direction, but he passed the flame in front of him and the acid hit it instead, sending a burst of fire up to the ceiling. *Interesting. The acid's combustible.* Blake backed away, and Lincoln kicked some of the Skittles closer to the demon.

His little nostrils flared, a greedy look in his eyes. Lincoln took a few wide steps back and the demon started to crawl down from the wall. When he hit the ground, he snatched a Skittle and gobbled it up, a thin sliver of drool falling from his mouth.

Lincoln kicked more toward him, the demon feverishly reaching out with his rat-like paws to pick them up and shove them in his mouth. He was kind of cute when he wasn't trying to blind us with acid. Lincoln charged forward, sword raised with blue sparks shooting off the tip. Blake came down on the demon with the flamethrower, at the same time Lincoln's sword took his head off.

Yikes.

The sight of his smoldering body hit me then, the severity of the situation setting in.

Lincoln spun on me. "Start talking!"

I winced. So much for possibly showing me preferential treatment. "Well..." I wasn't going to rat Shea out in front of Raphael, and I wasn't sure if Lincoln would protect her. I'd like to think he would, but I didn't know. So it was hoes before bros and all of that. But I was also a really bad liar.

"I opened a portal to Hell by accident," Shea confessed before I could speak.

I shot her an incredulous look. The last thing we needed was to get kicked out.

Mr. Claymore stepped forward, disbelief in his eyes. "You what? That's *very* advanced Magery."

Shea tucked a brown curl behind her ear. "Yeah...I might've read a book in your office I probably wasn't supposed to...and obviously I wasn't trying to open a portal to Hell. I was trying to open one to the library or something, to practice for the gauntlet."

Raphael surveyed the scene and shared a curious look with Mr. Claymore. "It could've been a lot worse. Portal opening is a fourth-year skill," he told Shea.

She winced, her cheeks reddening. "I didn't even know opening portals to Hell was a thing, or I never would've tried it."

He bobbed his head. "And you closed the portal all by yourself?" She nodded, and Raphael shared another look with Mr. Claymore, who nodded.

"Am I getting kicked out?" Shea was still holding her injured arm. She really needed to go to the healing clinic soon.

Raphael shook his head. "No, but I'm assigning you to an independent study with Mr. Claymore. One hour a week, on your own time."

Shea looked confused. "Okay..."

I was unclear whether that was a punishment or not. It seemed Shea was too.

Raphael's gaze roamed the room. "All right, let's reset the demon alarm. Noah, please walk Shea to the healing clinic. And Lincoln, I'd appreciate it if you oversaw this cleanup." He gestured to the room of dead demons.

"Yes, sir," Lincoln replied, then shot me a glare. As if it were possible for *me* to control Shea. Like it was my fault.

The room cleared out quickly, leaving just Lincoln, Blake, and me.

Lincoln crossed the space quickly and ran his eyes over me. "What the hell, Bri? You're supposed to be lying low. Now you're inviting demons into the training room?"

"You think I hatched this master plan?" I asked, with a hand on my hip.

His face softened. "No, but when you walk in to see your girlfriend fighting off a Hellhound, and a Snakeroot demon, it doesn't look good. You scared the shit out of me." He cupped my face gently.

I grinned. "Girlfriend?"

He rolled his eyes. "Whatever."

I leaned in to give him a quick kiss. When we separated, he sighed. "Seriously though, I was really worried. The alarm went off, you weren't answering your phone, and you weren't in your dorm. I freaked."

It was that admission that showed me how much Lincoln really cared. At first, I thought we might be some fling, but with each event that brought us closer and closer, the relationship felt more and more serious. Like a longer-lasting thing.

The door to the training room opened then. "Atwater! Healing clinic, now!" Noah barked, then shut the door.

Ugh. Duty calls.

CHAPTER 19

I raced to the healing clinic after Noah. "What's up? Is it overflowing in there?" I asked.

He shook his head. "No, but as your master healing teacher, I want you to heal Shea's arm. And she's in pain, so you need to hurry."

I stopped dead. "What? No way! I'll screw it up. You do it."

I'd only healed *very* minor things, like an infection from an ingrown toenail, Mrs. Greely's headache, and Shea's menstrual cramps. I was more of an assistant, really good at grabbing gauze and bandages.

He gripped my arm. "Demon injuries are very common in the war zones, and if you're given a healer position in the Fallen Army, you'll need to know how to heal a Snakeroot acid burn."

My eyes widened as he dragged me across the quad.

"She's my best friend. If I mess it up, I'll never be able to live with myself."

He looked back at me with smoldering eyes and tousled hair. "I care about her too, ya know."

I thought they were just make-out buddies. "You do?" I questioned. Now was as good a time as any to probe him for info.

He smirked. "She's a bitch to me, keeps me in my place. I like that about her. She's…one of a kind."

Did he just call my best friend a bitch? But in a weird, cute way? I was choosing to focus on the "one of a kind" comment instead, because that was super sweet.

"She thinks you're a man whore," I told him honestly.

His grin widened. "I know. That's her pet name for me."

They had a weird-ass relationship, I'd give them that.

"Come on. Let's go help her," he urged.

When we stepped into her room, her fiery gaze pinned Noah to the wall. "Feel free to take your time. It's not like I'm dying in here or anything."

He rolled his eyes. "You'll be fine. Brielle's here to heal you."

Shea's eyes bugged out, sweat beading her brow. "What? Has she ever done this before?"

I winced. "Not really, but—"

"But I'm here, and I'm the best healer this school has. And a wonderful teacher." Noah winked at Shea.

Shea scoffed. "I'm glad your ego is still alive and thriving. Just hurry. It feels like it's going to fall off."

Oh God. The walls are closing in. I'm going to faint. I can't do this.

"Ready?" Noah asked.

I gulped. "Of course."

Rule number 1 of healing: Act confident even if you're scared shitless. A scared patient is a bad situation.

Noah positioned himself over my right shoulder with his hand on my lower back, pushing me closer to Shea. I sat next to her in the healer's chair, where Noah, or one of the other healers, usually sat.

She gave me that look that said "if you mangle my arm, I'll never forgive you."

"Bitch, I've got this," I told her confidently.

That made her lips curl. "You better, or you owe me a box of Cloud Nine Donuts."

Ha! That would be my entire two-week paycheck. "Deal."

Noah dropped a bucket at my feet.

Frowning, I looked up at my teacher. "What's that for?"

"You'll see. Activate your healing centers, and I'll guide you through the rest," Noah instructed.

Activate my healing centers. No big deal.

I stared at my palms, and then to the Raphael tattoo on my forearm. *Wake up.* I pushed the thought to my hands. I'd done it a whopping three times in my life, so I was hoping it still worked.

"Relax. Your power will automatically reveal itself in the presence of someone injured," Noah assured me.

I knew that.

I let my hand hover over Shea's bubbled and angry red arm; the skin stretched so taut it looked like it might burst. Sure enough, my palm started to heat up, emitting a faint orange glow.

"It's working!" I tried not to sound too rookie, but I was pretty excited.

"Of course it is." Cool, calm, and collected. That was Noah.

The orange healing light was different from the Celestial light I learned about in class with Fred. The Celestial light could be used as a weapon; this was always a healing tool.

"Now, assess her injury with your power, and take it into you. Not too much, and not too fast—like Lincoln did with your tattoos. Just go easy, or you'll be in worse shape than her."

Yeah, he'd lovingly drilled that into my head every day for the past four months. Low and slow was the healer motto. Healers couldn't heal without taking on the malady themselves; it was a Catch-22. The stronger the healer, the more serious the injury they could take on. If a beginner healer tried to heal a person dying of a knife wound, that healer could die. Noah was the strongest among all of the healers apparently, which made him the master teacher.

I started my breathing techniques, in and out. When I went in, I sucked a little of Shea's burn into me, through my hands. I knew it was working the second the stinging sensation lit up the veins in my arm.

My eyelids snapped open. "It burns."

"I feel a bit better," Shea confessed.

Maybe I wasn't going to screw this up.

Noah rested a hand on my back. "Good, now breathe through it. Your body was made for this. The blood of the Archangel of Healing runs through your veins. With training and focus, there's no sickness you can't expunge."

I was supposed to concentrate, but at his words, my father popped into my mind. "Can you heal cancer?" I asked randomly.

Shea squirmed in her seat, and Noah looked uncomfortable. "Cancer is...difficult to explain. We can talk about this in detail another time, okay?"

He knew. He must've read my file too because he was giving me that pity look. I just nodded.

Focus, you idiot. Shea needs you.

Closing my eyes, I placed my other hand over Shea's arm. Taking in a deep breath, I sucked more of the injury in through my palm.

If someone had given me the ability to choose any superpower, it wouldn't be flying, although that was pretty great. It wouldn't be manifesting a million dollars, although that would be great too. It would be to end human suffering from illness. Watching my father, the strongest member of my family, be reduced to skin and bones, to lose his dignity, to cry out in pain—it was life-altering. If I could learn to take that from people, I would.

If practicing and becoming stronger could afford me the ability to be a great healer like Noah, then that's the path I wanted to take after school. I didn't want to be some raging soldier, with a high demon-kill record like Lincoln. I wanted to heal people. And not just people who were deemed 'worthy'—I wanted to heal anyone. Whoever was hurt or suffering deserved an end to that. I didn't realize until right then just how passionate I was about it.

"Slow down there, killer," Noah said, tapping my arm.

My eyes snapped open, and suddenly the pain of a thousand burning suns ripped through my body. Nausea rolled into me and I whimpered. Looking down, I saw Shea's entire arm glowing with a powerful orange light. My healing light.

Her injury was completely gone. *I did that.*

Noah sighed. "You overdid it, as I thought you would."

I grabbed my stomach, groaning again. My mouth watered with the nausea. I was going to be sick.

Noah grabbed the back of my neck, and lightly pushed my head down over the bucket between my legs. "Out with it, before it starts doing damage."

"Wh—" Then I vomited burning-hot, green acid into the bucket. *Twice.*

When I was done, I wiped my mouth, and looked up at Noah. "Holy shit. How is that possible?"

So many questions. For starters, how did the acid go through my veins, into my stomach, and out my throat without damaging me?

He chuckled. "I told you, your body was made to heal, and you have a natural talent for it. I hope you'll think about majoring in healing studies next year."

I just nodded, then looked at Shea. "Does this mean *you* owe *me* Cloud Nine Donuts?"

"That was *not* the deal." She answered with a smirk.

Noah leaned over the bed, and kissed Shea's lips, pulling back only a few inches. "Cloud Nine Donuts are on me, beautiful. I gotta see if Lincoln needs help." He stood and left the room.

Shea's gaze followed him through the door with confusion, lips puckered, eyes squinted.

"He likes you. Like *likes you,* likes you," I teased.

She frowned. "He's never kissed me outside of his car. That was weird."

I tried to breathe through the last of my lingering nausea. "He said you were a bitch to him, and he liked that you always called him out." *Did I translate that right?*

Shea's mouth popped open. "He called me a *bitch*?"

"*No*, not like that. It was like a compliment. I think.

He likes that you don't bend over backward for him or something. Said you were one of a kind." I was awful at that kind of stuff.

Shea crossed her arms. "Whatever, he's probably dating five other girls at the same time."

"Well, why don't you ask him?"

She laid back in her bed and stared at the ceiling. "Because I don't want to know the answer."

Denial. It was a nice place to live.

It was probably a horrible time to tell her that Lincoln had called me his girlfriend, so I decided to stuff that away for a later date.

"Dude, you opened a portal to Hell."

She winced. "Oopsie."

Drowsiness descended on me then, the healing had totally drained me. Laying my head on Shea's arm, I sighed. "This is why we can't have nice things. I'm burping black magic, and you're opening portals to Hell."

Shea laughed, resting a hand on my head. "We'd be straight-A students at Tainted Academy."

I chuckled. She was probably right, and that was a bit depressing.

"We can't all be Tiffanys," I stated.

"The world can't handle any more Tiffanys," she assured me.

Ain't that the truth.

CHAPTER 20

The next month nearly killed me. There was a development in the war, and Lincoln was sent away for two weeks at a time, as was Noah. They weren't allowed to say, but I'd overheard them talking about an increase in demon activity and losing the eastern border of the city. Lincoln had assigned Carl in his place. *Carl* was a crotchety, forty-year-old Celestial with Archangel Michael powers, who had no sense of reason. He worked me like a dog, and had no pity when I was hurt.

I was walking home from my shift at the clinic—limping, really—when my phone buzzed with a text.

Lincoln: I'm home. Come to the trailer?

I pivoted and started in the direction of the parking lot, nerves bristling through me. I hadn't seen him in two weeks. I always had this random, irrational fear that he'd break up with me for no reason. Now after being apart for weeks on end, with only an occasional email here or there, that was all the more likely.

I knocked, even though I had a key so I could water his one sad succulent while he was away.

"Come in," he muttered.

I stepped up and opened the door, but Lincoln wasn't in the front room.

"Hello?" I called out, closing the door behind me.

"Back here," he yelled, his voice strained.

I set my bag down and walked back to the bedroom where we'd made out so many times, I'd lost count. The room where I was hoping he'd rock my world sometime soon. The second I saw the gauze on his abdomen, a few drops of blood coming through, I stopped breathing, all those sexy thoughts flying out of my head.

"You're hurt!" I ran to his side, sitting at the edge of the bed.

His hand grasped the side of my jaw and neck, pulling me down so my forehead rested against his. His dark hair was tousled against his forehead, and aside from his wound, he looked sexy as all hell.

He inhaled. "I missed the way you smell."

Then his lips landed on mine and I fell into him, careful not to touch his stomach. I held myself up, relishing the feeling of his lips on mine. God, I loved kissing him; it was electric and amazing.

"You're hurt," I repeated, finally pulling away.

He looked up at the ceiling. "I'll be fine after a few days' rest. Things are getting worse out there."

I'd asked for more details before and he never gave them, so I didn't bother now. "Carl is a total psycho. He's trying to kill me," I shared.

Lincoln laughed and then winced, clutching his side, but for the few seconds that he'd smiled, his whole face lit up. God, he was handsome. Dark unruly hair, strong jaw, intense eyes. He belonged in a romance novel, not by my side.

"He says you're getting better at your flying sword lunges."

"Ha! As if he would ever pay me a compliment. I nearly broke my ankle last week, and he told me to tape it up and keep going!" I huffed. Lincoln grinned, giving me a devilish look. "What?" I asked, raising an eyebrow.

"He was my trainer. I told him to break you and put you back together again."

My eyes widened. "Lincoln, he took you seriously!"

His eyes darkened. "Good."

Sometimes I seriously question the mental stability of this man. I frowned. "Is this just about me passing the gauntlet?"

He was quiet for so long that I almost asked again. "No."

Mild terror flushed through my veins. "What else is it about?"

His lips puffed out as he sighed. "Bri, there is a very real possibility that they will one day kidnap you."

Full-fledged terror burst through my veins, making my heart beat erratically.

Lincoln propped himself up on one elbow, wincing in pain as he did. "I would find you. I will *always* find you. In the meantime, I need you to be able to take care of yourself. I don't want to think that any one of them could have their way with you until I could get to you."

My eyes widened. *Oh God.* I'd never thought about that. I mean, I'd heard the stories, but...

"Okay" was all I said. All I *could* say in the face of such horrifying news.

I let my healing power come to the surface of my palm and stroked his arm, but his hand came out and grabbed my wrist. He shook his head. "No."

I frowned. "Why not?"

He ran his fingers from my temple to my jaw. "Because I don't ever want to cause you pain."

Lincoln pushed the inside of the elbow I was leaning on, so I fell on him. I caught myself before slamming into his face, but now we were a few inches apart. He grasped the back of my neck once more, holding me close.

"You saved me from the darkest time of my life. I'm going to take care of you. No matter what."

My throat tightened with emotion. Deep down, Lincoln was a passionate soul, a loyal friend.

He was freaking perfect.

I'm so in love with him.

The thought actually shocked me. I wasn't sure when it had happened or how. We were slightly dysfunctional most of the time, but damn, I loved everything about him. I knew that even if we broke up, he'd always make sure I was okay. There was so much respect and love between us. We'd somehow started at each other's throats and became closer for it.

Lying back in bed, he pulled me down with him. "Stay with me," he mumbled.

Shea was waiting to meet up with me so we could practice drills, and I had a paper due the next afternoon that I'd barely started, but I stayed.

Of course I stayed.

"The gauntlet is in ten days! Ten days and your future will be determined!" Lincoln barked as he swung a left hook right at my face. I honestly couldn't believe I'd survived my first year at Fallen Academy. Well, almost survived. The gauntlet would weed out the weak from the strong.

Yes, my boyfriend was trying to beat me up. *All the time.* I dodged the jab, then threw a hard knee into his inner thigh.

"If I fail, it's not the end of the world, Lincoln," I

told him. The pressure he was putting on me was getting to be enormous. I stepped into his body, pushing my pelvis into his. "And I'm pretty sure I can still get you to make good on your promise whether I pass the gauntlet or not."

His gaze went razor-sharp as his arms lowered. "If you don't pass, you no longer will be allowed to attend school here. That means you won't live in the safety and protection of the academy. You'll get kidnapped, I'll have to rescue you, and it's going to be a mess. Just. Pass."

Geez, that got dark quickly. "Yes, sir," I said, saluting him.

"Trust me, there are other perks to passing, but I can't talk about them. Let's just say your minimum-wage job at the clinic wouldn't be needed."

That made my eyes widen a bit. Money? If you passed the gauntlet, were you given money? "I'm listening." Damn, the bastard knew me inside and out. Money and Cloud Nine Donuts were strong motivators for me.

Lincoln grinned. "Just be ready for anything," he added cryptically.

I waved my fingers in front of his face in a spooky gesture. "I got this."

He took on a serious look, then dropped his gaze to the floor. "I asked Raphael if you could be exempt from competing."

I stepped back, mouth open in shock. "You what?

Why would you do that?" How embarrassing! He thought I couldn't pass on my own and needed special treatment?

'I'll show him what we're capable of!' Sera screamed from her place at my hip.

'Calm down. He's just trying to help,' I told her.

Lincoln ran a hand through his hair. "I can't tell you why, but…the gauntlet is dangerous. Especially for you."

Especially for me? What the hell does that mean?

"It's a school thing, so it can't be *that* dangerous," I said casually.

Lincoln just shook his head. "You'll see. Just keep training, and when you're in there, use everything you have. Including the black tie."

We'd affectionately named my dark magic 'the black tie,' since it ended up strangling the person I sent it after. But I'd never wanted to use that again, and he knew that. I'd gotten my four-watt-bulb hands to a stunning twenty-watt with a ton of practice; I figured eventually I could blind someone with it or something along those lines.

"I don't want to go dark," I told him.

He rested his hands on my shoulders. "You're not, but you do have dark magic, and you need to use it when necessary."

Fine. He has a point, I guess.

I nodded.

"Be back here at seven tonight. I have a special

training for you." He started to walk to the corner of the room, where his gym bag and water were.

"What special training thing? Not Carl, right?" Fear gripped me at the thought. I never wanted to train with that man again.

He chuckled. "No, not him. But someone very special is going to teach you a lifesaving skill."

I sighed. "Cryptic much?"

He chuckled. "Just be here."

With a chaste kiss, he was off, leaving me to my own thoughts.

It was four o'clock. What was I going to do for three hours?

I decided to pass the time doing pedicures with Shea and Luke back in our dorm.

"When are one of you going to go all the way with your boys? I need sex talk here," Luke pointed out, while painting lime-green polish on his toes.

I threw my hands into the air. "I'm beginning to think something is wrong with Lincoln. What guy in their right mind denies sex?"

Shea chuckled. "A guy who is like four years older than you, is afraid of breaking you, and has had a lot more sexual experience than you."

I scowled at her. "Noah is older than you, and more

experienced, and yet he tries to have sex with you twice a day."

Her grin widened. "More like three, if you include the sexting."

Luke winced. "Throw that poor guy a bone, girlfriend. If you don't want something more serious with him, then drop him."

Shea studied her red toenails intently. "Well, I don't know. Last night he got all weird and asked if we were exclusive, then told me I could borrow his car if I needed it. It was creepy."

Both Luke and I stopped what we were doing.

"In what universe is any of that creepy?" I asked. I needed to have a private talk with her. She did this a lot, the whole self-sabotage thing. Growing up without a dad, and with a drug addict for a mom had left its marks on her heart. She didn't trust anyone in this world except my mom, Mikey, and me. That needed to change, or she would die alone.

"Right now, it's fine. If he cuts it off, I can walk away unscathed," she replied.

"I get it." Luke answered with a shrug.

Shea's gaze keenly focused on him. "Maybe I'm bi. I feel like I could trust a chick more than a dude."

Luke grinned. "Can you imagine rubbing up on a girl's boobs?"

Her eyes widened in shock and she shook her head. "Ew."

He busted out laughing. "Then you're not bi. You're just scared of getting your heart broken."

"Okay, now that we've all questioned our sexuality, and determined we have relationship issues, I gotta go." I announced, standing.

They waved me off.

I was wearing flip-flops, yoga pants, and an old T-shirt. My muscles were sore as hell, so I was hoping this was more of a cognitive training than a physical one. I made it to the gym at seven sharp. If Carl was in there, I was going to kill Lincoln.

Opening the door, I gasped in shock as Archangel Michael came into view.

"Hello, Brielle," he greeted in his buttery voice. I had to look away for a second, his skin exuded too much light to look directly at him. The glow suddenly dimmed, as he approached me.

"Hi. Sir, if I'd known it was you, I would've dressed a bit better." I tugged on the hem of my oversized T-shirt.

He waved in dismissal. "Propriety doesn't interest me. Come as you are."

I shifted my weight and my muscles screamed in protest. Lincoln had gotten me a training with the most powerful warrior on the planet? I was going to die.

"I'm still sore from my other trainings, but I'll do my best," I hedged, kicking off my sandals and moving into a fighting position. I pulled Sera from my thigh holster and held her out before me.

Michael's eyes glittered as a smile danced at his lips. He was insanely handsome, and said to have taken a human wife, but that was just rumor. I'd yet to see her.

"No, no, this isn't that kind of training. I'm here to teach you about her." He pointed to the dagger in my hands.

'Finally, it's about me,' Sera sang.

I smirked at her comment.

"You two speak mentally, don't you?" he inquired.

I nervously chewed on my lip. I hadn't really told Shea, Lincoln, or anyone about my conversations with my knife. It sounded too weird out loud, so I'd just kept it to myself.

I nodded in acknowledgment.

Michael smiled again. "The seraph blade is an extremely rare weapon. I've never seen one on Earth, nor do I know how it could've gotten here."

I shifted my weight again, unsure what to say.

"It's a rare weapon, even in the kingdom of light. I've seen merely a few in all of my existence. The seraphim protect the Creator's throne with it."

Whoa. Suddenly fear spiked through me. Was he going to ask for it back? Maybe she'd accidentally found her way into the school cabinet, and he didn't think I should have her.

'I dare him to try!' Sera said boldly.

She had way too much self-confidence. If the Archangel Michael wanted my weapon, he was getting my weapon, and that was that.

"She...picked me, and I'd like to keep her..." I tried and failed to sound bold and confident.

Michael frowned. "Of course. I'd never dream of splitting you up. You're soul-bound. She'll help you through your life's purpose here on Earth. Only death can truly part you."

Sera and I sighed in relief at the same time. I wasn't sure that being soul-bound to a weapon was a good thing, but it was what it was. I couldn't imagine life without her at that point, as weird as that sounded.

"I'm here to teach you a fourth-year technique called weapon retrieval," he continued.

"Weapon retrieval?" I asked, not sure what he meant.

He nodded and began to circle me. "In the event that you and Sera are separated, I can teach you to call her back to you from up to a hundred feet away."

My jaw dropped. "Like Thor's hammer?"

He frowned. "Who?"

I waved it off as excitement bubbled inside of me. "Never mind. So how does it work?"

Michael stopped and looked at me—looked *through* me, it seemed. "The seraph blade is a soul weapon. I can see your light and hers, intertwined in a way that's similar to soul mates."

My eyes grew wide. "Soul mates are real?"

Michael laughed. "Of course they are. Humans love the concept of soul mates, but in reality, soul mate relationships are the hardest of your life. They challenge you and force you to grow much more than any other relationship."

I was having a freaking conversation with an honest-to-God archangel. *Tell me all the things.* I wasn't a religious person, but I was curious about something. And now seemed as good a time as any to ask.

"So...do Christians have it right? I mean..." I wasn't sure how to delicately word my question so as not to offend him.

Michael laughed. "No one religion has it *all* right. The Creator doesn't care which path you take to find Him, and *all* paths lead to Him."

Hmm, that kind of made my brain turn into a pretzel. I still wasn't sure where I stood on religion, but it sounded a little more tolerable after that.

I was about to ask him if dogs went to heaven when he reached out to me. "May I have her?" he asked kindly.

With a little apprehension, I handed her over.

The second she touched his palm, his face took on a look of surprise. "Magnificent. I can actually sense your energy within her."

"Umm, cool."

Michael studied the blade a moment longer, then set her on the ground. "Now, as a slow start, we'll have you call her to you from the ground, close by." I raised one eyebrow and he grinned. "Just close your eyes, open your energy, and call to her."

'Do you know what he's talking about?' I asked Sera. I usually let her handle things like this.

'Not really, but I can sense you, and I can sense you're not touching me, so I guess I could manipulate the energies around me to gravitate toward yours...if I tried.'

That was all way over my head.

'Okay, try that,' I replied.

I kept my palm open and took a deep breath in and out, praying she wouldn't cut my hand.

Then the cold steel slapped into my palm and my eyes snapped open.

"Holy shit!" I said, then realized I was in a room with an archangel. "Sorry." I winced.

"They're just words." He smiled.

Truth.

"That was easier than I thought!" I exclaimed, bouncing Sera in my palm.

He smirked. "Because she did all the work." He scooped her up from my hand, before walking all the way across the room.

'He smells good,' Sera told me.

My face scrunched up. '*What? You don't have a nose. That's ridiculous.*'

'And yet I smell him, and he smells so good.'

Okay, I'm not even going to go there.

When Michael reached the very farthest corner of the room, he set her down, and stepped back.

"Now, call her to you." He was wearing a wicked grin.

What kind of angel takes pleasure in someone's failure? Ugh, he's been spending too much time with Lincoln.

I widened my stance, held out both hands palms up, and took a deep breath. 'All right, Sera. Show him what we've got. Come to me,' I beckoned. I kind of felt like I was calling a dog, but it was best not to tell her that.

She was silent a minute, and I began to grow worried. 'I got nothing, sorry,' she confessed. 'I sense your general direction, but I can't move myself to you from this far away.'

That ruined the really cool vision I had of her flying to me from across the room. I'd take her in my hand, raise her to the ceiling, and she'd send out a burst of light to top the whole thing off.

"She can't do it," I told Michael.

He nodded. "But you can."

Oh Lord. This is going to be a long night.

Michael looked at me compassionately. "I was told that you're not the greatest at studies of light, is that correct?"

I chuckled. "That's putting it nicely."

He walked toward me. "Everything is energy, light. If you can *feel* that, you can do anything. When you learn to feel Sera's energy, and use your inner light to call to her, very little can keep her from you."

I chewed my bottom lip, pretty sure Michael knew about my...problem, the fact that I had Lucifer magic in my blood, and most likely his wings. "Umm...what if I don't have any light?"

Now it was the archangel's turn to chuckle. "Nonsense! I can see your light, and it's the brightest I've ever seen in a human."

His words shocked me. I wasn't technically a human, but I knew what he meant. "How...how can that be? I have black wings, and dark magic shoots from my mouth and strangles people!"

He didn't seem surprised at the truth bomb. He just shrugged. "You're like a bug zapper."

I frowned. "Huh?"

Michael placed a hand on each of my shoulders. "Those of us with greater inner light attract the most darkness. Don't ever forget that."

I wouldn't. It was the first time since I'd learned that I was essentially Lucifer's spawn that I'd been given hope.

Maybe I wasn't evil, destined to be evil, or whatever I was afraid of.

Maybe I was the brightest light Archangel Michael had ever seen in a human.

Yeah, I'll go with that.

CHAPTER 21

It took me *three days* to learn to call Sera from across the room. Michael had taught me as much as he could that night, and then only by sheer exhausting practice had I been able to do it three days later. I wasn't sure if I'd be able to do it in a life-or-death situation or in a room crowded with demons, but I'd keep practicing nevertheless, as it was a good skill to have.

Now, it was the day of the gauntlet, and I'd already thrown up twice. I'd always carried my nerves in my stomach, but once I'd puked, I was pretty unshakable.

I left the bathroom for the third time and joined Luke, Chloe, and Shea in our dorm room.

Shea made a face. "You okay?" She knew what was going on.

"I'm good now. Got it all out," I told her.

We'd all been delivered letters at six that morning.

'Choose your team of four to go through the gauntlet. Choose wisely. If one of you fails, you all fail.'

It was three o'clock, and classes were suspended for the day. Chloe had her long, thick black gloves on, and her hood covered up her bright red hair. We'd pulled closed the light-blocking curtains in our room so she could enter, and now she was pacing the floor.

"We've got this. We knew it was going to be a team thing, and we've all been practicing accordingly," she assured us.

Luke looked terrified. "If one of us fails, we all fail," he quoted ominously. "I can't go back to living with my parents. I can't."

I held my hands out in a placating gesture. "No one's failing. Trust me, Shea and I are homeless if we don't pass. We're banned from Demon City, and we have no money, so a lot's riding on this for all of us."

Chloe stopped pacing. "If we fail, I'm sure my dad will give us jobs at the club. We can all share an apartment or something."

A little bit of relief ebbed into me, and I saw the others' expressions settle a little.

"Yeah. Good plan," Shea offered.

"We're *not* failing," I told my team. "Luke, you're strong and powerful. Chloe you're strong and fast. Shea is a badass, who can open and close portals to Hell, and I can freaking *fly*. We are not failing!" I shouted.

Everyone stopped and looked at me.

Chloe grinned. "And that's why you're team leader."

We'd never officially talked about having a leader, or who it should be in the event that we were teamed up. I chewed on my lip nervously at the idea of being in charge of our fates at the academy.

"Definitely," Shea echoed, and Luke nodded.

A knock came at the door, and we all froze. The gauntlet wasn't for four more hours. We were to meet in the parking lot and get loaded onto buses and go to God knows where.

Luke started for the door, but I jumped up to intercept him. My intuition was screaming, though I couldn't pinpoint why.

"Hang on," I urged, then stepped in front of him, and leaned against the door. "Who is it?"

"Delivery. Cloud Nine Donuts," a young female voice answered.

I grinned, chastising myself for being paranoid, and pulled open the door to a young woman, wearing a Cloud Nine Donuts hat with a box and card. Luke snatched the box out of her hands, and I took the card.

"It's all paid for," she told me, then turned and left.

I ripped open the card.

Good luck today, babe. You got this.
    Love,
    Lincoln

Babe? Love? Lincoln didn't talk like that. We hadn't said *I love you* yet, and he didn't call me *babe*. He'd send something like: *Woman, remember your training or I'll kill you. You have to pass.*—L

"Stop!" I shouted as Luke licked his fingers, having finished one off already. The girls had the donuts poised at their mouths. "I think it's a trap," I told them, and Chloe and Shea dropped their donuts.

Luke looked positively green before he hunched over and started to moan.

"What's wrong?" I ran to him.

"My stomach!" he cried out, before bolting for the bathroom.

Just then I heard giggling at the door. A very, *very* familiar and annoying laugh.

Tiffany.

"I'm going to kill her!" I shouted, going for the door.

Shea reached out and stopped me. "Let's not get suspended right before the gauntlet. We need to let it go. I'll work on a counter spell to the sick spell Luke took. Let. It. Go." That was real rich coming from Shea. She was always down for a fight.

"She's right," Chloe added. "We can't do anything to compromise passing this test. Only 65 percent of Fallen Academy students pass their first year."

I hated logic and reason. I'd already had the fight with Tiffany five times in my head, and it was going to be *good*.

"Let's focus on getting Luke feeling better," Chloe urged me.

Breathe in. Breathe out.

'I could blind her. Just go out into the hall and hold me up,' Sera egged me on.

I was pretty sure that, for an angel weapon, she had no angelic conscience.

'Let's let it go. For now,' I told my partner in crime.

"How do we help Luke?" I asked Shea, deciding to take the high road.

She walked to the bathroom door. "Luke, I need to know more about what's happening, so I can make a counter spell."

His muffled voice came back through the door. "Imagine explosive diarrhea, and then multiply that by ten!"

Shea winced. "Okay. Got it! Hang tight."

She paced the room, mumbling to herself, pulling out books, and checking jars of dried herbs. The healing clinic was freaking closed today, of course, the entire staff having moved to the gauntlet site. Most of the teachers were off campus too. If Luke was going to get help, it was going to be from us.

"Okay. Chloe and Bri, you need to go to Mr. Claymore's office and ask him for one ounce of dried carob, two ounces of agrimony, and three ounces of barberry. If he's not there, break in and get them."

My eyes widened. "Don't you have a key? You're his assistant."

She shook her head. "He took it away after I read that book and opened the portal."

Damn.

"What will all those herbs do?" Chloe asked, nervously eyeing the bathroom.

Shea rolled up her sleeves. "I'm going to constipate the shit out of him. No pun intended."

"I'm dying!" Luke screamed from the bathroom.

"I'm going to fix it!" Shea yelled back. "Go!" She shooed us.

"One carrot, two alimony, three burur. We got this!" Chloe said confidently.

Shea's eyes bugged out. "Oh my God, no. Let me write it down or you'll kill him."

She scribbled it on a piece of paper and then we left the room. I told myself that if Tiffany was in the hallway, it was meant to be and I should give her a beatdown, consequences be damned. But she wasn't. *Damn.*

I turned left to go out into the common room when Chloe grabbed my arm.

"It's still light out, so I can't go outside. This way." She pulled me toward the back of the hall, somewhere I'd never been.

I'd forgotten about the sun allergy and what it must've been like to live in constant fear of going outside during the day.

"If the sun hits you…?" I started.

"A few seconds will give me hives, but more than

ten minutes and I'll die of anaphylaxis," she explained casually, like it was no big deal.

"Oh God," I muttered, horrified. I hadn't known it was that bad.

She shrugged. "It is what it is. I get strength and speed, and you should see me jump off a twenty-foot roof. Barely hurts."

I gave her a sly smile. "You have a way of looking on the bright side."

We'd reached a tall, black lacquered door with a big moon symbol on it when she looked back at me. "My whole family are Nightbloods, so it doesn't faze me."

Pulling out a key from around her neck, she unlocked the door. It creaked open, a damp smell hitting me almost immediately.

"Is it true the tunnels are underground?" I asked, suddenly claustrophobic.

Chloe nodded and grabbed my arm. "Come on. Luke needs us, and the gauntlet is in three hours!"

Right. For Luke. I stepped into the hallway and the door closed behind us, sealing out all light.

"Can you see in this?" I asked her, reaching out before me. It was literally pitch-black, not even a glow from underneath the door.

"Yeah, can't you?" her voice came back to me from somewhere up ahead.

"No." I was starting to feel a panic attack coming on.

She grabbed my hand. "Ten steps down," she explained.

I counted them slowly as I walked. *Holy crap, it's so freaking dark.*

When we reached the bottom, she informed me that we were now underground, and then dragged me through the twisting tunnels.

"Hi, Melee!" Chloe greeted, and my eyes widened.

"There's someone here?" I asked. It only occurred to me then that I could use my phone's flashlight. I pulled it out of my pocket and turned it on.

A brunette swam into view and smiled at me.

"Celestial," Chloe told her by way of explanation.

She smiled. "Welcome to the tunnels."

"Er, thanks," I muttered, relieved that I could now see the walls and shapes before me. The walls were made of a burnt red brick, and there were no lights, which I thought odd since lightbulbs didn't burn Nightbloods. I guessed it kept their night vision sharp or something along those lines.

We made a few more turns and then climbed a flight of stairs until we reached a door that read 'Magery Wing.'

"This should spit us out right into the hallway that holds Mr. Claymore's office," Chloe stated.

I nodded, clutching my phone and the list of herbs.

She pulled out her key again and unlocked the door, swinging it open a few inches, but we stopped when we heard a familiar voice.

"But, sir, last year a student died in the gauntlet," Lincoln argued.

My whole body froze, and Chloe squeezed my hand.

"Yes, a horrific outcome. Yet, we tell the students of the danger, and give them the option not to participate," Raphael retorted.

"But, sir, if you could just exclude Brielle. I'm afraid the demons are out for her. The gauntlet could be especially dangerous for her," Lincoln pleaded.

I angled myself so I could see them. They'd stopped in the hallway, where they were alone. Except for us.

Raphael put a hand on Lincoln's shoulder. "Son, you already asked, and my answer is no. I know it's hard for you to accept, but you can't save Brielle from her fate. The Fallen Army is the only thing keeping the demons from taking over Angel City. We need new recruits. We need the upper hand, or the world will fall into darkness. Lucifer creates a hundred new demons a day, unleashing them onto Earth, and they already outnumber us greatly." Raphael sounded on the verge of tears. He hated his own words; I could sense that.

"I know that." Lincoln sounded dejected. "But can't you just pass her into second year?"

Anger flared in me that he thought I couldn't pass the gauntlet.

Raphael shook his head. "She's the greatest weapon we have in this war. We must train her like everyone else, or we'll only be handicapping her."

Lincoln looked resigned. "Yes, sir," he answered in a clipped tone, then turned on his heel.

"Lincoln," Raphael called out after him.

The tall Celestial turned back, and my heart broke at the anguish in his face. He was only trying to protect me.

"Brielle is a lot stronger than you think. Stronger than most of us," Raphael confessed, and his gaze swept over the door where we stood.

Chloe and I sucked in a breath, and stepped backward, but then came the sound of retreating footsteps, and they were gone.

Chloe grasped my hand. "You okay?"

I stared at the ground, emotions ping-ponging through my body. "I dunno."

What the hell had I just overheard? Did Raphael know we were standing there? It felt like he had.

The thought of Lucifer creating a hundred new demons a day made me sick. Growing up in Demon City, they didn't mess with us much, but I knew they were constantly attacking Angel City, and other pockets of civilians.

"My dad says Lucifer won't stop until we're all demon-bound slaves," Chloe whispered.

Like I had been. Like my mom was.

"That's not going to happen," I told her through gritted teeth. For the first time since I'd heard the prophecy, I hoped it was real. I would love nothing more than to kill that abomination. Assuming it was possible.

"Come on. Luke's counting on us," I murmured.

When we got to Mr. Claymore's office, it was locked. Of course. But with two strong shoulders into the door, Chloe knocked it right off its hinges. We made quick work of grabbing the herbs, and left a note explaining it was an emergency, and we'd pay for the door.

When we finally made it back to the room, Shea was wincing in front of the door as Luke shouted obscenities.

"I'll kill her! I'm going to rip all of her hair out, and then strangle her with it!" he screamed.

If Tiffany survived the gauntlet, she definitely had a beatdown coming, that was for sure.

"We're here," I called out to him, hoping it was going to work, and he'd be okay in time for the gauntlet. We'd already chosen him as our teammate, and I wasn't going to let him fail.

Shea spun from the door and inspected our herbs. "Good job."

Chloe and I both sighed in relief that we'd grabbed the right ones.

My best friend went to work grinding the herbs into a stone bowl and waving crystal wands over them. Then, a bright purple light shot from her hands and a puff of smoke rose up from the bowl. I peered over her shoulder after it cleared and saw a purple lozenge inside it.

Whoa. Being a Mage was pretty badass.

"He's not going to poop for a week, but this is the only thing I could think of," she explained to us.

I nodded. "Just do it. We'll figure the rest out later." *Maybe we can give him prune juice tomorrow.*

Shea went to the door and slid the lozenge underneath. "Eat this. It should stop the spell."

"Thank God," his muffled voice replied.

Then we waited. After a few minutes, I heard the sink running and then the door opened. Luke was sweating, looking pale and like he'd lost five pounds.

"I need food. And once I've regained my strength, I'm going to find Tiffany." His voice was shaky and weak.

"It's awful, I know, but we just overheard Raphael and Lincoln talking, and the gauntlet sounds really dangerous. Someone died last year. Let's focus on getting you better, and then we can worry about Tiffany after we pass," I assured him.

He crossed his arms, jaw clenched, seemingly seething with rage. "Fine," he said after a beat.

Shea met my eyes, a question in hers, but I didn't elaborate. The gauntlet sounded like it was preparing us to be in the Fallen Army, and it seemed entirely real. Not like a drill.

I appreciated Lincoln's attempt to keep me safe, but like Raphael said, I couldn't be coddled; it would do me no favors in the long run.

It was time to face the gauntlet.

CHAPTER 22

After Luke ate a rack of ribs and half a dozen dinner rolls he was looking much better. He said his tummy would cramp every so often, but then it passed, which was a good sign.

Now, we were waiting out in the parking lot in a huge, white silk tent. There was a small stage, and on it was Archangel Michael. Around the perimeter were over a hundred Fallen Army guards, Lincoln being one of them. He looked so handsome in his black uniform. The winged insignia showcasing his Celestial heritage, with four stars to mark his rank, was proudly displayed on his chest.

There were about a hundred and fifty of us in the entire first year class, all standing around in our specially assigned Fallen Academy suits, loaded with weapons, unsure about what the hell this gauntlet thing was.

Michael stepped up to the edge of the stage and held his arms wide. "Thank you all for coming to the end-of-year graduation test, which has earned the name 'the gauntlet.'" He spoke without a microphone, yet his voice boomed to all corners of the tent.

We quieted our conversations and stood with rapt attention.

"What we haven't told you yet, is that the gauntlet is actually an admissions test into the Fallen Army," he declared.

People started to murmur and cast glances at the soldiers around the room.

Michael waited until everyone quieted before he spoke again. "Over a decade ago, when we first started Fallen Academy, our aim was to teach you to use your powers and then send you out into the world, but that changed as the demons took over more and more territory. Now, we're in a fight for survival, and the truth is the school was always built as a military academy."

That earned more murmurs. I didn't know why the news felt shocking, but it did.

"Graduates were offered jobs in our army, fighting demons, defending humanity," he continued. "But we can no longer wait four years for you to graduate and join us. So, seven years ago, I came up with the idea for the gauntlet, a real-life military test where if you pass, you will be given a job as an entry-level enlisted soldier in the Fallen Army."

Whoa. We're joining the army? Today? At nineteen years old?

He put his hands up. "But of course, this is voluntary. If you don't want to join the Fallen Army and help curb the overabundance of demons, then you're free to leave right now. You will be unable to attend second year at the academy, as we don't have the resources to train civilians anymore, but you will be given temporary housing, and a job placement coordinator. Hopefully, this will make it a smooth transition for you as you get out into the world with your new powers. We hope the one year of training here has served you well enough that you can manage your new life with your new skill set."

Now everyone was full-on talking and looking around the room in shock.

Shea turned to me. "So going through with the gauntlet means we're joining the Fallen Army?"

I swallowed hard, my eyes meeting Lincoln's. He just nodded. If he could speak to me, I knew he would say that joining the army was the safest thing to do.

"I guess so," I replied.

Chloe pulled her hood back, as it was pitch-black out now and we were in the safety of the tent. "I've wanted to join the Fallen Army since I was five. I'm totally in."

Luke nodded. "The army saved my cousin. They used to live on the border. Demons took over their farm, but the army pushed them back. I'm in too."

Shea's stern gaze connected with mine. "I'm with you. Whatever you want to do, I'll follow you."

I'd never entertained the idea of joining the Fallen Army. I'd always thought I'd be a college student and the rest would just work itself out. I could tell by Shea's face that she really wanted to join. Fallen Army soldiers were salaried. They had apartments and cars, and it was the smartest thing to do financially. It also felt morally right. Now that I'd lived the past several months in Angel City, I saw the damage the demons did, the way they terrorized the innocent.

"I'm in," I told them all, and Shea grinned.

Michael cleared his throat. "If you've chosen to leave, please walk to the back of the tent, as the rest of this conversation is private. If you choose to stay, know that tonight's test will be fought with real demons."

That had more than a few people walking to the back of the tent, where Rose, the school seamstress, escorted them out. To my dismay, I saw that Tiffany had chosen to stay.

After about twenty students left, Michael addressed us all again. "We're honored to have you brave students here tonight. The gauntlet will be a test of everything you've learned here at Fallen Academy. You'll each be called forward and assigned a lieutenant to explain it all in detail and watch over your test. Then you'll be asked to sign a waiver. This test will weed out the weak from the strong. Godspeed, and grace be with you."

Fear started to gnaw at my gut. Maybe I didn't want to be a selfless Fallen Army warrior, saving the innocent from the demons. Maybe I just wanted to be a civilian and go about my life, waiver-free.

"We've so got this. We've been training, and Brielle is an amazing leader," Chloe said. She always seemed to be able to find something positive to say.

"Totally," Shea agreed. "And I heard everyone in the army gets a monthly stipend, even if you're finishing school."

Luke chuckled. "Good to know where your motivation lies."

Shea shrugged. "I'm not ashamed of my love for the green."

I stayed silent, though in my head, I was mapping out the next three years of my life and beyond. If I didn't take the opportunity, this 'job interview,' what would I do with my life? Who was going to hire a Celestial with black wings? The demons would probably successfully kidnap me, and I'd be killed.

Taking a deep breath, I called to Sera, who was in my boot holster.

'You with me?' I asked her.

Her reply was quick and firm. *'We got this,'* she told me with a fierceness I wished I possessed.

Time to pump up my team.

"Let's do this. The gauntlet is our bitch tonight." I put my hand forward with a wicked grin, and Chloe placed hers on mine. Shea and Luke were next. "Worst case, we bartend at Chloe's dad's club for the rest of our lives," I continued.

Luke raised his eyebrows. "Honey, worst-case is we all become demon food tonight."

I blanched. "Fallen Academy on three. One. Two. Three."

"Fallen Academy!" we all shouted.

Everyone stared at us like we were idiots.

Screw them. I have a solid team with good camaraderie. Bring it.

"Brielle Atwater and team!" Lincoln shouted from his place on the far wall. He was holding a clipboard, and looking menacing with his sword on one hip, and a sleek black gun on the other.

We walked over to him slowly. There was one other group standing with him, and my stomach sank to see it was Tiffany's. When we reached his area, he nodded to all of us. "I'm Lieutenant Lincoln Grey, and I'll be in charge of your gauntlet training tests. It's my job to make sure no one gets hurt, but it's your job to pass the test."

Tiffany stood taller, pride blazing in her eyes, as if she wasn't scared shitless inside. Maybe she wasn't.

Lincoln kept stealing glances at me, but his expression remained hard. "You each have a team of four, and you'll each have to battle four lower-level demons to pass the test," he continued.

The other group's members' eyes widened, Tiffany included, and Lincoln nodded.

"That's right. We're going outside Angel City, into the war zone, where demons we've been capturing all week have been set up in abandoned houses and buildings. We don't tell the students ahead of time because that makes it less likely for the demons to ambush the training exercise. Once you sign your waiver, you'll be magically barred from speaking about the details of the gauntlet ever again. You won't be able to warn future students who come along or sell secrets to Demon City. If you agree with all of this, then sign here, in blood. I'll explain the specifics once we're all on the bus."

What is it with these people and their blood?

He handed waivers out to each of us. When he got to me, our hands brushed, and my eyes locked with his. His face held so much worry. I tried to tell him with my own expression that I was going to be fine, but I wasn't sure whether or not I pulled it off.

My waiver had my name printed on it. As I started reading and scanned the words 'possible death may result,' I just pricked my finger on the tiny needle taped to the signing pad, pressed it to the paper, and shoved the form back at him.

Once he had all the forms, he handed them to a squat, redheaded woman who saluted him, and then he faced us again. "Get on bus number four. I'll meet you there to explain the rules," he told both groups.

"Bus loading this way!" a large, older Fallen Army soldier called from the back of the tent.

We started to move in that direction when Lincoln caught my arm, holding me back. "My magical gag has been lifted for a few hours. I just wanted to tell you that there are soldiers all along the perimeter of the buildings. You say the word, and they'll barge in and end the training. Don't be a hero."

I frowned. "You don't think I can do it?"

That hurt. *Bad*.

His face fell. "No, that's not it at all. I think that since I met you, demons have had it out for you. I think there's a very real chance that the demons in your training will know who you are and… I don't know, maybe I'm just being paranoid. Just be safe, okay? Joining the Fallen Army is the best thing for you, but if you feel you're in grave danger in there, you pull the plug, all right?" He reached for my face but thought better of it. We were in a roomful of his colleagues, after all.

By pull the plug, he meant fail. There was no way that was happening.

Crossing my arms, I looked him up and down with my cockiest glare. "I'm going to pass the shit out of this test."

A slow grin crossed his face. "That's my girl." He winked.

Three winks. I was collecting them and committing them to memory.

We walked quickly to an all-black, short bus marked with the number four. There were over two-dozen buses from the looks of it.

As I stepped on with Lincoln, I saw there were about eight Fallen Army soldiers sitting in the back. I recognized Chloe's brother, Donnie, as one of them. I knew he was in Lincoln's brigade. They both probably requested our team. One quick glance at Luke told me he was totally freaking out to be on the same bus as him.

After I took a seat next to Shea, the bus took off.

This is happening.

I'd never been outside Angel City or Demon City. The war zones were dangerous, from what I knew. People were killed there daily, food was in short supply, and demons were constantly wreaking havoc on the innocents. Rape, murder, and God knew what else happened on the regular out there. Growing up in Demon City, we saw the somewhat civilized side of the demons. They didn't attack their own kind or in their own territory, so all of this was going to be new to me.

Once Lincoln finished talking to the bus driver, he stood, staring down at all of us. "All right, will the two team leaders raise your hands," he bellowed.

Nervously, I extended my arm into the air and looked to see the other team had, of course, selected Tiffany. Her Light Mage insignia was glittering on her uniform.

Bitch.

I prayed Shea could brew up a diarrhea potion that would make her ass explode.

Lincoln nodded to someone in the back, and a young brunette in her early twenties stood, walking over to the blond Light Mage. I recognized her from the beach, but I didn't know her name.

"The leaders will be fitted with a magical device. If at any time they deem the training has become too dangerous, they can press the button and my team will burst in and save the day. At that time, your entire team will fail the gauntlet, so only press it if someone's in mortal danger."

We all shared nervous looks. I could see now that Lincoln had a matching device on his wrist.

He held on to the rail at the top of the bus as it turned and headed out of the city. "Everything we do in the Fallen Army, we do as a unit. A team. If you can't work as a team, you have no place in this army." His eyes fell on Tiffany.

Ha. Take that.

"There are eight lower-level demons loose in an abandoned industrial building, four for each team. It'll take all of the skill sets you've learned here at the academy, and all of your teamwork, to kill them."

I glanced over and saw Tiffany blanch. She'd probably never killed a demon. None of them had. Not that I had any demon kills on my record, but I'd nearly killed Shea's boss, and we'd fought those demons in the gym, so we were more prepared than most.

"Once you've killed all four, you may exit the building, and join us. We'll send anyone who's injured to the healing tent, and then we'll all celebrate," Lincoln explained.

Tiffany grinned, high-fiving her sheeple like she'd already won.

The bus had reached the edge of the city already, the ominous concrete walls rising up like sentinels in the night.

"A final word of warning. Passing the gauntlet is not worth a life. If at any time you feel anyone on your team is in mortal danger, you push that button. I will have no lives lost on my shift. Do you understand?" His eyes bored into each one of us, lingering on me the longest.

We all nodded nervously.

"The correct response is 'sir, yes, sir,'" Lincoln informed us smugly.

Oh hell no. I was not going to have to start taking orders from him, and calling him 'sir,' was I?

Everyone else shouted, "Sir, yes, sir," but I mumbled it. I had major problems with authority, which probably wouldn't serve me well in the army. I'd definitely have to work on that.

We were passing through what used to be Burbank, California. I tried not to gape at the sight of the blown-out houses, scorch marks up the walls, abandoned cars, and half-burned lawns. A few soldiers patrolled the street with a spotlight, but otherwise it was deserted. Off in the distance, a massive explosion rang out, causing all of us to jump.

Lincoln nodded. "Demons love blowing shit up. You'll learn that. This area of the city is pretty deserted, so it's considered somewhat safe, but ten miles out, it's still an active war zone."

"People live out here?" I asked, horrified and suddenly super grateful for my cushy life at the academy.

He nodded, looking out into the wasteland of burned homes. "Most couldn't afford to leave. Then, Angel City erected the wall and started filling up. By the time they decided to join us, the demons had taken hold."

Oh God. Are they trapped out there? I felt sick just thinking about it.

The bus pulled into the parking lot of an abandoned industrial building, the number four spray-painted on the side. It rose up four stories high, some windows were blown out and the roof looked ready to cave in.

"This is us. An old sewing factory. A big staircase splits the building in two. Tiffany's team will take the left, and Brielle's team will take the right. The demons were released in there about an hour ago and are magically bound from exiting any of the doors or windows, so they're going to be pretty pissed," Lincoln stated.

Great.

The bus doors opened then, and Lincoln started to walk out.

I stood, looking down at my team. "Double-check

your weapons, and make sure your suits are fully zipped up. We're bound to encounter another Snakeroot demon." They nodded, making sure their skin wasn't exposed where it didn't need to be.

Tiffany rolled her eyes. "Let's go. Don't screw up," she barked at her lackeys.

Her three teammates jumped up and trailed after her, pushing past us as they went.

When Tiffany passed Luke, I saw him visibly flinch as his hands balled into fists.

"Don't worry, she's going to get her payback." I whispered to him.

He took a deep breath and nodded.

We all stood and exited the bus as the rest of the Fallen Army soldiers trailed after us. They started to take up a perimeter around the house, pulling out their weapons, and looking up at the ominous building. I glanced up at one of the windows and saw a shadow pass across it.

Lincoln threw a duffel bag at my feet, and another at Tiffany's. "Headlamps, glow wands, and lanterns. The building has no power."

Awesome. Fan-freaking-tabulous.

I knelt down and unzipped the bag, distributing the items to my team before I put on my headlamp, and then stuck two glow wands in my outer thigh pockets. I used a carabiner to hook one of the lanterns to my waist.

"Luke, beast out. I want to go in full power," I instructed, and he nodded.

Lincoln looked at me with a slight grin. "Good call."

"Thank you, *sir*." I raised an eyebrow.

That only made him grin wider. *God, he's so gorgeous. Why won't he deflower me already?*

"Can we start now?" Tiffany asked, crossing her arms over her chest.

Maybe I could hurt her during the training exercise, and make it look like an accident.

Lincoln scowled at her. "We'll start when I say we start," he snapped.

Each and every member of my team sported a gleaming smile at his words.

Tiffany's mouth popped open in shock as she stared at Lincoln, then turned her back to him.

Lincoln clearly didn't want anything to do with her, and she needed to learn that real quick. Their families might've been friends, but that's where it stopped.

Luke walked around the other side of the bus to strip down and shift. I noticed Donnie, Chloe's brother, break away from his place, near the front door where he'd been talking to another soldier.

"Good luck, sis," he said, pulling her in for a side-arm hug. He was *super* good-looking, not the least bit feminine in demeanor, but Luke swore he was gay. I guess that would teach me to stereotype.

She smiled. "Thanks. Did Mom make you request to watch over me?" She put one hand on her hip.

He looked down at her with a wicked grin. "Of course."

She chuckled, showcasing her fangs. "Well, we're going to do great. We have a solid team."

Just then, Luke padded out from behind the bus. His huge brown bear, with large, black, curled horns, always had me awestruck and terrified simultaneously.

Donnie's gaze swept Luke up and down. "Yes, you do," he agreed appraisingly.

Walking over to Luke, I fitted a headlamp around his horns.

"All set?" Lincoln asked me.

I nodded. *Now or never.* I was either about to become a member of the Fallen Army, a cocktail waitress at Chloe's dad's club, or…dead.

Lincoln barked an order at his team, who readied their weapons and stood in a rigid stance, clearly ready to break into the building and save our asses at a moment's notice. Then, he walked over to the steel door and opened it. Only lurking darkness awaited us inside, which sent my stomach roiling.

Tiffany walked up to Lincoln, sashaying her hips, and he handed her a key. "Stay on the left side. Good luck, and don't forget to use your button if needed."

She grabbed the key and rolled her eyes. "Save your

recovery team for Archie. We'll be fine." Then they started into the building.

Every time she opened her mouth, my hatred of her grew deeper and deeper, like a cavern.

I was next. With one last settling breath, I took the key from him, his fingers caressing mine. Looking up, I met his gaze and wished I could kiss him.

"Your wristband has a GPS tracker so—"

"We'll be fine. See you soon."

He nodded, pulling his hand back, but looking anything but convinced.

"Let's do this," I told my team, then walked into the dark opening.

A bunch of first-year students were about to take on four demons.

No *big deal.*

CHAPTER 23

The moment we slipped the key into the door on the right side of the stairs, I smelled it. Sulfur and oil. *Demons.*

"Good luck, Archie," Tiffany's catty voice called from above me, as her team slipped in the door across the hall.

"Watch your back, bitch!" Shea spat venomously, Luke growling at her side. A big-ass, scary bear growl.

Tiffany's face tightened in fear for a second, but then she slammed the door shut.

"Whoa, okay. Got the aggression going. I like it. Now let's take it out on the four demons inside," I said to Shea, then pushed open the door.

Luke was the first one in. He brushed past me, head down and horns ready to ram anything that got in his way. His spotlight spread out through the space, but I saw nothing but dusty, half-broken sewing desks.

Chloe was in next, Shea beside her, and I brought up the rear, closing the door and locking it behind me. I didn't want any of these suckers getting out and failing us. Magically locked in or not, I wasn't taking any chances.

I opened the carabiner at my waist and pulled the lamp out. Clicking it on, I rolled it into the middle of the room.

"There!" Chloe shouted as movement crawled along the far-right edge of the wall. The little bastard passed into the light, and I saw tiny, bat-like wings for a split second.

"It's a Yew demon!" I shouted, and then Chloe was off, like a hawk seeking prey as she cut through the room.

Yew demons spit fire. If you got them going, they wouldn't stop until the whole place was up in flames. Their only weakness was that they were pretty much blind and super slow, going off sound.

Chloe was fast enough to distract him, zipping to his right. When he heard her coming, he spit a stream of fire into the air ten feet from where she'd been standing. He didn't even sense her as she reached up and yanked him down by one wing. With a screech, he flapped madly as she pinned him to the ground. The little bastard spit fire onto the old hardwood floors but nothing alighted, and then Luke was there. Chloe maneuvered the Yew demon so Luke could take the small, bat-like creature into his mouth. Then he shook his head vigorously until we heard the snapping of the demon's neck.

I knew there were three more in the building, so I didn't pay too much attention to the Yew demon. Luke and Chloe had him. Instead, I spun in a circle and scoped out the rest of the space. The front area was pretty open and led to a main room full of sewing desks, but the back part, past Chloe and Luke, seemed to have an office and another stairwell.

Luke glanced up from his kill, and I walked over to pat his round rump. "Good boy," I cooed.

He reached around, head-butting my leg, and I laughed. "Okay, okay. Sorry. Awesome job, you badass."

He hated being treated like a pet, but I wasn't sure how else to talk to him in his animal form.

"Come on. I think this place is four stories high, so there's probably one demon on each floor," I said to everyone.

I grabbed the lantern, and we walked slowly to the back of the room where the office was. Pulling Sera from my boot, I peeked inside the office room. A quick scan told me it was empty.

"This is going to be easy-peasy," Chloe announced as she started up the stairs.

"Don't get cocky!" I shouted after her, running to catch up. "Hang back a second." I placed a hand on her chest and stepped in front of her.

The lower-level demons were Yew, Snakeroot, Larkspur, and Castor, the latter being more dangerous than the others. Though any one of them could kill us, burn our faces off, or make our lives a living nightmare.

"You did a great job with the Yew demon, but let's be cautious," I urged. We'd reached the top of the steps, where there was an opening to another level.

She nodded and let me take the lead into the room. I gripped Sera firmly in my right hand, then stepped inside.

The second I crossed the threshold, nausea rolled into me, making my mouth water as bile churned in my belly.

"Lark...spur," I said between dry heaves as the rest of my team burst into the room, flashlights shining.

Larkspur demons made you physically ill while in their presence, weakening you the longer you stayed near them. Ten minutes in the room and I'd be puking my brains out, unable to do a damned thing to defend myself. I already felt the body aches setting in, like a really bad case of food poisoning, or the flu.

'*Sera, help,*' I called, holding my dagger in front of me. Larkspur demons were a menacing seven feet tall, and they packed a punch. If I could illuminate the room, there was no way he could hide.

Sera's light shot out of the tip of her blade and burst like a firework at the ceiling.

Oh shit.

The light had also shown him where we were. From his place near the far-left window, he was now running at us.

"*Infirmi!*" Shea yelled, and a spark of yellow shot from her palm, slamming into the demon's gut. His legs buckled, and he started to fall forward. Luke made a distressing sound from behind me, and I took a split second to glance over my shoulder at the Snakeroot demon riding his back.

What the hell! My eyes widened. There were two of them on that floor. I felt like I was going to throw up, but I had to push all that aside and deal with this, or we were in some deep shit.

"Chloe, help Luke!" I shouted, my mouth full of saliva. Then I advanced on the Larkspur demon with Shea at my side.

"I weakened his legs, but it won't last." she said, then turned over and retched on the ground.

Wasting no time, I leapt onto the demon's back as he was trying to stand and shoved Sera between his shoulder blades up to the hilt. The moment I sank the blade into his flesh, he roared and arched his back, using his incredible strength and speed to try and buck me off. I kept my hold on Sera as my body was flung up and outward, in a forty-foot arc across the sewing factory.

This landing is going to hurt. Wait, I have wings!

At the last second, my wings shot out, and I got all of two flaps in before I crashed into the far wall. I hit with the entire left side of my body, minimally slowed by my wings, and sank to the ground. Doing a quick assessment for anything broken, I tried to stand. My left hip was pinching fiercely, but it didn't feel dislocated at least.

Looking back over to the fight, I saw Chloe chasing the Snakeroot demon while Luke was panting on the ground. The Larkspur demon had his hands around Shea's throat.

"Shea!" I roared and burst forward from where I stood. Launching into the air, I felt pain shoot into my left hip, but as soon as I let my wings take over, I was fine. Flying across the room, I slammed into the demon's back, knocking him off Shea.

'Keep me in him long enough and I can obliterate him!' Sera ordered.

She was in battle mode, and so was I. I wouldn't lose any friends tonight, and I would not fail this test.

The Larkspur demon hit the ground at an awkward angle and I fell on top of him, plunging Sera into the closest part of his body I could reach, which happened to be his groin.

Take that, you bastard.

Then I crawled over him, straddling his abdomen and trying to pin him down long enough to allow Sera to work. Being that close to him was making me feel like death, my whole body breaking out in chills as nausea rolled into me like waves crashing against a shoreline.

His face contorted in rage, his thick, gray leathery skin bunching into a menacing, pug-faced look. I thought I had his arms pinned, but then I realized he'd just been letting me pin them as his left arm shot out and his fist connected with my jaw. Pain exploded in my ear and neck, a scream of surprise tearing from my mouth.

I went berserk then, raining blows from both fists along his face, neck, and anywhere else I could reach. Just like Lincoln taught me, I pushed my upper body weight into each blow to make them as powerful as possible.

Suddenly, the demon's body started to heat beneath me, making the backs of my thighs hot. With wicked speed, his arms shot up into my armpits, and then I was launched off him. I crashed into the ground near Shea, who was heaving on the floor on all fours. Same with Luke's bear. Only Chloe and I were left, and we were barely functioning.

I shot back up into a standing position and charged him again. He was sitting up, about to pull Sera out of his groin. And he was…glowing, his skin appearing as though it contained a small fire beneath it. Beads of sweat dripped from his brow, and he was screaming in pain.

He wrapped his hands around Sera's hilt just as I leapt into the air and delivered a perfect flying kick to his forehead. His upper body snapped back as Sera's magic flooded his system. I landed, looking down at him. Light was pouring off his skin, ebbing out of his pores like golden lava.

'*Step back. He's gonna blow,*' Sera informed me.

I lunged backward, tripping over a desk just as a cracking sound filled the air, and his body exploded outward, sending meat and shards of light splattering across the room. He was destroyed from his knees to his neck, just his head and feet left.

That sudden, violent sight finally did it for me. I hunched over and vomited onto the ground.

"Help!" Chloe shrieked.

Shit. I'd forgotten that she was dealing with the freaking Snakeroot demon.

Shea suddenly burst into a standing position—looking better now that the nauseating Larkspur demon was dead. She brandished her circular blade and made quick strides across the room to help Chloe, as I tried to regain my equilibrium. Chloe had the little sucker pinned under her boot like last time, holding his wriggling body tight. Her black shoe looked to be bubbling—she'd been hit with his acid.

Shea slid on her knees and thrust the blade across the creature's stomach. A flow of green acid instantly spewed out onto the floor, sending a stream of phosphorescent steam upward. Chloe leapt backward just as the acid started to eat through the wooden floorboards.

The Nightblood was panting, her hair messed up, parts of it pulled from her ponytail. "I take it back. No more easy-peasy."

Yeah, no shit.

"Everyone okay?" I asked.

Luke was looking better; he was standing now and had quit panting. I was pretty sure Chloe was the only one who hadn't thrown up.

"I feel much better now that it's dead." Shea pointed to the Larkspur demon's remains.

My eyes fell to Chloe's boot, which was smoking.

"Chloe, take that off or the acid will eat through it to your foot. Trust me." I had the scar to prove it.

She quickly did as I asked, and I took a deep breath, assessing the next challenge. "Okay, there's one more demon left. My educated guess is that it's a Castor demon."

Castor demons were the most dangerous of the four. They created these little energetic bursts or waves that knocked you on your ass. Getting within two feet of a Castor demon was damn near impossible, and their skin was thick like armor, not much able to pierce it.

"Chloe, you're our best bet to get close to him. Luke, if you can charge in fast and hard, then hopefully we'll have the element of surprise. Shea and I can try to take him out once you've stunned him."

Chloe nodded, rolling her neck and pulling her sword from its scabbard. "I can do that."

Luke nodded his big bear head.

I took another breath, still shaken from the violent death of the Larkspur demon. "Okay. Let's head up to the next level."

I grabbed Sera from her place on the floor and wiped

the Larkspur demon's blood and guts off on the calf of my pant leg. Then I praised her for doing a good job with the demon. I wanted her to know I appreciated her, since she seemed to have feelings and all that.

Slowly and quietly, we took the steps one by one, partly to be stealthy and partly to drag out the inevitable. I was tired, my hip hurt, and I wanted a full-body massage with a four-hour nap. But I wasn't a quitter.

I reached the doorframe and the stench of brimstone hit me like a truck. It was like a smoky vinegar taste that I'd grown up smelling only around the highest-level demons. Fear tightened my gut as confusion rolled into me; maybe the smell was left over from whatever demon lived here before. There were still two floors left, so this one could very well be empty. Regardless, I pulled Sera from her holster once more, not wanting to take any chances, and stepped into the space. I crouched down, rolling the lantern into the center of the room and then glanced around, trying to see if there was a demon or not.

In the far-right corner of the room, I saw a hunched-over, shadowy figure.

Frowning, I looked at my team and motioned for them to follow closely behind me, instead of my initial plan to charge and stun him. I tiptoed slowly and carefully over to it. With each step, I tried to make out what it was, and why it was playing dead. Maybe it wasn't a Castor demon; maybe it was another Yew demon, or Larkspur.

As I got closer, I saw the shape and size of the body

definitely matched a Castor demon, but it was still just hunched there, playing dead.

On my hand signal, Chloe zipped through the room like a bolt of lightning and pounced on him, ramming her sword into his rib cage as Luke burst past me to finish him off.

The demon didn't move.

"He's dead," Chloe said, as Luke slowed his approach. The Nightblood rolled the demon over to show his face. His eyes had turned white, and he definitely wasn't breathing.

Lincoln said we had to kill four demons, so if this one was already dead, then there had to be another. I spun around. "It's a trick. There's still one in here."

A noise from the back of the room had me spinning again. There, in the middle of the room, was a purple and yellow glowing blob, a circle of colors suspended in the air, growing bigger and bigger each second.

"Uh, Shea…is that?" I asked.

Shea stumbled backward. "A portal."

I chewed my lip, glancing at my GPS bracelet. "Is this part of the exercise?"

The opening was as big as a door now; only a black and gray stone wall could be seen behind it. A wall not from that building.

Maybe it was a trick. Perhaps a Light Mage was going to portal in another demon from an adjacent building to mess with us.

"It must be," Chloe offered, moving into a fighting stance.

I snapped my wings, letting them stretch and prepare to fly just as a figure stepped from the portal and out into the room.

Everything within me revolted at the man before me. The hairs stood on my arms and legs, and I felt my knees go weak. He was six feet tall, with dark glossy hair, black sinister eyes, and pale, thin skin. He was handsome in a scary way, his looks screaming danger, but the thing that terrified me the most were the black angel wings on his back. Identical to mine. On his forearm was a tattoo, a skull with a sideways crown, and black wings behind it.

"Hello, Brielle." His smooth voice made my insides shiver. He looked to be in his early thirties, but the way he carried himself was that of a person much older.

'*Run. Call for help,*' Sera urged.

I swallowed hard. "Who are you?" He wasn't any demon I'd ever met.

He grinned, showcasing a full set of white teeth, but the look in his eye was assessing me, as you'd assess a good meal.

"I go by many names, but I prefer Prince of Darkness," he crooned.

That was all I needed to hear.

Reaching over, I pushed the button on my bracelet, then stepped in front of my friends, stretching my wings out to shield them.

"*Run!*" I told them, holding Sera in front me.

I was standing before the freaking Devil himself.

Lucifer.

He tipped his head back and laughed. The haunting sound echoed off the walls, and made my stomach roil with nausea. His hand lifted, and he waved two fingers toward himself. At the same time, my feet started to unwillingly be dragged in his direction. My body rose a few inches off the floor, controlled by an unseen force, and I was floating against my will right toward the Devil.

No.

"You know, I think it's unfair that the others have branded you, and yet I've been left out of the fun." He eyed the visible tattoos on each arm.

"*Infirmi!*" Shea screamed and thrust her hand out, shooting a spell at Lucifer.

He laughed harder, black smoke leaking from his mouth. "That's cute," he cooed.

Shea's spell disintegrated a few feet from him. Chloe grabbed hold of my shoulders and tried to pull me back, while Luke rose up on his hind legs and roared.

Lucifer slammed his palms together and black mist shot out. All three of my friends went flying in different directions, each crashing into the nearby walls, and sinking into unconsciousness. I tried to move but couldn't. Trailing my eyes over each of my friends' chests, relief flooded through me that they were all breathing.

I had reached him now. Twelve inches from the maker of evil.

'*What do I do?*' I asked Sera as my knees wobbled in fear.

'*I don't know.*'

Oh God. She'd never said that before. I was totally screwed.

Lucifer's eyes narrowed at my blade. With one flick of his wrist, Sera was torn from my hand, and sent sailing across the room, hitting the ground with a *clink*.

"You're the one from the prophecy." His eyes glittered in excitement.

The portal was still behind him. If I could possibly kick him through and somehow close it, maybe I had a chance.

"Just leave me be. I won't hurt you. I'm just a kid," I pleaded. I knew it was useless to try and gain empathy from the Devil himself, but I couldn't stand there and do nothing.

He grinned, stepping closer. "You think I'm scared of you?"

The stench of oil and vinegar burned my nose.

His hands lit up, a glowing red that pulled my gaze down to where they rested near his waist. "No, no, no, my child. You're the first and only human creation of mine. I want to mold you into the great and dark warrior you can be."

Those glowing hands were freaking me out. I

tried to squirm, but it felt like I'd been molded into a statue.

Taking a deep breath, I remembered my training with Archangel Michael and tried to call Sera to me, sending my energy out behind me to brush against hers.

"I want you to be endowed with *all* of your powers, my child." He slammed his hot palm right into the center of my chest, gripping my arm with his other hand, and pinning me in place.

A shriek tore from my mouth as pain like I'd never felt before ripped through me. A dark heaviness coated my skin, like a wet blanket, as sadness enveloped me. Mind-numbing depression crawled into the corner of my mind, and I screamed harder as I tried to fight it. Rage built within me at the unwanted violation. I felt that darkness searching inside of me, looking for an outlet. I'd kept it pent-up for so long, trying so hard to be good and full of light, that I wanted to burst.

Another flare of red surged from his palm to my chest. I let it all go. I screamed, as agony and rage swirled within me, letting the dark, ugly monster inside of me loose. A huge, black, inky blob crawled up my throat and flew from my mouth, wrapping around his neck, and the lower half of his jaw.

Shock marred his features but was quickly replaced with absolute pride. His eyes glittered as he assessed me with complete adoration.

No.

He snapped his fingers, and the black necktie fell from his throat as if it was made of paper. Then he took his hand from my chest and beamed at me. "You'll do great and terrible things in my name," he declared, his voice reverberating off the walls.

Fuck that.

With the last reserve of energy I had left, I wrapped it around Sera and pulled. My legs were still frozen to the spot, but when she flew across the room and into my hand, I was able to move my arm and thrust her at him. Lucifer saw my jab coming and sidestepped it, grabbing me by the neck and trying to pull me with him into the portal.

At that moment, Lincoln and his team burst into the room, screaming my name. He took one look at the Prince of Darkness standing in front of the portal to Hell and the blood drained from his face.

The Mage girl in their group shouted a bunch of words in another language, and a bright blue star shot from her hand before it burst across the ceiling, sending little sparkles of glitter over everything. When they touched Lucifer's skin, he cried out and pulled his arm back, releasing me. I was still thankfully on my side of the world, him in his, but my toes were inches from being in Hell, literally.

"Come, child," Lucifer beckoned and thrust his arm out again, latching onto mine. Lincoln leapt into the air and came down on the Devil's outstretched arm with his sword, cutting it clean off.

I fell backward on my ass, the Devil's spell over me broken. The Mage girl jumped in front of Lincoln and started to close the portal as Lucifer sat on the ground, blackish-crimson blood spurting from his forearm.

The arm Lincoln had cut off suddenly levitated through the portal, and Lucifer caught it in midair, smirking at me.

Then the portal closed.

Everyone turned to stare at me, eyes wide in shock. I glanced behind me to see that Shea, Luke, and Chloe were all stirring, waking up. Thank God.

On the ground, panting, I managed to look up at Lincoln, who was gaping in horror at my chest.

"Wha—" I looked down and a sob tore from my throat.

There, branded on my chest, was a skull with a sideways crown, the black wings behind it.

"He's marked you," Lincoln said with mild revulsion, as if that made me evil. As if it made me a devil as well. Then his face quickly changed to something more compassionate, trying to mask his initial reaction, but it was there, I'd seen it.

I clawed at the tattoo to no avail, leaving red streaks on my chest.

"What does this mean?" I asked him, and he gave me the same look of pity people had given my father.

Lincoln crouched down and reached out for me, but I recoiled. He sighed, staring off at the floorboards, unable to meet my eye. "I think it means he's fully activated your dark powers."

My dark powers. As if I owned them and had chosen them. A black cloud crossed over my soul then, and I knew I'd never be the same again.

My greatest fear had been realized.

I'd gone dark.

CHAPTER 24

I COULD HEAR THE HUSHED VOICES ARGUING INSIDE the room as I sat outside the door to Raphael's office. As much as they tried to keep quiet, I heard everything.

Once again, I'd been whisked away from the revelry like a freak, just like at the Awakening ceremony.

"He branded her!" Lincoln shouted venomously.

"Hang on, we don't know exactly what he did," Archangel Michael's strong voice cut in.

"Raphael, you're not going to kick her out, right? Her team killed all of the demons. Four demons dead. That means they passed the gauntlet." Lincoln's voice was sharp, threatening.

Technically, the fourth demon was dead when we got there—compliments of the Prince of Darkness, I assumed—but I was going to go with it.

There was only silence for a moment, and I started to get nervous.

"Of course I'm going to pass her. Everyone needs to calm down. She's innocent in all of this. What Lucifer may or may not have done doesn't matter. Let's not alienate her any more than she already is."

Bless him.

"She carries his mark over her heart. That's very deep, dark magic," Mr. Claymore said. I hadn't even known he was there. I'd been in shock since the Devil himself opened a portal in the middle of my school exam and branded me with dark magic, so I figured I was allowed to be a little out of it.

I looked down at the mark and tears welled in my eyes. The skin was angry and red from me scratching at it, hoping I could peel it off. But it was no use.

"But you can get it off, right?" Lincoln asked, a mild hysteria tinging his voice.

Silence. Moments and moments of silence.

"I don't think so, but I'll try. My magic is no match for the Prince of Darkness," Mr. Claymore sighed, resigned.

I drew my knees up to my chest and cradled them. I wanted my mom to wrap me in her arms and stroke my back while singing "Twinkle, Twinkle, Little Star." But she was in Demon City, and I was stuck here.

"Let's all just take a breather and keep an eye on her. See if anything…manifests. We can take it from there." Gabriel was the level-headed one, the peacemaker.

"Manifests?" Lincoln asked.

I replayed the way he'd looked at me the moment he'd seen the mark on my chest. Fear and horror had marred his beautiful features, filled his shining eyes.

"Let's just take everything one day at a time. Be here for Brielle, and whatever she may need from us," Raphael stated.

"Permission to take the rest of the night off, sir." Lincoln's clipped tone was back.

"Permission granted, son," Michael replied.

Raphael's office door opened, and Lincoln stepped out, light pouring out of the room with him.

He looked down at me curled up on the ground and scooped me up, one arm under my knees and the other behind my back. Cradling me to his chest, he started walking me to the parking lot in the direction of his trailer.

"I can walk," I mumbled, but I didn't really want to walk. I didn't want to be alive right now. Everything felt too hard.

"No," Lincoln simply stated.

Ever since Lucifer had put that mark on me, a depression had settled at the edges of my mind, waiting to pounce if I let down my guard. So, I let him carry me—covered in demon blood and guts—across the parking lot, past his motorcycle, and to his door.

He set me down gently, and then unlocked his door. "You can shower. I'm going to make us something to eat," he murmured.

It was like ten at night, and I wasn't hungry, but I couldn't turn him down. I gave him a weak smile and nodded. We didn't have many dates where Lincoln cooked for me, both of us busy most nights with my school and clinic job or his work with the Fallen Army.

Dinner at ten o'clock? Why not?

I trudged through his trailer and went into the tiny bathroom, closing the door and locking it. Resting my forehead against the back of the door, I took two deep breaths. The night had not gone how I'd expected. Then again, who really expected the Prince of Darkness to show up and brand them? Just…wow.

Yep, I'm in shock.

Turning on the water, I started to strip out of my smoky, bloody, demon-coated clothes.

Screw this day. Screw it hard.

Stepping under the water, I felt a little bit of the tension leave my shoulders. I wasn't alone. I had Lincoln, Shea, and everyone else on my team. I had a good support group. I was going to be fine.

When I grabbed the soapy loofah, and ran it over my chest, a sob stilled in my throat.

The mark.

I'd forgotten about it for three seconds, but there it was. Never in a thousand years would I have guessed that anything could be worse than the death mark the Dark Mages took. But there I was, marked without even a needle by the Devil himself. The sadness I'd felt before when he'd branded me ramped up a notch. I furiously scrubbed at the mark, but it only hurt my skin.

I couldn't hold back the tears anymore. My body. He'd done something to my body against my will. I felt so violated. My tears turned to sobs as my chest ached with emotion, a physical pain spreading throughout my limbs.

Grief.

Would my dark powers grow stronger? Would I ever find my light like Fred, Lincoln, and the other Celestials had? Did Lucifer break me?

"Bri?" Lincoln's voice was laced with concern as he called to me through the door.

I tried to control my weeping, but I couldn't; I'd opened the floodgates, and now it was like a free-for-all. I turned off the water and slowed my breathing, trying to rein in what I was feeling.

"What's wrong? Are you hurt? I mean, physically?" Lincoln sounded panicked. I wasn't a crier. I'd fainted and thrown up on him when he'd had me work out too hard, but I wasn't a big crier.

"The mark" was all I could say in between my weeping.

His reply was instant. "It doesn't matter. I mean, it doesn't matter to me. I still…love you. No matter what."

Shock and hope ripped through my body, chasing the pain and sadness away.

Lincoln just said he loves me.

He loves me.

I wrapped myself in a towel and threw open the door. "What did you say?" Maybe I hadn't heard him right. The L-word was a big deal, and I could very well be hallucinating in my fragile state.

He grinned and ran a hand through his hair. "I freaking love you, Brielle. I have for a while now, but...the last people I said that to were my parents, and they got killed, so...I don't know. I—"

I stepped forward and shut him up with a kiss.

Lincoln Grey loves me. I shoot black death chokers from my mouth, and have been personally branded by Lucifer, yet Lincoln Grey still loves me.

He tasted like strawberries, and despite the craziness of the last five hours, pleasure pooled in my belly as heat traveled between my legs. The L-word had done something to me.

Lincoln pulled back and gave me a lopsided grin. "Aren't you supposed to say it back?"

I laughed. "Oh please, we both know I've been in love with you for months."

That made him chuckle as he reached out and stroked my chest, right over the mark, just above my towel. "Lucky me."

I think we both became aware that I was dripping

wet, naked except for just a thin towel, at the same time, because all of the air seemed to suck out of the room. My breathing slowed as heat throbbed between my legs.

And I dropped my towel.

YOLO.

His eyes widened, desire flaring in his gaze. "Brielle."

I took a step toward him, one hand on my bare hip. He'd never seen me completely naked before. Pretty close, but not the full deal.

"Lincoln, I'm a woman. I may only be nineteen, and I may have less sexual experience than you, but I am a woman. And I know what I want." I stepped closer so my tight nipples were pressed against his chest. Even with his shirt on, I could feel the warmth from his skin.

His breath came out in a ragged gasp. "Are you sure? Now?" His words were gentle, and sweet. He didn't want to take advantage of me in a vulnerable situation, but I needed him. I needed our love like a life raft in the ocean. Now more than ever.

I nodded.

He snaked a hand out and slid it down my spine to cup my butt. With a light squeeze, he pulled me into him. My pelvis pressed against his, and my arms went around his neck, as we started to walk backward into the bedroom.

Once inside, I shifted my hands from his neck to the button on his pants. My mouth was hungrily feasting on him as my body heated, preparing for what was going to happen. I'd never felt this way about anyone in my entire life. Physically, emotionally, spiritually, Lincoln lit me up inside. He was my other half, which was probably why we butted heads, but dammit, I loved the guy so much it hurt.

And now, to share a moment so special with him, it completed something in me, something I hadn't realized was feeling unfinished.

Lincoln laid me down, his lips on the curve of my breasts. With an outstretched arm, he rummaged through his nightstand drawer and produced a condom. As he peppered my skin with kisses and licks, I felt my desire ramping up to epic proportions.

Our bodies pressed together then, moving in rhythmic motions. I moaned every time his skin came back to touch mine. I trailed my fingers down his back and lost all sense of time; it was just Lincoln and me, stuck in this moment of love, pleasure, and complete trust.

My back began to arch as my body started to unravel. "Lincoln," I moaned.

His hands clenched as he reached that place with me, and I felt every last piece of darkness flee from my soul.

I am light.

I am lovable.

This mark does not define me.

Our breathing slowed and then he laid down, curling me into his chest. We stayed there for some time, just being together in the moment.

Suddenly, a charred smell hit my nose. "What's that smell?" I asked.

Lincoln bolted from the bed. "I burned dinner!"

Laughter erupted from my chest. It looked like cereal was on the menu.

Sitting in a clean pair of Lincoln's boxers and an oversized shirt, I took a bite of the crunchy cereal, and pinned my lover with a glare.

"So hit me with it. Did Tiffany's team pass?" I asked.

He chuckled. "That's all you care about right now?"

Priorities. I needed to know if I'd be spending the next three years of schooling with that demon. I nodded and took a sip of cranberry juice.

He sighed. "She did. One of her girls has a nasty acid burn on her back, but they passed."

Dammit. That bitch.

I growled. "So, what now? Fallen Army?" I wasn't sure what joining entailed.

He smirked, and leaned in closer, leveling me with a sinister gaze. "Boot camp over the summer. Run by yours truly, Drill Sergeant Lincoln Grey."

I dropped my spoon into my bowl.

"Oh shit."

TO BE CONTINUED...

ACKNOWLEDGMENTS

Wow this book was so fun to write and took so many people to make it happen. Big thanks to my beta readers, Steven Smithen, Lela Eder, and Megan Mayes. Thank you to the team at Bloom for editing this book and taking a chance on me and my words. A HUGE thank you, as always to my loving and supportive family. The time I spend with my characters is time away from you all and I'm so grateful you understand this passion I have for writing. Lastly, to my ARC team, Leia Stone Wolf Pack, and all my readers, thank you for being so loyal and enthusiastic about my books. I heart you all bad. <3

ABOUT THE AUTHOR

Leia Stone is the *USA Today* bestselling author of multiple bestselling series, including Matefinder, Wolf Girl, The Gilded City, Fallen Academy, and Kings of Avalier. She's sold over three million books, and her Fallen Academy series has been optioned for film. Her novels have been translated into multiple languages and she even dabbles in script writing.

Leia writes urban fantasy and paranormal romance with sassy kick-butt heroines and irresistible love interests. She lives in Spokane, Washington, with her husband and two children.

Instagram: @leiastoneauthor
TikTok: @leiastone
Facebook: leia.stone
Website: www.LeiaStone.com